BROOKLYN VALENTINE

RACHEL A LEVINE

Brooklyn Valentine

iUniverse books may be ordered through booksellers or by contacting:

iUniverse
1663 Liberty Drive
Bloomington, IN 47403
www.iuniverse.com
844-349-9409

ISBN: 978-1-4502-3207-4 (sc)
ISBN: 978-1-4502-3208-1 (e)

Print information available on the last page.

iUniverse rev. date: 07/22/2023

For Rivke, my very own *"really"* love.

CHAPTER ONE
The Airport

"What am I, Sollie, 'The Unforgiven'? It's two years already. Either forgive me or shoot me," Manny had complained the other day.

"Who said I don't forgive? I forgive," he had said.

"Get outta here. You hold onto a grudge like it's a life preserver."

Sitting in Friday night rush hour traffic to the airport, Sal had nothing better to do than to consider what Manny had said. Sal had agreed to give someone a tour of Brooklyn for the first time in two years. Two years since his tour business had collapsed, and with it, his dream of getting out of the cab-driving business. He wasn't sure why he'd agreed to do it, but maybe it was to prove to Manny that he was letting go of that life preserver. But now he was tired. It had been a long day and he was starting to be sorry he let Manny rope him into this. What good could come of it? And what did he even know about this woman he was picking up? Nothing. Except Manny had said she was rich and from Wisconsin. Two years ago Sal would have been overjoyed to have a rich customer. Now it didn't matter. One rich customer was too little, too late. Why couldn't Manny have recruited customers like this when they were still in business? Maybe if he had, they would still be in business. Crap, there it was again. The grudge.

So now he was stuck in traffic, and once he picked her up to take her back to her midtown hotel he'd be stuck in more traffic. And then he'd have to pick her up tomorrow morning for a tour of Brooklyn. More traffic. He started to think about ways out. The woman wasn't really coming to New York for the tour anyway. It was just something to do to kill time. But she had pre-paid. And that meant she was really interested. And that appealed to Sal. He was a sucker for people who were interested in his home town. Still, he was torn. If the tour was a success, he would feel crappy about the business having failed. If it was a failure, he would feel crappy about wasting the day when he could've slept late, and then hung out with Bennie and helped him make valentines for his entire third grade class.

The traffic dulled his senses and made him restless all at the same time. He hated being late, and he didn't even know what this broad looked like. He got to the airport, parked, and ran to the terminal, hoping she hadn't given up on him and taken a cab into the city. He scanned the baggage carousel area, but there were only a few passengers looking pissed off that their luggage wasn't there. He left the terminal and headed for the cab stand. There was a long line.

"Yo! Terry? That you?" he called out.

She turned toward him. "Yes?"

He walked toward her. "Sal Iorio. I guess I missed you in there," he said, thrusting out his hand.

"Sal? Manny said your name was 'Sol'. And I thought you were supposed to meet me at the gate," she answered, with a quick glance at his waiting hand. "You're late."

"Sal, Sol, what's the difference. I'm just glad I found you," he said, and pulled his hand back, seeing she wasn't planning to shake it anytime soon.

The next cab in line pulled up and the cab driver leaned out his window, bumping his large turban against the frame. Sal laughed as the driver said, "Get in, Miss. I take you."

"It's okay. She's with me," Sal told him.

"Next in line for cab. She come with me," he answered.

Sal approached the cab, and as he did so, the man reached over to his passenger seat and picked up a knife encased in an exotic sheath. He waved it at Sal. Terry gasped and stepped back.

"It's a free country, Pal. Isn't that why you came here in the first place? There's enough for everyone," he said and gestured toward the rest of the people on line.

The cab driver cursed him in a foreign language, put down the knife, and inched his cab up in line.

"Scarcity mentality. That's his problem," Sal said to Terry, who was struck dumb. "Here, let me take that." He reached for the one large duffel bag she carried.

Terry took a deep breath and handed it over. It was windy. Her hair was disheveled, and the noise was overwhelming.

"The car's not far. Or would you rather wait and I'll bring it around?"

"I don't mind walking."

"Sorry about the scene there."

"Are you always so hostile to immigrants?"

"Hostile? Are you kidding? That guy just doesn't get it yet. A couple more years here, he'll be fine. Right now he's still fighting for territory," he said as he took a good look at her. Her fine blonde hair was flying straight up, and her glasses were slightly askew.

"All my grandparents were immigrants. You know the potato famine in Ireland? In Italy, in the late eighteen hundreds, it was a string shortage. A very severe string shortage, which would explain why my father's mother hoarded string."

"Are we almost there?" Terry asked.

"Right over here," Sal motioned. "You know what else she hoarded? My grandmother? Paper bags. She used to have a box labeled 'Torn paper bags.'"

"You're pulling my leg."

"Swear to God."

Terry seemed unsure.

They walked down some steps, and entered the short-term parking lot. Sal put Terry's bag in the trunk as she opened the back door and got in. He almost protested and insisted that she get in front, then decided against it. Give her a chance to relax, get to know him, and then he would suggest it.

"So, where're we going?" he asked.

"The hotel."

"The hotel? Okay. I guess that's one limiting factor."

"Just a moment. It's the Waldorf, or ... wait, that was last time. I know I wrote it down somewhere," she said as she fumbled through her purse.

"Take your time. I've always wanted to witness an archeological dig," Sal said as he looked in the rear-view mirror and watched her rummage through her things. She seemed like all the ditzy tourists he'd ever picked up. He put a tape in his cassette player and headed out of the parking lot.

"Okay, it's the Marriott Marquis on -"

"Broadway and forty-fifth."

"Exactly. Thank God someone in this city is competent," she said as she put everything back in her bag and pushed her glasses up on top of her head.

"Sounds like you've been here before."

"Many times."

"Well, it's a great city."

"I've seen most of them. They all lose their novelty after awhile."

"Not this one. I've been living here my whole life, and I'm still asked to take people places I've never even heard of. Besides, there's novelty in never knowing *where* I'm gonna go. Someone gets in, they tell you where to go. Then they get out, someone else gets in, and voyla, I'm off again."

"'Voyla?'" I think you mean 'voila.'"

Sal made a motion with his finger as if he were scoring a point on an imaginary scorecard. "Got another one."

"Excuse me, are you mocking me?"

"Not at all. I just knew you'd correct me."

"And how did you know?"

"A cabby gets to be a good judge of people."

"So, you think I'm a snob."

"Oh no. If you were a snob, you *wouldn't* have corrected me. You would have been smug about it and told your friends about the dumb cabby who pronounced 'voila', 'voyla.' But you corrected me because you're a real person."

"And you're a sneak."

Sal caught her expression in his rear-view mirror. She had that semi-dazed look so many people have at the airport. He figured it was just a temporary feeling of being a little lost. But since he didn't travel much, he wasn't entirely sure. He looked again and saw her staring out the window.

"So, how come you want a tour if most cities are so dull?"

"I've done the Manhattan thing, Statue of Liberty, Empire State Building ... even a walking tour or two. Your brochure sounded interesting. I always wanted to explore the other boroughs of New York, but I didn't know where to begin. I'm interested in the different ethnic neighborhoods, too."

"Yeah, well, I'm an ethnic myself. In fact, I'm two ethnics, Italian and Jewish. Hey, here's a joke for you: What do you do for a living when you're half Italian and half Jewish?"

"You drive a taxi."

"That's pretty good! But wrong. You work in the diamond district cutting rhinestones," he said, laughing at his own joke.

"I'll trust that that's funny."

"It is. You know, Jews work in the diamond trade and Italians are into glitz."

"I'll have to take your word for it."

"Does this music bother you?" he asked suddenly.

She hadn't even really noticed it. "Ummm ... I can't make up my mind."

"You don't know if it bothers you? That's not the same question as, 'Do you like it?'"

"I understood the question."

"You have to think about whether it bothers you?"

"Yes. Is that so unusual?"

"Most people, they know if they're bothered by something or not. If you have to think about it, you're not bothered," he said. But she didn't respond. "It's Carmina Burana by Carl Orf. It's choral music. A lot of people make the mistake of taking it too seriously."

"And why is that?"

"Why do they make that mistake? You mean, with this particular piece or with music in general or with -"

"Just my luck to get the only taxi driver in New York who actually speaks *too much* English."

"Now, *that* was funny. So, what do you want to do on your tour besides meet the natives?"

"What do you suggest?"

"Anything in the brochure that piqued your interest?"

Terry sighed. Was she tired or was he annoying her?

"Take Coney Island. Now, I'm not saying it's like it used to be, but it's still worth seeing for historical and cultural reasons. And then there's all the other neighborhoods. I can teach you something about the history. You'll even get to meet some real live natives and eat some great ethnic food. No extra charge for the *agita*."

"Agita?"

"Indigestion."

"Sounds like a full day."

"Isn't that what you wanted?"

"Yes."

"You sound unsure."

"I guess I wasn't aware that your business had folded so long ago. Manny made a brief reference in our last conversation, but by then I had already paid."

"You saying you want your money back?" Sal asked, shocked.

"No, no. It's not that. It's just ... are you sure you have the time to do this?"

"Sure. I can pretend I'm still in the business."

"What happened to your business? Your partner, Manny, didn't say much."

"He's not my partner anymore. What happened is: nothing happened. Then we ran out of cash."

"You were probably undercapitalized."

"That simple, huh?"

"I see it all the time."

"No kidding? What business are you in?"

"Real estate," she said, without explaining. Then she leaned her head back against the seat. "Do you mind if I smoke?" she asked, as she reached into her purse for her cigarettes.

"Sorry, it's not allowed."

"Not allowed? By whom?"

"It's company policy."

"But isn't this your taxi?"

"You got it."

"So, if you own the taxi, then you set the rules, don't you?"

"Right again."

"So what company are we talking about?"

"My company."

"Jeez Louise. Don't tell me you're one of those health food fanatics who believes they can live forever if you only eat foods starting with the letter Q and only on alternate full moons?"

"It's actually alternate gibbous moons, if you must know."

He thought he saw her smile slightly.

"Do you usually work on Saturday?" she asked.

"Frequently, yes. Why?"

"Maybe I'm imposing."

"Don't be silly. This is New York. You're being way too polite!"

"You're probably stuck in this cab all week. Why should you have to work tomorrow just to show me around Brooklyn?"

"Just? I don't think you realize how much there is to see in Brooklyn. Did you know that one in eight Americans were either born there or lived there?"

"Note the past tense. They all move out and become dewey-eyed from a distance."

"*I* didn't move out."

"Yet."

"You got a crystal ball in your bag, or what?"

"It's a fact that most Americans don't remain in the place they were born." She paused, as if thinking. "And that fact alone fuels thousands of businesses … including mine."

"Well, I'm a lifer."

"Like a jail sentence?"

"It's called *commitment*."

"To a geographical location?"

"For your information, *home* is not just the intersection of latitude and longitude," he said. "Listen, I gotta get us out of this traffic. I'm gonna take another route. It might not be direct, but at least we'll get there some time today."

"Fine."

Sal took the Queens Boulevard exit, but it was just as slow as the highway. "It's rush hour. There's no fast way."

"I'm not in a hurry anyway."

"You hungry?"

"Actually, yes."

"Then let's stop for a quick bite."

"How about the White Castle we just passed? Fast food is my weakness."

"You know what I think? I think the words 'fast' and 'food' shouldn't be allowed in the same sentence. Correction - not even in the same paragraph or -"

"Point taken. So what do you suggest?"

"There's a great little kosher pizza place used to be right around here. Can't be far."

"And pizza's not fast food?"

"Yeah, but at least it's kosher."

Sal turned a few corners looking for the pizza place, finally found it and parked. He got out and held the cab door for Terry. As she stood up, he realized she was really tall. Had to be about five nine. She had brushed her hair in the cab. He got a good look at her and was surprised to realize she was pretty. Her hair was shoulder length and light blonde, her eyes a light amber. She was only about a head shorter than he was, which he liked. But she looked tired, and her clothes were a little rumpled.

He opened the door to "Jerusalem II Pizza And Falafel." The place hadn't changed. There were the same diamond-shaped mirrored tiles all over the walls and the same five Formica tables with plastic chairs that he remembered. Of course, there were a lot more cigarette burns in the countertop than he remembered. And, sure enough, there were the required travel posters of Israel, complete with yellowed scotch tape.

"Don't you love that smell? You gotta try their falafel. Not at all greasy. They use olive oil so you don't have to worry about the fat. It's a monosaturate, which is actually good for you."

The pale young man behind the counter asked for their order. He couldn't have been more than twenty-one.

"What happened to Moshe?" Sal asked.

"Moshe Waldman?" the young man asked.

"Yeah. He used to own this place."

"He sold it last year. To my father."

"Is the falafel still so good?" Sal baited.

"You tell me," the young man answered without expression.

"The lady here's an out-of-towner. Never had falafel before. I'm trying to impress her," he said with an obvious wink.

The young man made a face that told Sal he was being placated, and went to work on their orders. Good old Moshe would have played along.

"He's no Moshe," Sal said quietly to Terry. "Moshe and I used to have these wild theological discussions. He came from Israel. I think he even had a relative in the Knesset. He knew something about everything, Moshe."

They were standing side by side at the counter, staring into the mirror on the opposite wall. Sal ran his hand through his short dark hair. Maybe it was too short. He never liked how it got spiky when it was like this. And, he could see he needed a shave. He could never go more than eight hours before he started to look like a bum, and he felt self-conscious standing there, next to Terry. Not that she was dressed so great herself. Still, in *her* eyes he figured he probably looked like some low-life New York cabby who didn't even bother to shave before going to work.

"And how do *you* know so much? I don't get the feeling that you're a Ph.D who's driving a cab because he can't get a job," she asked.

"I'm an autodidact."

"An auto-what?"

"Autodidact. Self-educated."

"You didn't go to school?"

"Dropped out of high school at sixteen. It's a long stupid story."

"Is the condensed version less stupid?"

"The condensed version is that I thought I was hot stuff working for my uncle in construction and making what I thought was good money. So what did I need school for?"

Terry nodded as if considering what he said. "That's certainly the condensed version."

"The rest is ...." he paused and sighed. "Nothing worth talking about."

"Good. Let's eat," she said as she took her plate of falafel and turned toward the tables. "An English-speaking, autodidact cabby who listens to classical music, eats kosher food, and lectures me about smoking and low-fat diets. It's going to be an interesting trip," she said with a smirk, but was she making fun of him?

He brought his tray over to a small table and sat down. Terry joined him.

"So," she began, between bites of falafel, "how do I know that I can trust you for an entire day in the remote recesses of Brooklyn?"

Sal laughed. "You know, most women worry about that, but none have ever come out and actually said anything."

"And how do you know what most women worry about?"

"I have women friends who tell me things," he explained between bites.

"And I have men friends who tell *me* things."

"Oh yeah, like what do they tell you?" he asked, intrigued.

"I'll wager I know the very first thought any man has when he meets any woman."

"Okay. What are you betting?"

"This meal. If I'm wrong, it's on me."

"You're on," Sal said.

Terry took a sip of her drink. "The very first thing a man thinks when he meets a woman, *any* woman, for the first time is," she paused for effect, "'*Would* I have sex with her?'"

Sal burst out laughing.

"And the *second* thing?"

"'*Could* I?'"

Sal choked on his Coke.

"Looks like dinner's on you, Mister Autodidact."

CHAPTER TWO
Park Slope/President Street

After dropping Terry off at the Marriott, Sal headed home. It was eight o'clock. He had planned to work even later, but changed his mind. Driving in rush hour traffic always knocked him out. Terry sure as hell seemed like a snob at first. But there was something tough about her too. A rough edge. A woman in real estate probably had to be tough. And it had to be high-end real estate if she was rich. Sal's Uncle Eli used to do that kind of thing down in Brazil. It was a fluke. He wound up there as a young guy in the Merchant Marine and went looking for a synagogue to say Kaddish for his father. The few Jews down there took him in immediately. Somehow one thing led to another, and before long he was helping them get loans from banks in America and keeping a small percentage. But, like his mother used to say, "A small percentage of a lot of money is still a lot of money." And then Eli invested in real estate.

Maybe Terry was as rich as Eli? Nah. She definitely didn't give that impression. If she was rich, why didn't she have a limo waiting for her at the airport? Why was she wearing such ugly clothes?

He took the FDR south to the Brooklyn Bridge and headed home, to Park Slope. Bennie should be in his PJs by now. Hopefully, Pop hadn't had any trouble giving the kid his bath and washing his hair.

"Hey! Where are you guys?" he called as he walked in. The downstairs was dark and quiet. A ray of light from the streetlight outside made its way in the front window and illuminated the old brick fireplace with its crowded mantel full of photos, toy cars, Lego blocks, and a small Lladro statue his mother had loved. He lingered a moment, considering the still life on his mantel and the scraps of red and pink construction paper strewn about the floor. Bennie must've been making valentines.

He walked into the dim living room, to the mantel, picked up the statuette of a mother and her child, and ran his hand over it. It was still so smooth. He used to love to touch it when he was a kid. It hadn't been on the mantel since his mom died, fourteen years ago. Pop must've set it out recently.

"Up here," his father called out.

Sal slowly walked up the long, steep staircase. The banister was loose again. He'd have to fix it again. The truth was, the whole house needed work. An old brownstone like this needed more attention than a child.

"Hi," he said, as he walked into the large old bathroom, warm and cloudy with steam.

"Look, Papa, I'm at the car wash," Bennie said as he buffed his bare behind against the bath towel his grandpa held around him.

Bennie had a thing for car washes. For brushes of all kinds, actually.

"Pretty neat," Sal said as he sat down in the barber chair his dad had installed in their bathroom after he retired. Sal had protested, but Joe had insisted. He wanted to make a little extra money cutting hair at home. Eventually, Sal had to put the kibosh on it, though. Somehow, instead of having fewer customers after closing the beauty parlor, Joe had more. People loved to come over, drink wine or tea, and chat with him. It was more a social club than a business, and there were just too many people coming through the house for Sal's comfort. Joe liked the company, but it made Sal nervous. Now Joe only cut the hair of a few old men he had known for years. It was safer for Bennie this way, Sal felt.

"Shake the towel, Grandpa," Bennie ordered. "Make it like the car wash."

Joe slowly moved the towel back and forth. "Some kid, huh?" he said to Sal. "Today we saw … how many Bennie? Four or five sweepers?"

"Six! We saw the little one by the hospital too!"

Bennie was obsessed with street sweepers. Since he was three he got excited watching them, and if he saw one off in the distance he made Sal chase it.

"Did you ever see that little one by the hospital, Papa? It only has one brush."

"Nope."

Joe put down the towel. "That's enough, Bennie Boy. Grandpa's too tired now." Then he turned to Sal. "He won't let me give him a haircut," he said, gently grabbing Bennie's bangs in one hand and making a snipping motion with two fingers of his other hand. "Two snips! One, two, and it's over," he said. But the boy pulled away. "What's the matter? You don't like Grandpa to cut your hair anymore?"

"It tickles," Bennie complained.

"So, I'll use powder," Joe offered.

"I think he's allergic to the powder, Pop," Sal said.

"You don't look so good, Sweetheart," Joe said to Sal as Bennie dashed out of the bathroom, completely naked.

"I'm a little tired."

"Did you eat any dinner? I made a nice sauce."

Sal stood up. "I'm not hungry. I'll put Bennie to bed. You go rest."

"You could use a haircut too," Joe said.

"A haircut? Look how short it is!"

"Not a *real* haircut. A shape. A style. Or something," he gestured at his son's head, indicating disapproval. "You're using conditioner, like I told you?"

"It doesn't make any difference," Sal said.

"Now you're the barber in the family? Here, let me do something," he said as he approached Sal, reaching for his head.

"Hey! Not tonight, okay? It's late."

"You want me to tuck him in? I thought you'd want to study a little," Joe offered.

"I'm too tired to concentrate. Go watch your nature shows."

Joe went downstairs and turned on the television. Sal knew how exhausting it was for the old man to care for his son every day after school. It was only on Wednesday afternoons, during Bennie's Hebrew School, that Joe got a little break during the week. At seventy, Joe was incredibly spry, but still no match for Bennie. It wasn't the physical work that exhausted Sal, though. It was the emotional work. The listening. The explaining. The constant thinking about what the little boy was doing and feeling and needing. He remembered his mother saying to him, just after he got married, that to a child, a parent is the sun, moon, and stars. And if you couldn't be as constant and predictable as that, then it was better to wait until you could be. So he waited until his relationship with Angela would be like that. Only it never was.

Sometimes being the sun, moon and stars to Bennie overwhelmed him, so he didn't really understand why he wanted another child. But even through his fatigue and frequent self-doubt, he knew he did. Badly.

Sal called out to Bennie, "I'm cleaning up the bathroom, and then I'm coming right in to tuck you in. Okay?" The little boy didn't answer. He waited. Then called out again. Still, no answer. He walked into Bennie's room. It was dark and there was a lump under the covers. The little boy was hiding. It was an old game they played and, though Bennie still loved it, Sal sometimes found it tiresome. Still, he hadn't seen the boy all day and he'd missed him. Obviously, Bennie felt the same way.

"Boo!" Bennie shouted and leaped out from under his blanket.

Sal scooped the skinny little kid up into his arms, taking in the delicious smell of his clean wet hair and powdered body. He was small for eight, his skin was still the virginal soft skin of a baby, his forehead still wide, his nose still the small button he was born with. And his eyes: he had Angela's large, luminous blues.

"I didn't know ghosts were ticklish," Sal teased.

Bennie jumped back into his bed.

"Papa, I know there's no such thing as ghosts, but," he paused, with a serious look, "what happens if a dead person wants to come back for a little while just for a visit?"

Sal covered up his son good and tight. Even though he was eight, Bennie still liked being swaddled, just like when he was a baby, and also demanded to sleep with all his stuffed animals and old worn-out baby blanket. Being small to begin with, Bennie looked much younger when he was asleep.

But where was this question coming from? Sal wondered. His son understood that death was forever. They had discussed it many times. He and Joe had agreed not to bullshit the kid. You bullshit your kid about the big things, they never trust you about anything.

"You think dead people want to come back, Bennie?"

"Maybe."

"Why would they want that?"

"They might want to see their family again."

"Dead people don't want anything, Bennie. They don't think. They don't feel. Being dead isn't much fun, but dead people don't know it, so it's okay. If you're afraid of something, then just tell me."

"I'm not scared, but I think Grampa wants Grandma to come back."

"Why is that?"

"He talks to her picture sometimes."

"He misses her," Sal explained.

"I know. I heard him tell Janet."

"Who's Janet?"

"Courtney's grandma."

"Who's Courtney?"

"My friend from across the street."

"Did I ever meet her?" Sal asked.

"I don't know. But her mother died a long time ago.

"Really? She lives with her grandmother?"

"Yeah. Her father lives in Jamaica, though." Then he paused. "Papa?"

"Yeah?"

"Do old people get married?"

"Sure. Sometimes. If they find the right person."

"But then, why do they get married if they're gonna die soon?"

"No one's getting married and no one's dying, Bennie. Those are really big changes in people's lives. And usually, especially with marriage, there's plenty of notice." He paused, then added, "With death you sometimes get notice too."

"Did you and Grandpa get notice with Grandma?"

"Yeah. Pretty much."

"I hope we get notice with Grandpa," he said.

"Grampa's not dying so soon, if that's what you're thinking. He's a healthy guy, and he's gonna live a long time."

"What if he doesn't?"

"Well, everyone's gotta die. We talked about all that, didn't we?"

"Yeah. But what if he dies before he gets married again?"

Sal started to answer and then stopped himself. He wasn't sure what to say anymore, and he was tired. He got in bed next to Bennie and kicked off his shoes. As he stared up at Bennie's ceiling, he smiled. He had painted it sky blue, and, with some huge sponges, he had painted white clouds on it because that was what Bennie had wanted. And, after Angela left, he went out of his way to make the boy happy. If a ceiling that looked like a sky did the trick, it wasn't much to ask.

"We can't know when someone's time is up, Bennie," he said, finally. "You know what I told you about that, right? You gotta love a person a lot *every day* because we never know when their time is up. Every day is important. You can't say 'Today isn't as good as tomorrow because tomorrow I'm going to a birthday party and today I'm not,' right? What did I teach you?"

14

"Carpe diem."

"Exactly. What's special about *this* moment? With me and you together, and Grampa watching television downstairs?"

"I like listening to the TV downstairs. It sounds far away. And then I try to listen to it for as long as I can before falling asleep."

"Yeah, I know. I used to like to do that too. And sleeping in my parents' bed -"

"Can I, Papa? Please?"

"Oh crap, what did I say that for? Not tonight, Bennie. I'm going to sleep early." He braced himself for a showdown: begging, crying ... but Bennie too was tired.

"Sal? Sal! Phone call!" Joe called up the stairs.

"Be right there," he called back. "Listen, Bennie, maybe tomorrow night we'll cuddle up together and watch a Godzilla movie in bed, okay? The video store got one I don't think you've seen. Now I gotta go see who's on the phone." He stood up and stepped back into his shoes, then bent down and kissed the boy on the cheek. Bennie reached up his skinny arm and draped it around Sal's neck, pulling him in closer. It was the gesture of a lover. The first time Bennie did it he was shocked, and then moved to tears. Joe told him he too had done this as a little boy. Children can be that passionate. That was something Sal never knew. Children's emotions had always struck him as shallow and fleeting. But now he knew better.

It confused Sal that during intimate moments with his son, he found himself wanting more children and wondering what they might look like. Somehow, in his heart, he felt that Bennie was really supposed to be one of many of his children, part of a larger family that he should have created already. He had to catch himself sometimes when he described Bennie as his "oldest." He knew these other children only existed in his imagination, but they seemed so damned *real*.

Sal felt Bennie's hands patting his hair, as if comforting him. He had to gather the two small hands in his and remove them in order to stand up. "See ya tomorrow, Big Boy," he said gently. He kissed the boy again on his forehead and started to leave.

"Papa?"

"Yeah?" Sal asked, pausing in Bennie's doorway.

"If Grampa gets a new wife, would Grandma still be my grandma?"

"You mean Grandma in heaven? Sure! She's always gonna be your grandma even though you two never even met. No matter what happens, she's your grandma. Now go to sleep or you'll get up too late to watch your cartoons."

"It's a woman," Joe mouthed, as he handed Sal the phone.

"Yeah, what's up?" Sal said into the phone.

"Is that how you answer your phone?" she asked.

"It's my house. I'll answer the phone any way I like." Then he paused. "I hope this isn't a crank call 'cos I'm kinda cranky already," he said, and motioned to his father to turn down the volume of the television on the counter. Joe had been watching it as he made his tea.

"This is Terry," she said.

"Oh, hi."

She was quiet for a moment. "I was thinking about the tour tomorrow," she said and stopped.

"Yeah, and ...?" Sal asked.

"I've been giving it some thought, and I'm not sure I feel comfortable with the whole thing."

"What '*thing*'? You mean *me*. You're not comfortable with *me*. I can understand that, I'm a total stranger. Even though we just had a nice supper in a restaurant, I can understand -"

"*That* was a restaurant?" Terry laughed.

Sal could see that his father was sticking around on purpose. Joe didn't want to miss his TV show, but he was curious. He was probably thrilled there was a woman calling, *any* woman. He was fishing around in the closet for some cookies to go with his tea. Trying to look busy.

"Look, I'm not gonna jump your bones, if that's what you mean. I told you, I'm strictly business."

Joe's eyes widened.

"That's not what I'm concerned about," Terry said.

"And I'm not crazy or violent. I never hit anyone in my entire life ... well, except Dennis Annunziata in the eighth grade. But he - "

"I'm not afraid of you, Sal."

"So what's the story? You called Manny and he made a special deal for you and -"

"And I'm not sure it was a great idea after all."

"What happened? Was it the falafel? My lousy jokes? I know it wasn't my road rage 'cos I don't have that. You know what I suffer from? 'Road Disbelief.' I just can't friggin' *believe* half the stuff I see on the road every day. Remember that show, 'How'd They Do That'? I'm always wondering: *why'd* they do that? Now *that* would be an interesting show."

Terry was silent.

"Maybe I talk too much. You want me to shut up?"

"No. It's not that," she said. "I mean, yes, you do talk too much, but I don't mind."

"You're not afraid of me, and you don't mind my talking too much. So, what is it?" he asked, not sure he wanted an answer.

"I think I should just spend a quiet weekend alone. I have a lot planned for next week."

"You want to spend a *whole weekend* alone in a hotel room watching over-priced movies and drinking five dollar thimbles full of Ginger Ale while staring at a bed the size of the Queen Mary? What do people do in those rooms, anyway, that they need a bed that's wider than it is long?"

"I'm sure I don't know."

Why was he fighting so hard? Why *not* just let her off the hook? What the hell did he care? He'd give her her damned money back and sleep late for a change. Still ... there was something that bothered him about her change of mind. Was it really possible that someone could be *that* worried about imposing? Only one way to find out.

"Okay, look. It's your call. But just for the record: I am more than willing to do this. I am *eager* to do it. In fact, I am *dying* to do it, to tell you the truth. I miss doing it. So you'd be doing me a favor."

Joe suddenly turned from the counter and gave Sal a look.

"Okay," Terry said.

"You serious?"

"Yes. Why?"

"I didn't think that would work."

"You were lying?"

"No! I was just trying to figure out if you were really that polite or if it was really something else."

"If it were something else I would have told you, believe me."

"Okay. Great. Fine. Be ready at eight. I'll pull into the cab line by the entrance to the theater. Be sure to be waiting for me."

"Eight o'clock in the morning? Are you serious?"

"Yeah, I'm serious. I'll have to get up at six-thirty. But you can sleep later."

"Look, tomorrow isn't a work day. Can't we make it a little later?"

He heard her sigh again, and also noticed Joe sitting at the table, eating his anisette cookies and sipping his tea. His father gave him a look. It meant, "Be nice. This is a *woman* you're talking to."

"If you really think we need to get started that early, then eight is okay."

"It's a big borough."

"Okay, I'll see you at eight."

"Listen, Terry, wear comfortable shoes and dress in layers and bring an umbrella in case it rains and -"

"Sal."

"Yeah?"

"I'm from Wisconsin, remember? I know how to dress for the cold."

"Is it that much colder in Wisconsin?" he asked.

"Is this the general level of conversation I can look forward to? Talking about the weather?" Her tone was more teasing than sarcastic.

"Hey, you gotta keep up your end, you know."

"You never said that was part of the deal."

"Hell, one of us better be interesting or it's gonna be a long day," he said, finding himself enjoying the conversation.

"I have a feeling it's going to have to be you," she teased.

"You think I'm interesting?" he asked, flattered.

"It's more that you have the potential."

"I have the *potential* to be interesting? You mean since I talk so much I'll eventually hit on something that actually interests you?"

"You know what is decidedly *un*interesting?" she asked.

"What?"

"This conversation. It's giving me a rash. I'll see you tomorrow," she said, and hung up.

"Is this lady a customer?" Joe asked.

"I'm giving her a tour. She's from out of town." He sat down and looked more closely at his father. "You look tired, Pop. Is Bennie giving you trouble?"

"Bennie?" he laughed. "Bennie is what keeps me young," he said, and dipped his cookie in his tea. "So, maybe you'll like this woman," Joe said.

"Whatever."

"What 'whatever'? Why don't you go out anymore? You used to." He paused, then said, "I'll make you a tea," and got up. Sal didn't stop him.

"I'm getting too old to chase women."

"Who says you should chase? There's a nice woman right here on the block who likes you," he said as he filled the teakettle and turned on the gas.

"Location counts with real estate, Pop, not women."

Joe opened the cupboard filled with colorful tea boxes. "What kind you want? You got so many here. You never drink them."

"It doesn't matter. Whatever you grab. And if you're talking about Mochelle, I'm not interested."

"What's wrong with her?"

"She's not that bright, and her parents aren't exactly cooking with gas either. What kind of name is Mochelle? I bet they spelled the name wrong on her birth certificate and didn't even realize it."

"Who cares how she spells her name? What's the matter with you?"

"It's not just that. You can't have a discussion with her. I took her out for dinner once, remember? To a fancy restaurant. I told her she could have 'carte blanche' and she asked, 'Is it good?'"

"So, she doesn't talk French, what do you care?"

"Then we were talking about politics, and I said something about the president having veto power, and you know what she said?"

"What?"

"She said, 'Who's Vito?'"

"You want Kissinger? Maybe Einstein too?"

"You and Mom talked about everything."

"We were married thirty-five years. When *you're* married thirty-five years you'll talk about everything also!"

"I want someone I can make conversation with. Do you realize she's only eighteen years older than Bennie?"

Joe put the Red Zinger tea bag in the mug and sat down again.

"Twenty-six is a grown woman! What's wrong with you? Always finding fault. When was the last time you went out with a woman, eh? You're a handsome man. If you let me fix up your hair - "

"Forget about my hair, will ya? I had dinner with a woman just tonight, for your information."

Joe's bushy eyebrows shot up. "Really? Who? Someone I know?"

"The woman for the tour tomorrow."

"Ah!"

"Stop with the 'ah.' We were stuck in traffic and we were both starved, so I pulled over. That's all."

"Ascoltami, Sweetheart, please. You're always rushing around. Life passes people by who pass *it* by. Believe me. I know. How can *you* be too old for anything when I'm seventy and I'm ready for anything?"

"You had a different life than me."

"Had? It's all over now? Look how you talk. When I was your age - "

"When you were my age mom was still alive and you had a great relationship."

"So? You'll have a great relationship too. Why not? You're entitled."

"Yeah, but what can I offer a woman? A kid that's not hers, an over-sized, broken down old house, and a small paycheck."

"What did I offer your mother when I asked her to marry me and I was only nineteen years old and living at home?"

"I thought you were twenty-one when you got married?"

"I was. Our parents made us wait. A good thing because when I was nineteen I had nothing, but by the time I was twenty-one I had *next* to nothing. See? Things change," Joe said with a small smile.

"Twenty-one and without a kid. I'm forty-three, Pop. And I have responsibilities."

"Sweetheart, in ten years, ten *short* years, that responsibility will get up and march out that door and go to college. And what will you have then? A lot of gray hair and a lot of tea you never drink!"

"Bennie likes the pictures on the boxes," Sal said. "So, you're telling me to get married already."

The teakettle whistled. Joe pushed himself up out of the chair and turned off the flame. He poured the water into the coffee mug that said "World's Best Dad" and brought it back to the table. Placing it in front of his son, he said, "Already? What is it, five years?" he asked, without sitting down.

"Six."

"Six years. Okay, I won't say 'companionship' since you hate when I use that word. But you need a person who's for you and you're for her. That's all." He stood next to Sal.

"It's been longer for you," Sal stated, building his case.

"Fourteen years," Joe said, softly. "I should have remarried a long time ago."

"Yeah? You think so?"

"You don't?"

"We've done okay, just us three. We made a home and a life for Bennie. It's not so bad. Except ...."

"Except what?" Joe asked.

"I wanted a larger family. You know, more kids."

Joe shook his head. "You don't have the time to look for a wife, but you want more kids? What's the matter with you?"

Sal ignored him. He shouldn't have said it. He knew it made his father a little crazy every time he mentioned it. But sometimes he just needed to say it. As if in the saying, the solution would show itself.

"I saw the statue is back on the mantel," Sal stated.

"Yeah, yeah. It doesn't make me cry now."

"That's good, Pop."

"Life goes on. Don't wait so long, Sweetheart. Like I did."

"It's so complicated," Sal said, breathing deeply, feeling tired just thinking about the whole process of meeting and dating women.

"*You're* making it complicated."

"Adults don't make new friends past a certain age. People are closed up. Too busy. Too set in their ways," Sal said as he poured sugar in the tea and stirred.

"A single woman wants to meet a man, and a single man wants to meet a woman. It's like when you turn on this radio," Joe said, walking to the counter and clicking on the old plastic radio. There was static. "The waves are out there in the air, invisible." He waved his graceful old barber's hands. "Until you turn on the radio, you don't even know about them. But that's why we have a radio, right? So we can find the waves."

"There's an analogy in there somewhere," Sal said, and got up. He walked to the counter, turned off the radio, and patted Joe on his shoulder. "But I'm too tired to find it."

"Just try a little bit, okay, Sweetheart?" Joe asked, and petted Sal on the cheek. Sal nodded his head.

Joe went back to the table and cleared his own cup and saucer. He was still such a handsome man, even at this age. His white hair was as thick and wavy as ever. Sal often wished he had the same hair. Instead, his was coarser and a little wiry. Joe's eyes were still a clear brown. And he was still a decent height, too. Like Sal, Joe had started out at six foot two. Even after some shrinkage, Sal figured Joe wouldn't disappear the way some old folks did. Yeah, he looked pretty good, Sal realized. Even better lately somehow.

"I bought Bennie a little box of chocolates, for Valentine's Day next week," Joe said, placing the dishes in the sink. "Not too big. I know you don't like him eating too much junk."

"It's okay, Pop. He's expecting it." He and his father had been buying Bennie chocolates for Valentine's Day since the boy was two years old. And, of course, they always got him a card with a cute little furry animal on it. Preferably a kitten. They had stopped buying stuffed animals because his collection was growing at such an alarming rate that soon enough they'd need a separate room just for the toys.

"Maybe next Valentine's you'll be buying for someone other than Bennie," he began. But Sal cut him off.

"Was Bennie talking about death today, Pop?" he asked, as he sipped the tea off the teaspoon, testing to see if it was still too hot.

"To me? Not a word. Why?"

"He's all of a sudden worried about missing dead people and them missing their families."

"Maybe he misses *his* family," Joe offered.

Sal took an anisette cookie from the tin. "Angela?" he asked.

"Who else?"

"So, you think I did the wrong thing? Now he's getting older?"

"I don't know, Sweetheart. If I didn't know Angela, maybe I'd think so." He paused, then walked over to the table and sat down. "But you forget? I knew Angela."

They were both quiet, listening to the hum of the refrigerator and the rumble of the hot water heater. The television played silently on the counter.

Joe reached across the old kitchen table and patted his son's hand, then stood up and walked to the counter, reached behind the toaster, and pulled out an envelope.

"Yeah, I knew Angela too," Sal said, softly.

Joe sat back down at the table and handed the envelope to Sal. "This came," he said.

Sal took the opened envelope from his father, held it momentarily, then took a deep breath. He knew what it was without looking, and even if he didn't, Joe's eyes said it all.

CHAPTER THREE
Marriott Marquis/45ᵗʰ & Broadway

8ᵗʰAV. - 43-44 STREET 29/04/09

"Sweetheart, come on, wake up! Aren't you supposed to pick someone up this morning?" Joe asked, as he leaned over Sal's bed.

"Holy crap!" Sal shot up and looked at the clock. It was seven-thirty.

"You want me to make a little breakfast you can take with you?"

"No, I gotta fly," Sal said, as he jumped into his clothes.

"At least a cup of coffee, something -" said Joe as he followed Sal around the large master bedroom.

"Pop, I can't wait. I'll pick something up. Where's my watch?"

The old man shuffled around the messy room, moved a pile of National Geographic magazines, gathered together some stray dollar bills, and held up the watch.

"I always tell you. If you put things in their right place, you can always find them."

"I don't have a right place for my watch," Sal said as he scrambled toward the bathroom with Joe right behind him.

"I'm not talking about building another wing. Just a spot. A spot where you always put it. Like where I always put my denture glass," Joe persisted, as he handed the watch to Sal.

"Okay, I'll put my watch in your denture glass from now on."

"Don't be such a wise guy."

"You see my keys?" Sal asked, then squeezed some toothpaste onto his tongue, spread it around his teeth, and rinsed.

"Downstairs, on the hall table. Where else? Every night I find them, I put them there. Is this something new? Only for the last nine years. Why can't you remember that? What's so hard?"

Sal tiptoed past Bennie's room and went into the bathroom, where he started to shave.

"What's the plan for Bennie today?" he whispered to Joe, who stood in the doorway.

"He's gonna play with Courtney, across the street," he whispered.

"Yeah, he mentioned her. He's playing with girls now?"

"She's a lovely little girl. A little younger than him, but you know how girls are."

"He doesn't mind playing with girls?"

"Why should he mind?"

"Is she interested in street sweepers?" Sal asked. "Because that's what Bennie wants in a woman."

"She manages to get him interested in other things," Joe said.

Sal checked himself in the mirror. His dark eyes looked rested and he was neat. His jeans were clean and fit him well. He tucked in his denim shirt and buckled his brown leather belt with the Model T buckle. Maybe it was corny, but he loved it anyway. Stepping back from the mirror to get a more complete view, Sal was pretty pleased with what he saw. For forty-three, he wasn't bad to look at. He didn't have a pot belly like most guys his age, he wasn't losing any hair, and he had good muscle tone.

"So, he's played with this girl before?" Sal asked.

"Sure, sure. They're good friends."

"I gotta run, Pop," he said as he sprinted down the stairs.

"Be nice to this lady, Sal. You didn't talk so nice to her last night. She's a paying customer, and remember, you gotta keep your eyes open."

Translated, that meant Sal should consider her as wife material. Was he imagining it or was Joe getting pushier about this stuff lately?

When he was merging onto the Gowanus Expressway from the Prospect, heading toward the Battery Tunnel, Sal reached into the back pocket of his jeans for his wallet and realized he had forgotten it. Now he'd have to take the Brooklyn Bridge and get across town. No question about it, he'd be late. Maybe only by fifteen minutes if the traffic wasn't bad, but it was terrible. The BQE was crawling, of course, and there was a stalled car in one lane. Then he realized he'd have to stop back home to get his wallet. Crap. Did he have to invite her in? Would it be rude to make her wait in the car?

When he pulled up to the Marquis, he didn't see her. But he was half an hour late. Maybe she got pissed off and left. Leaving the car running, he got out and looked around. He considered running inside and phoning her up in her room, but he didn't know her room number. In fact, he didn't even know her last name. Great, just great. Now, how long should he hang out?

"Looks like we compromised," Terry said, as she approached, almost unrecognizable. Her hair was pulled up off her face, her make-up was fresh, and her light amber eyes were clear and rested. She wore jeans with a pink cashmere turtleneck, and a black leather jacket tied at the waist.

"How's that?" he asked, a little flustered.

"You said eight, I said nine. It's eight-thirty," she said as she reached for the back door handle.

"I'm sorry I was late, Terry, I-"

"*You* were late? I thought *I* was late," she said as she turned back around to face him.

"You mean you just came down, now?"

"Yes."

"You mean you were half an hour late?"

"Yes. I said I was sorry. But you were late also, so -"

"Yeah, but *I* couldn't help it. Traffic, broken down cars, and -"

"I couldn't help it either. My wake-up call never came," she said as she opened the back door and started to get in.

"You're sitting in the back? What am I, a chauffeur?"

Terry backed out, slammed the door shut, and turned around to face Sal. "You know, you're awfully contentious for a man who only yesterday convinced me that he actually *enjoyed* doing this," she said, her face beginning to look a little pinched.

"Yeah well, maybe now *I'm* the one having doubts."

"I'm beginning to see why your business failed. With that attitude."

"*My* attitude? Just because you're used to being chauffeured around - "

"How do *you* know what I'm used to?" she asked.

"How the hell could you be late after you agreed -"

"I had no control over it!"

"And what am I? The God of Traffic?"

"Who told you to take a route with the potential for traffic?"

"'Potential for traffic'? This is New York!" he shouted.

Terry must have realized she was still holding open the car door, so she slammed it. "Who told you you were even remotely qualified to give tours of a city if you -"

"Who told *you*," he cut her off, then stopped. They were in a full-blown argument, and he knew it was his fault. "Who told you to be so damned attractive all of a sudden? I don't do well with very attractive women."

She had trouble switching gears. He could see it. Her anger came to a dead stop, like a car at a light. Then she looked confused. Then she burst out laughing.

"It's true. Plus, I don't become a human being until my first cup of coffee, Sal said."

Terry opened the front door and got in. He walked around to the driver's side and got in also.

"How long do I have to wait for this transformation to occur?" she asked.

"I'll grab a cup at home. I have to stop there anyway. I left my wallet."

Terry didn't answer.

"Last night you looked pretty, I have to admit. I mean, even with that God awful wrinkled outfit. But I didn't realize that you were such a knockout. I'm sorry, it just makes me nervous."

"You have a talent for conversation-stopping," Terry said.

They were heading downtown on Broadway.

"I've always found this interesting," she added, looking out the window.

"Broadway? Yeah, I guess."

"Do New Yorkers go to the theater much?" she asked. "Or is it mostly out-of-towners?"

"I don't know about New Yorkers. But *I* don't."

"Why is that?"

"I don't have the time."

"Even on days off?"

"I spend them with my son, Bennie."

"How old is he?"

"Eight."

"He's lucky. A lot of fathers would rather play golf."

"Like yours?"

"Yes. What about yours?"

"Joe? Joe liked to play bocce when I was a kid growing up. He used to go all the way to East New York and play under the El with all these other Italian guys in tee shirts."

"Bocce?"

"Yeah, it's a game where you basically roll a ball and then try to hit that ball with the other balls. Whoever comes closest wins. Joe used to take me with him, but I got bored. So I'd go hang out with my friends, playing handball."

"He liked having you with him?"

"Oh, sure. He was always wanting me to tag along with him. I used to work in his barbershop too, when I was a teenager. For pocket money. I give a mean shave and shampoo."

"Your father was a barber?"

"Yep. Hey, you ever notice how all barbers have the same philosophy of life? I used to think it was just Joe, you know? No matter what he was talking to a customer about he always ended by saying 'Whaddya gonna do? You gotta live and let live.' "

"What about stylists?"

"Oh yeah, them too. Because they're all just glorified barbers. You find me one barber or stylist who doesn't say something like 'You gotta look the other way' or 'You gotta mind your own business' or 'It takes all kinds' at least once in your conversation, I'll pay you good money." He paused. "You have a hairdresser?"

"On again off again. I don't have the patience for salons."

"So, am I right? Does your hair dresser say things like that?"

"I don't get the same one every time, and I tend not to make much conversation."

"Why is that?"

"I don't know, actually."

"I'll tell you why. It's because you know they're gonna say something stupid like, 'It takes all kinds.' Why make conversation with someone who sums up everything with something like that? I only know one barber with a real opinion."

"Is that so?"

"Yeah. Jorge. He used to work for Joe, and he'd say all this negative stuff. One time he said to me, 'Sal, Brooklyn is a negative experience.' I said, 'Jorge, you're fifty-five years old, you've lived here your whole life. That's not exactly what you'd call an *experience* anymore. That's called a *life*.'"

"And what did he say?"

"'You gotta live and let live.'"

Terry laughed. "Was your father always a barber?"

"Pretty much. Eventually he opened a real beauty parlor because he figured that was where the money was. Women spend a lot more time and money on their hair than men do."

"He was right."

"Joe is usually right. I'll give him that."

"He's still alive?"

"I hope so. I left him home with Bennie."

She smiled. A real smile. And it made Sal feel good. Maybe it would be okay that she was so good-looking.

"So your father cares for your son. There's no wife?"

"No more."

"Divorced?"

"Yep. You?"

"Never married," she said, and then, after a brief pause, "do you mind if I ask why you got divorced?"

"No. But the real question is why did I get married?"

"For the same reason everyone else does. It's not such a mystery."

"It is to me," Sal said.

"They're running for shelter."

"That simple, huh?"

"For most people. It almost was for me."

"Almost?"

"Almost."

"But you didn't."

"No. I didn't."

"And you don't regret it?"

Terry paused, thinking about her response. "I only have one regret, and, well ...."

"Okay, I'll bite."

"Being childless."

"Oooh. I see," Sal said, and then stopped himself from asking the dozen or so things that popped into his head.

They were silent for a while as Terry observed the streets of the city and Sal tried to decide how far to push the conversation. How far did she *want* him to push?

"Do you find it difficult being single?" she asked.

"You mean with a kid?"

"Actually, I meant, do people seem to be uncomfortable about you being single and even give you a hard time about it?"

"Oh yeah, sure."

"Does it bother you?"

"Only when my pop does it, for some reason. It's like he's in some God-awful hurry for me to get married again. But it's different when you've been married once already."

"Really? How?"

"You know all the traps."

"You don't think someone who has never been married can see those traps by observing other people's marriages?"

Sal thought for a moment. "Nope. No way. You can see people getting divorced and you can hear about why it happened, but you can't know first-hand how they walked into those traps. That means you gotta be thinking, somewhere, in the back of your mind, that they could have avoided it. And, that *you* probably would have avoided it if it was you. Once you walk into a trap yourself, you know for real that you couldn't have avoided it. That makes getting married again kinda scary."

"It would seem equally valid that people can learn from those mistakes and so feel more hopeful about a second marriage."

"New marriage, new traps. Old lessons are null and void."

"So, there's nothing to be learned from a failed marriage?"

"Nope."

They were approaching the Brooklyn Bridge. Terry stuck her head out the window again.

"So, whaddya think?" Sal asked.

"It's smaller than I expected. But it's lovely."

"In its day it was a real big deal ... like going to the moon was for us."

"Really?"

"Oh sure. Until then people had to take a ferry across, and when the river froze they couldn't get to work. It's an incredible thing considering they didn't have the machinery and technology we have today. And, it was the tallest structure in the city, so when you walked across it, it was probably like being on top of the Empire State Building is for us."

"When was it built?"

"It was finished in eighteen eighty-three."

"You just happen to know that fact?"

"I was really into the Brooklyn Bridge during the centennial in nineteen eighty-three. I joined committees and everything. I don't remember much detail, but I'll always remember the date it was finished."

"What's that other bridge?" she asked, pointing.

"That's the Manhattan Bridge. And that one, farther up, is the Williamsburg Bridge."

Terry watched as a train slowly made its way over the Manhattan Bridge.

"Do trains go over this bridge also?"

"Not anymore. They used to, though. And trolleys too. But that was a while ago. Like nineteen forty-five or fifty or something like that."

"Is that because it's not strong enough?"

"What's the matter? You worried it's gonna collapse or something?"

"I have a touch of phobia about water."

"Well, we're not in the water. We're on the bridge. Do you have a touch of phobia about bridges too?"

"Only if they go *over* water."

Sal laughed. "Why didn't you tell me? I coulda taken the tunnel."

"That would've been even worse. It really is a grand old piece of architecture," she said, and then took a deep breath. "Now get me the hell off it."

CHAPTER FOUR
Park Slope/President Street

They made small talk as Sal negotiated the roads and tried to figure out where the hell he could have left his wallet. If he was lucky, Joe had spotted it and put it aside, knowing he was coming back. But if Joe had found it, he would've beeped him.

Sal turned the cab onto President Street. The brownstones were lined up like tired old soldiers trying their best to look spiffy. Some had their original stone exteriors, others had been painted or even covered with siding. But, in general, the block still had a gracious look, even with the small piles of dirty snow scattered everywhere.

Sal pulled up in front of his brownstone.

"Nice old place," Terry said.

"Thanks. Listen, I'd invite you in, but -"

31

"Oh that's okay. I wouldn't dream of imposing on your family."

There it was again. Her concern about imposing.

"You wouldn't be imposing. It's just that .... you know what? Come on in. You wanted to meet some natives, right? Well, Joe and Bennie are as native as they get."

"Oh no, really. You don't have to -"

Sal turned to face her. "Look, Terry, we gotta get something cleared up right now, okay? I don't do stuff I don't want to. I'm no push-over. And I don't think we're gonna have much fun today if I have to keep worrying about *you* worrying that you're imposing."

Terry held up her hand to stop him. "Okay. Point taken." She opened the car door and got out.

"Pop! We're here!" Sal called out as he opened the front door.

They could hear the Elton John song "Bennie and the Jets" coming from upstairs.

"You seen my wallet?" Sal called out.

Joe came to the top of the steps already neatly dressed, with shaving cream on his face and a straight razor in his hand.

"Now the wallet? What's the matter with you?" He went back in the bathroom and rinsed the cream off his face, then came back out.

"That answers that question. Where the hell'd I leave it?"

"Papa, you're back!" Bennie said as he ran down the stairs, still in his PJs.

"Just for a minute, Bennie. I came back for my wallet."

Joe came downstairs. "I'm Joe Iorio, Sal's father. Come. Come inside and make yourself at home," Joe said as he placed one arm partly around Terry's back and escorted her into the living room as if he had expected her.

Sal raced around the downstairs, then gave up and headed upstairs.

"I told you, Sal, a million times. Just pick a place for it. Did I say to build a whole wing? No, just a place. Everything in its place," Joe shouted up at him from downstairs. Then he turned to Terry. "Right, Terry?" he asked.

"I agree wholeheartedly."

"So, I hope he's giving you a good price. If he doesn't, you tell me. I didn't raise a son to be greedy."

Terry smiled politely. "He's been very fair, Mister Iorio."

"Mister? I'm so fancy I need Mister? Call me Joe."

"I like your aftershave, Joe. Old Spice?"

"You like it?" he said, a bit flustered.

"I think most women like Old Spice," she said, enjoying watching him blush a little.

"Well, this is just for me and Bennie. We're spending the day together."

"Aren't we going over to Courtney's, Grampa?" Bennie asked.

"Of course. That's what we have planned," he answered, and then, rather abruptly, "Now go eat your breakfast I made for you, Bennie."

"Will Janet make us roti again? For lunch?"

"We'll see. Now go eat."

Sal came downstairs waving the wallet. "Under the blanket. Should have looked there first."

"In *bed*? You went to sleep with your pants on?" Joe asked.

"I dozed off reading. I wondered what was poking me all night."

"He falls asleep with his clothes on, forgets to set the alarm, he's late, he can't find anything, doesn't eat breakfast, and runs out the door," Joe started his litany.

"Ready?" Sal asked Terry.

"Why don't you let me make you a quick little breakfast. A little eggs and - "

"We got a lot of ground to cover, Pop," he cut him off. But he could see that Terry was interested.

"Always in a rush. That's the problem. Instant this, quick that."

"Thank you for the offer, Joe," Terry said, holding out her hand.

"At least come back for supper," Joe insisted, as he held Terry's hand. "I have the sauce all ready, and I left out the meat. You'll pick up some macaroni, and I'll make a nice salad." Then to Terry he said, "Now he's a vegetarian."

"Being kosher is not the same as being a vegetarian," Sal said.

"Okay, okay. If I leave out the meat from the sauce then we can make garlic bread with real butter, right?" he asked.

"No meat in the whole meal?" Sal asked.

"Not a drop."

"May I use the bathroom while you two gentlemen work out the dinner arrangements?" Terry interrupted.

"Sure. Top of the steps, make a right, and it's -"

"I'll show her!" Bennie yelled and came running in from the living room. "If you lock the door it might not open, and then you'll get stuck in there," he said as he led Terry upstairs.

"We're not coming back for dinner," Sal whispered to his father when they were alone.

"You're gonna spend money on a meal when I can make something just as good here?"

"She's just a paying customer, Pop. I don't even know her."

"By the end of the day you'll know her."

"Why should I bother? She's from Wisconsin. You know where that is?"

"Am I stupid? Of course I know. My cousin Al lived in Chicago his whole life, and you know what? He wrote me all about it. I can even read!"

Bennie left Terry in the bathroom and ran back downstairs to eat breakfast. When she was finished, she lingered in the upstairs hallway, glancing in each bedroom. Taped along the corridor wall was a time-line, which was obviously some kind of school project of Bennie's. It began with the birth of his father, Sal, forty-three years ago, then his mother, Angela. So, that was her name. Born in nineteen fifty-seven. That made her just three years older than Terry. A gorgeous little girl with curly black ringlets all over her face, and deep blue eyes. At nineteen she was very thin, dressed sexily in a mini-skirt and tight top. And there, in nineteen eighty-seven, was Bennie.

Terry passed Bennie's room and immediately noticed the painted ceiling. The same blue sky as Sal's cab, with the same fat white clouds. She paused at the entrance to a bedroom she knew immediately had to be Sal's. His clothes were strewn about. The bed was unmade. Yet there was a sense of style to the room. Someone had hand-stenciled an interesting geometric border along the top of the walls. On his bookcase, which was stuffed to overflowing, were small picture frames, all with pictures of Bennie through the years. There was also an assortment of tiny antique glass bottles in all shapes and colors. On his night table she noticed a Hebrew workbook that a child would probably use. Maybe he and Bennie were working on it together. In the far corner of the room was a large potted tree that might be fichus. Hung all over the tree, hanging from strands of bright wool, were tiny metal cars, Tinker Toys, and other small objects she couldn't make out from where she was standing. Bennie's work, no doubt.

"I love that barber pole!" Terry exclaimed, as she came down the steps. "Is it from your old shop?"

"Sure it is. It's the original. It was there when I bought the store in.... " Joe stopped to think. "Nineteen forty-seven. Or maybe forty-eight, so who knows how old it really is."

"Did it ever revolve?" she asked.

"Of course! It still would if my son would let me do the wires right."

"It's bad enough we gotta have a barber pole outside our bathroom. We don't need it to revolve also."

"See what I mean?" Joe said, then turned to Sal. "Pick up some fresh macaroni at Scarola's, whatever kind you and your lady friend like, and call and tell me what time you think you'll be here."

As they were turning to leave, Bennie walked up to them holding a broken toy. "The little mustache brush fell off the street sweeper," he said as he handed the tiny street sweeper to Sal.

Sal took it and examined it quickly. "All it needs is some glue."

"I told you we'll buy glue later," Joe told Bennie. "We have no more."

Terry reached for the small toy. "May I see it?" she asked. Sal handed it to her. She examined it for a moment, then said, "Once a Girl Scout, always a Girl Scout," and stuck her hand into her purse. After fishing around she came up with a small tube of nail glue. "Always prepared," she said, as she sat down on a step, put down her purse, and searched inside for her glasses. Bennie scooted over to her and sat down.

"Why do you have glue in your pocketbook?" he asked.

"I don't know. I gave up on false nails years ago," she said, as she delicately squeezed the tube, coaxing out a small pearl of glue and then running it along the edge of the tiny brush. "This may hold it for today, but I wouldn't play too roughly with it. When you have a chance, pick up some Crazy Glue. It's great for non-porous surfaces like this," she said as she stood up.

Bennie was delighted as he took the toy from Terry.

"Let it set for about twenty minutes, okay?" she said.

Bennie put the toy street sweeper on the step.

"That's where you put it? You want it should get broken again?" Joe scolded.

Terry picked it up and placed it on the hall table. "I think it'll be safer here," she said, smiling at the boy.

"Can you fix my GI Joe too?" he asked.

"Enough, Bennie. We gotta go now," Sal admonished.

"When they come back for supper Terry will try, right?" Joe asked Terry, avoiding his son's eyes.

"Of course," she agreed. "And we'll pick up some glue in our travels today," she added.

Bennie was clearly pleased, but Sal wasn't. "Be good to Grampa, and remember, best behavior on your play date. Okay?" he said to his son, and bent down to kiss his cheek.

"Play date? I thought we were going over to Janet and Courtney's, Grampa?"

"We are."

"Who's Janet?" Sal asked.

"Courtney's grandmother," Joe explained.

"Oh yeah, right."

"Janet's gonna make us roti," Bennie offered.

"Yeah? She cooks for you?" Sal asked.

"She gives him lunch if he's there at lunchtime," Joe explained.

"They're the new family across the street?" Sal asked.

"New? They're here eight months already. Now you go and have a good time," Joe said.

"So long," Terry said. "Nice to meet you."

They closed the door behind them and headed down the front steps. Sal sighed heavily. What an ordeal. But the morning was clearing up, and the sun had just begun to shine, and his wish for a mild day seemed to be realized.

"Sweetheart," Terry said.

"Huh?"

"Joe called you 'Sweetheart'."

"Yeah, he always called us that."

"Us?"

"Me and my brother, Ike."

"Where does *he* live?"

"Long Island."

"I've never heard a grown man call another grown man Sweetheart," she said softly, more to herself than to him.

They got into the cab, Sal pulled away from the house, and headed down President Street.

"So your son likes Elton John."

"Huh?"

"It was on upstairs."

"Oh yeah. He likes that one song, 'Bennie and the Jets,' for obvious reasons. Sal started singing the lyrics: "He's got electric boots, a mohair suit -"

Terry interrupted him. "Isn't it '*She's* got electric boots?'" Terry asked.

"Crap, I think you're right! Let's just keep this between me and you okay?"

"My lips are sealed."

"Damn it! I forgot the coffee again. If you don't mind, we'll stop at Manny's before we head out."

"Fine with me. So, is dinner included in the price of the tour?"

"Sure. You can even pick the place. But I would suggest -"

"I meant, *Joe's* offer of dinner."

Sal was stunned. "First you're afraid of imposing, now you invite yourself to dinner?"

"I guess I'm a fast learner," Terry smiled. "And I didn't invite myself. *Joe* invited me." This was some gutsy broad, Sal thought. Then Terry asked, "Does Joe go out much?"

"What do you mean, 'out'?"

"I mean, does he see women?"

"Nah! He's too busy with Bennie. Why do you ask?"

"Well, he's a handsome man, and he was so neatly dressed."

Sal shrugged it off. "He's always been meticulous. Not like me, I guess."

"Does he always wear aftershave?"

Sal pondered her question for a moment. "Yeah, I guess. He's got that same bottle of Old Spice on his dresser forever."

"He looked like he was getting ready for a date."

"A date! Are you kidding me? Who would Joe go on a date with?" He changed the subject: "You ever hear of Flatbush Avenue?"

"I think so. Why?"

"We're on it. Manny's place is up the street."

"So I'll finally get to meet Manny."

"He's running his own store now. Cards, candy, nuts, and stuff," he said as he began to maneuver the cab into a parking spot. "In a desert of insanity, Manny is like ...." he considered for a moment, "an oasis of madness," he said, adjusting the steering wheel and turning off the engine.

CHAPTER FIVE
Manny's Candy & Nut House/ Flatbush Avenue

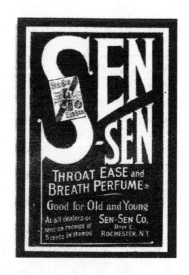

"Hey, Blood! What's the story? Hey, here's Terry!" Manny said from behind the counter.

"Just make with the coffee, Manny, and skip the welcome wagon," Sal said, glancing at the candy counter. "No licorice pipes today? What's the story? It's the one thing I ask."

"I told you, they're hard to get. One distributor. The guy was doing gummy candy years ago, for some reason he couldn't make a penny. Now everything's gummy: Coke bottles, bears, snakes."

Terry stared as Manny spoke. He was an absolutely huge man with a cafe-au-lait complexion. And he was totally bald. His sleeves were rolled up so she could see that both of his arms were covered with tattoos. She got the distinct feeling that most of the rest of him was covered with them also. His clothes were pretty normal, though - jeans, a flannel shirt, sneakers. He was eating something with an incredibly strong odor. She tried to place it.

"I told this guy a hundred years ago he was on to something, and he ignored me. Said Americans eat chocolate. Europeans eat gummy stuff. Well, *he* was wrong, *I* was right. Surprise! You know what I'd like to see, Sollie? Gummy historical figures. Make it educational. Then parents would let their kids eat more of it, ya know? Like gummy Abraham Lincoln."

"Say hello to Terry, Manny."

"Hey, Terry, what's up? How's this guy treating you?"

"Sal's a perfect gentleman, I assure you."

"'Sal'?" Manny looked at Sal suspiciously. "A Bar Mitzvah boy named Sal? Well, listen, '*Sal*,'" he began, sarcastically. "I wanna share something with you."

"You like the word 'share' in this context?" Sal asked Terry. "In this context it means he's gonna lay a trip on me."

"If you could hold onto a buck like you hold onto a grudge, we'd still be in business."

"If you could've held up your end, we'd still be in business."

"I managed to get the friggin' brochures all the way to Wisconsin, didn't I? Here's the evidence," he said, pointing to Terry.

"Yeah, two years too late," Sal accused.

"Well, better late than never," Manny answered.

"Screw that. Every time I come in here for a lousy cup of coffee, I have to hear this."

"So why do you keep coming?"

"It's free."

"Nothing's free, my friend. Now you gotta listen. You see all this Valentine's shit? Cards and stuff? It's a week before Valentine's Day, right? And I still got most of it. You know why? Half the people who get married in this country split up. There's millions of people walking around on Valentine's Day sad. Sad people don't buy nothing. But these same people, Sollie, they all have pets. You know how many people own pets in this country?"

"How many?" Terry asked.

"More than fifty percent! Can you believe that! I read it in <u>American Demographics</u>." Manny noticed Terry eyeing the candy in the case. "What do you like, Ter? You want some Licorice Allsorts? Here, let me get you some. Don't mess with the pink ones." He scooped up a huge amount of candy and poured it into a large plastic bag.

"Don't you think that's a little excessive?" Terry protested.

"Don't worry, Sollie will help you eat them, especially since they're free."

"What is that you're eating?" she asked.

"This stuff? Sen-Sen. Want some?" he asked, and, at the same time, plucked a small packet from a candy rack and handed it to her. She sniffed it, wrinkled her nose, and handed it back to him.

"I love the stuff. But it doesn't sell much anymore. So, like I said, fifty percent of everyone's getting divorced and more than fifty percent of everyone's got a pet."

"So now you're gonna tell me they're the same people, they get divorced, and then bingo, they get a pet?" Sal teased.

"A real wiseass. Let me show you something. Come here," he said as he stepped out from behind the counter and headed down a narrow aisle. He moved very gracefully, almost prancing on the balls of his feet. To Terry he seemed like a dancing bear.

Terry and Sal followed him down the aisle filled with red and pink cards and heart-shaped boxes. The back wall was covered end to end with valentines also, but these all had pictures of pets. They were organized by category: dogs, cats, birds, turtles, snakes, hamsters, mice.

"I don't even want to know," Sal said, as he surveyed the wall.

"I do. What's the idea, Manny?" Terry asked.

"See, Sollie? This lady has some brains. The idea is that I'm the only guy selling pet valentines in all of Brooklyn."

"That's not hard to believe," Sal said.

"Pet valentines have always been *from* the pet, these are *to* the pet. The guy who sold me these, at first, he didn't want to. You know why? He said I would lose my shirt. He didn't want to set me all up with them and then have to take them back. His commission and all that happy horseshit. The guy's a nobody. Walks around in a friggin' miasma, and he -"

"Miasma? What is that? You hear that, Terry? That was for you."

"The guy's got his head up his ass half the time. Telling me anything that has to do with pets won't sell, for God's sakes. I told him last year, I said give me whatever stock you have, I'll sell it and if I don't I won't stick you with it. You can keep your commission and buy the Jacuzzi. So he gave me what he had and I sold out! I mean it! This year I told the guy I needed more and so he gave me all this. It turns out it's all old stock, Sollie. They 'found' it in their warehouse. Never sold it. No one would even look at it a few years ago. And I can't get enough!"

Terry was browsing the cards as Manny spoke. She picked up a card from the Reptile section and read it: "'To my favorite boa. I love you moa and moa.' Very nice sentiment."

"A card to a snake? You mean people actually buy this crap?" Sal asked.

"People love their pets, Sollie. Pets don't overspend on your credit card or divorce you when your hemorrhoids stop you from seeing <u>Terminator Two</u> on a Saturday night."

"You wanted to show me valentines, you showed me valentines. Now we gotta go. Terry, you want a coffee?"

"Yes, please. Light and sweet."

"Just a sec. Maybe Terry wants to hear my proposition?" Manny asked.

Terry turned to face Manny, immediately interested, which bugged Sal. He thought for sure she was smart enough to know a kook when she met one.

"Okay. Here it is. It's a week before Valentine's and I'm selling these suckers like crazy. By Valentine's I'll be sold out.... except maybe for a few chameleons and spiders. They go in and out of fashion. If I sell out, like I expect, I'm gonna expand. And I need a partner. First I want to create 'Pet Day.' Like Mother's Day and Father's Day and Grandparent's Day. But I don't know how to get it started. I need some ideas and definitely some publicity. You know anything about that?" he asked Terry.

"Well, I'm not a PR expert, but I've come up with ideas for my company."

"Good enough. So here's the rest of it," he said, this time with his voice lower and checking the store to be sure no one else was around. "The other thing that I'm selling like crazy is stuff to do with astrology."

"You're really getting in on the ground floor of that trend!" Sal said, sarcastically.

"Will you shut up? I'm not even addressing you anymore. He thinks because I sell nuts that *I'm* nuts," he said to Terry.

"Come on, Manny. Astrology? It's been done. It's *all* been done."

"For *people* it's been done," he said. Then in a whisper, he added, "Not for pets."

Sal burst out laughing. Terry said nothing, but Sal could see in her expression that she was amused, maybe worse, intrigued. Manny saw it too.

"Terry, people would pay real money to get a horoscope for their pet. Trust me, I know."

"I believe it."

"See, Sollie? She believes it." Then he turned to her. "Do you really believe it?"

"I think you're on to something. But how would you offer the horoscopes?"

"I was thinking like having an astrologer come into the store on a special day, let's say on Pet Day, and advertising it, and having people bring in their pets to get their horoscopes."

"Well, it could work, but the Health Department might object. After all, this is partially a food establishment."

Manny waved it off. "I'm not worried about them. They're already on the payroll."

Sal could see the flicker of surprise in her eyes. Maybe now she'd stop listening to this fool.

"Besides, I would close the store to regular business on that day. Not sell any food."

He handed the two coffees to Sal.

"We gotta go," Sal said and started for the front of the store.

"I made some flyers, Sollie. Nothing fancy. I'm no artist. But I figure you ride around a lot, you could stop here and there, you could put them up for me, okay? I'm stuck here six days a week."

Sal didn't respond. He opened the door for Terry.

"Nice to meet you, Manny," she said, as she left.

"I'll see you guys later," he said.

As they got in the cab, Terry stopped and stepped back. "I forgot something," she said, and turned to go back.

"What is it?" Sal called out the window, but she didn't answer. He turned on the engine and waited. When she came back he could see that she was holding a bunch of flyers.

"You actually took those things?" he asked, as she got in.

"Why not? It's a great idea."

"It's one in a series of 'Great Ideas'. The last thing that screwball needs is encouragement."

"What do you know about business? Yours failed."

"I was in business with *Manny!* And how long do you know him? A few months? Or even maybe a few weeks? No. You know Manny all of - ." He stopped to look at his watch. "Twenty minutes. You know how long *I* know Manny? Thirty years. I won't even entertain this discussion."

"Then you're being a fool," she said, calmly, rolling up the flyers and sticking them back in her purse, then turning to face him. "Would you like to guess how many houses I sold last year, Sal?"

He was taken off guard by her change of topic. "No idea, I can promise you."

"Thirty. And of those thirty houses, twenty-four of them had nice-sized backyards. Of those twenty-four, nineteen had dog houses in those back yards. And, in every one of those nineteen cases, *every single one*, the buyer not only noticed the dog house, but commented favorably. Do you know one woman actually got emotional over it? It reminded her of the house she grew up in. She could have bought that house for much less than she did if she had tried. But she didn't. So, when Manny talks about how emotional people are about their pets, I listen."

"Yeah, and when *I* tell you not to listen, you still listen, right?"

Terry's expression said it all, and Sal knew immediately that he was out of line. It was like he was back arguing with Angela.

"I believe I've had enough," she said as she unlocked the cab door.

"Don't," Sal said. "I shouldn't have said that."

"Who do you think you're talking to?"

"I'm sorry, okay? I was out of line."

"To say the least."

They sat in silence. Terry was very still and stared straight ahead. Angela would have cursed him, screamed, gotten out and slammed the door no matter what he said or did. Being sorry was never enough for her.

"Look, I'm sorry, okay? I just seem to go on auto-pilot like I was still with my ex."

"You fought a lot?"

"You could say that. And she always made it worse."

"*She* made it worse? Why was it her fault?"

"Because she didn't know how to fight."

"I didn't know there were rules."

"Well, there are. And she broke them all," he snapped.

"One day remind me to ask you what the rules are. In the meantime, here's *my* rule: don't get hostile with me again. I am not Angela. And ... you're not Charles."

"That's *your* ex? Charles?"

"Yes. I guess he broke the rules also, and, he would never apologize when he was wrong. So, I appreciate your apology. But I won't accept your hostility."

"Let me make a note of that," Sal said, and pretended to be writing on a piece of paper. "Apology okay. Hold the hostility."

Terry made a snide expression. "Now, can we continue this discussion about Manny?"

Sal finally took the lid off his coffee and sipped it. It was still way too hot, so he opened the cab door and spilled some out. "Be careful for the coffee. It's still hot," he informed her. "Okay, here's the deal about Manny. It's not that his ideas are wrong or crazy or anything," Sal said as he sipped. "In the IQ department he's got us all beat. The guy reads about twenty magazines a week. And he retains it all. That's what's really amazing. But in twenty years, with all the schemes he's had to make money, none worked. And I don't intend to get sucked into this one."

"Did you lose a lot of money?"

"Only everything I had saved at the time, plus some of Joe's and even Schmuli's," he said as he turned on the engine. "And, contrary to what *you* think, I am *not* a fool. He thinks I'm unforgiving. I'm not. I'm just trying real hard to undo some past mistakes."

"Is that why you're getting a Bar Mitzvah now?"

"You don't *get* a Bar Mitzvah, you *become* a Bar Mitzvah." He paused. "How'd you know about that?"

"Manny called you the Bar Mitzvah boy."

"I didn't notice."

"You weren't paying attention."

"I can't afford to pay too much attention to Manny anymore. Besides, what's my Bar Mitzvah got to do with this?"

"Can I share something with you?"

"You and Manny are just dying to share with me today," he said, but stopped himself. There was something in Terry's tone that softened him. It wasn't her trying to one-up him, or prove he was a jerk, like Angela used to. "Okay. *You* I'll pay attention to."

"It's important to learn a lesson from your mistakes. But I think it's more important to be sure you're learning the *right* lesson."

He decided to say nothing until he was sure it wouldn't come out angry or sarcastic, because, even though he didn't like what she was saying, at least she was being sincere about it. Still, he couldn't help but wish she would just take his word that Manny was a nut job, a *genius* nut job but still, a nut job, and then they could just drive around on this wonderfully bright winter day and enjoy Brooklyn.

Finally he sighed deeply and said, "You think I'm learning the wrong lesson here somewhere?"

"It's a possibility. All I'm saying is that you've tuned out Manny so completely that you may miss a really viable idea when it comes along."

"Yeah, but once you start *hearing* Manny, then you start *listening* to Manny. Once you start *listening* to Manny, you get into trouble."

She smiled a small smile. But still, there was that seriousness.

Terry sighed and sipped her coffee. The morning sun lit up her profile, and her light brown eyes were illuminated. She looked delicate in that moment, her skin radiant, her whole self a little far away. Out of reach.

Sal forced himself to turn away from her and concentrate on driving. He forgot that the cab was already running and turned the key again. The screech of the engine startled them both, and Sal smacked himself in the head with his hand. "Schmuck! Do you know I have *never* in my whole life done that! Whenever I see someone *else* do that I think 'What a jerk!'." He put the cab in gear and pulled away from the curb. "Now, I'm the jerk."

There was an awkward silence for a while, as Sal tried to figure out how to lighten things up. They had been making idle chatter almost from the minute he picked her up yesterday. Now it was like ... like there were things being left unsaid, on purpose.

"You wanna know how me and Manny became friends?" he offered, finally.

"Sure," she said, as she ate her candy and sipped her coffee.

"I made a big effort back in junior high school. I figured if I was his friend, maybe he wouldn't beat the crap outta me."

"Was he in the habit of beating people up?"

"No, but I didn't know it. I took one look at him and figured it was better to be a friend than an enemy. Turns out Manny doesn't have too many enemies."

"That's not surprising."

"But he doesn't have too many friends, either."

"Why is that?"

"Why's that? Take a look at him. He clears the whole sidewalk every time he walks outside. He's what you might call an intimidating individual. What would you do if you saw a guy like that coming at you?"

"Where I come from that would be as likely as getting kosher pizza."

Sal laughed. "I bet you don't get to meet too many people like me and Manny, huh?"

"The only 'ethnic' I knew growing up was my father's partner. He was Jewish."

"How'd they ever manage to get together?"

"What's the difference?" she said a little abruptly. "What's our next stop?"

Sal took the hint and dropped the father subject. "You'll see when we get there," Sal said. "And do me a favor, will ya? Don't worry about anything. Don't have any major insights, and don't make any lifestyle decisions on this trip, okay? Just drink your coffee and try to enjoy yourself. You think you can do that?" he teased.

"I'll work on it," Terry said, which struck Sal as funny, but a quick glance in her direction told him she was being absolutely serious.

CHAPTER SIX
Brighton Beach –

Sal drove to Ocean Parkway, turned left, and headed out towards Brighton Beach. It was a largely Russian community, situated on the same peninsula as Coney Island. Sal had considered living in Brighton at one time. He loved the idea of being right on the water in one of those apartments with a great ocean view. Just after Angela left, he actually considered buying a co-op in one of the largest, most luxurious buildings on the beach. He spent several weekends looking at apartments and then walking on the boardwalk trying to make up his mind. That's where he met up with the Polar Bears. And they were the ones who told him to forget the whole idea of raising a kid in an apartment, even an apartment with a great view of the ocean.

"Why did Manny say not to eat the pink ones?" Terry asked, as she popped another piece of candy into her mouth.

"What's that?"

"He said not to eat them. Why?"

"I didn't hear him say that -" Sal began, but stopped himself when he saw the look on Terry's face. "Okay, okay. I know what you're gonna say. I wasn't listening. I don't know why he said it. I wouldn't worry about it though," he added.

"Good," she said, as she reached her closed hand across the seat. "Then you can have them."

"Gee, thanks. If I drop dead suddenly, grab the wheel and remember my dying words."

"Yes?"

"There's no right on red in Brooklyn."

Terry laughed and dumped the pink candies into a tissue. "This is a nice area," she noted.

"Yeah, it is. Ocean Parkway used to be real exclusive. Doctors and professionals. Right around here are mostly religious Jews. I think they're Lebanese. They're going to shul now."

"Temple?"

"Yep. And just over a few blocks, in Borough Park, are also Orthodox Jews. In Williamsburg there's another whole community. They're mostly Satmars."

"Is that a specific branch?"

Sal laughed. "I wouldn't call it a branch ... well, maybe. Yeah, I guess it's like that. It's a sect of Hasidism. There're other sects, too, like Lubovitch. They all have different beliefs and follow their own rebbe. You know, a teacher."

"Do you know much about it?"

"A little here and there. My best friend, Schmuli, is Orthodox."

"Really?" she asked, shifting her position slightly to look at him.

"Sure. We grew up together. I was the Shabbos goy for his parents."

"The what?" she asked.

"*Shabbos* is the Jewish sabbath - "

"I know what Sabbath is," she said.

"Well, did you know you're not allowed, by Jewish law, to work on the Sabbath and that turning on a light is considered work?"

"No."

"So they used to have non-Jews come in and turn on the lights for them. A *goy* is a gentile. I was the sabbath goy for Schmuli's family."

"But I thought you were part Jewish?"

"I am. But obviously we weren't religious. I mean my mom married an Italian."

Terry paused to consider what he was saying and Sal paused also, watching her process what he said. He was starting to get used to these sudden silences, and he was also starting to like that she wasn't stubborn or competitive. She was tough, no doubt about that, but there was also something soft about her, something reassuring in the way that she listened so carefully to him. Well, she listened to Manny too, actually. But still, it was nice that she really paid attention. Who else did he know who did that? No one.

"What I like about this part of Brooklyn," he started, and noticed Terry snap to attention, "is the wide open feel to it. Where I live it feels more like a city to me. Out here, as we get closer to the shore, it feels like suburbia."

They were on Ocean Parkway and Avenue Z. The Parkway was three lanes in each direction, with a small service road on each side. The houses were either elegant two-family brick or large, ornate apartment buildings. Some even had circular driveways. The islands that separated the service roads from the main roads were lined with trees and benches.

"In nice weather, people are out here all day long, bullshitting, strolling with their babies, eating ice cream. Some of the old men play chess. It's real nice. When I was a kid, before air-conditioning, people would sit out here all night with radios, listening to the ball game. They'd bring out bridge tables and eat whole meals. My parents and some friends even barbecued out here once. I remember one really hot summer night, when I was a little kid, my parents took me and Ike and walked the few blocks out to Ocean Parkway for a 'picnic' dinner. We thought the heat would break once it got later, but it didn't, so we stayed out a long time.

I got so tired I fell asleep on a bench. I remember being carried all the way home by my pop, and my mom nagging him about his back and how he should put me down," Sal said, becoming more involved in the memory as he told it.

"Anyway, so much for the good old days."

"You speak so fondly about your childhood," she said with a smile. "It's nice to hear."

"It was a great time, believe me. Most people have all kinds of lousy memories. Not me. Not one," he said as he turned on to Brighton Beach Avenue.

"You were very, very lucky," Terry said and turned to look out her window.

Yeah, he could go on and on telling Terry all about his life. It was easy. She seemed interested. But she didn't offer much information about herself. That's how she was different from just about everyone else he knew. She didn't bend his ear about her life, her opinions, her ... *anything.*

"How about you?" he asked. He had parked the car and turned off the engine. He turned to face her.

She pulled her gaze away from the window, turned, and saw him sitting, expectantly. "I guess I wasn't so lucky," she said without emotion and got out of the cab.

Sal hesitated a moment before joining her. Why'd he have to go flapping his jaw about how great his childhood was? Come to think of it, why was he mouthing off about himself so much anyway? She probably thought he was a selfish jerk. And even worse, he probably made her feel bad, too. She seemed to have some bad memories or something.

"Brr! It's much colder here!" she announced, as they walked up the street toward the beach.

"Put on something warmer."

"This sweater is pretty heavy. I'll be okay."

"Yeah, but at least cover your head. All your body heat escapes through your head."

"I thought that was an old wives' tale."

"Do I look like an old wife? I'll go get you a hat from the cab," he said, and ran back before she could stop him. When he handed it to her, Terry laughed.

"I'll look ridiculous!" she protested, holding up a brown tweed cap with earflaps.

"Nah, around here you'll fit right in," he said, and waited for her to put it on. When she didn't, he took it from her and plopped it on her head. "Now tie it up!" he insisted. But again, Terry hesitated.

"I'll get hat-head," she protested.

"Better hat-head than the flu," he argued.

"I don't know ...." she said and reached for the cap.

"It's just me, okay? What's the big deal?" and he pushed the hat back down on her head, pulled the strings under her chin, and tied them up tightly. He did it quickly, avoiding her eyes, before he could stop and think and realize that he was probably completely out of line again. But she didn't pull away. Instead, she slipped a finger under the bow, gently loosening it.

"So, do I look ridiculous?" she asked.

"Nah," he said, as he stood back and considered. "You really wanna know what you look like?"

"What?"

"A schmuck with earmuffs."

At this Terry broke into convulsive laughter, which struck Sal funny, and he started laughing also.

"I've never heard anything like that!" Terry said, gripping her stomach. Her eyes were watering.

"My grandmother used to use that expression," Sal said, "and I always wondered what she meant by it. Now, I know," he teased.

The ocean wind blew stray newspapers across their legs as they stood on the street corner.

"Come. The entrance to the boardwalk is this way."

They walked the two blocks to the beach, the wind getting stronger as they approached.

"People forget that Brooklyn is part of Long Island. We're surrounded by water. This is the Atlantic," he said, as they climbed the ramp to the boardwalk.

They stood quietly for a moment, taking it all in. The sun had slipped behind the clouds, turning the beach into a study of gray, slate blue, and white. The squeaking seagulls and the motion of the tide were the only sounds they heard.

In the distance Sal could make out a small group of people.

"Follow me," he said.

They walked along the boardwalk, saying little, watching the clouds blow over the ocean. Terry kept the hat on. Sal had to stop himself from chuckling every time he looked at her.

"Are those people sunbathing?" Terry asked, pointing to a group of women sitting on the sand, leaning against a brick wall, their faces tilted upward with sun reflectors held under their chins.

"You got it. And those other people, over there?" he pointed. "They're my Polar Bear buddies."

"I don't believe this."

"You thought I was making it up?"

"No, no, it's not that." She stopped.

"Hard to believe anyone would do this kind of thing, huh?"

"Exactly."

"I just got over a cold or I'd go for a swim myself. Let me introduce you to my friends," he said, as they approached the group standing down by the water's edge.

They were all men, all wrapped up in large overcoats. It was hard to guess their ages, but they were all fifty-five plus. All except Sal.

"Sollie!" one of them said as Sal approached. "You come, the sun disappears." He hugged Sal tightly. He was a short, rotund man with a warm smile and blue eyes.

"This is my friend, Terry," Sal said to the group.

"You like to swim in the winter also?" another man asked.

Terry laughed. "I don't even know how to swim."

"Whoever doesn't teach a child to swim should be arrested!" he said, pointing his long finger at her.

"Ivan is very passionate about the water," Sal explained. "This is Dmitri, and this is Ivan, and this is Igor," he said, introducing them each to Terry.

"Nice to meet you."

"The others are out there," Dmitri said, pointing to the ocean.

Sal and Terry turned, shielded their eyes with their hands, and scanned the ocean. Finally they spotted two figures far away, swimming slowly toward shore.

"Ah ... here's Irving!" Ivan said, indicating a small old man approaching from the boardwalk.

Irving walked up, said little, and began to remove his coat.

"Where you going?" Ivan asked him.

"Where you think?" he answered, as he shed another layer of clothing.

"No swimming today, Irving. Remember, the doctor said ...." Ivan began.

"I come, I swim," was all Irving said, and then he kicked off his shoes.

Ivan gave Sal a pleading look. But Sal wasn't sure what to do. Irving was eighty-five years old and swam in icy water most of his life. With that, Sal's beeper went off.

Sal looked at the beeper display. "It's my friend," he announced. Then he turned to the old man. "Listen to me, Irving. You can swim, but only if I go with you. Otherwise, no dice."

Irving made a face, but shrugged his shoulders, indicating his agreement.

"I'll be right back," Sal said. "I gotta return this call." And he walked up the beach toward the pay phone on the boardwalk.

"You can use my cell phone," Terry said and handed it to him.

"Thanks," Sal said and dialed. Then he started wandering all over the beach to get a good signal.

"In Russia we are walrus. Here, polar bears," Irving said to Terry.

"He means in Russia they *call* us 'walruses' and in America they call us 'polar bears.' Also, no ice statues," Irving added.

Terry looked puzzled.

"In Russia, in winter, people make very large ice statues of all kinds. Here they do not."

"Why is that?" she asked.

"Is not cold enough."

"That's hard to believe," Terry said.

"Must be cold all the time. Otherwise everything melt."

"You sit mit the vimin?" Igor asked Terry.

"Excuse me?"

"He asks if you would like to go sit with the women," Ivan explained, pointing to the row of sunbathing women.

Terry wasn't sure what to do. She didn't want to insult anybody.

"Come, I'll introduce you," Ivan said, finally, and led the way. "You and Sal are serious?" he asked, as they trudged through the sand.

Terry was confused. "About what?"

"I see," he said, realizing he had made a mistake, and said nothing more. Terry was relieved.

The women were seated against the wall, all wearing heavy, shapeless coats and pants with boots. And their hats! Some even more ridiculous than Terry's. All of their uplifted faces were oily with suntan lotion. Their eyes were closed as Terry and Ivan approached, and she had a moment to notice how deeply wrinkled most of them were. Of course, they were also very tanned.

"Ladies, I'd like for you to meet a friend of Sol's. This is Terry."

Their eyes flew open, almost in unison, and they took her in. Then, one by one, as they each decided they had seen enough, they each closed their eyes again and resumed their sunbathing positions, their faces tilted upward. It would have been comical if she weren't feeling so self-conscious.

Ivan pointed to the first woman in the row. "This is Selma, and this is Irini, and this is Rita, and this is Natalie. Now everyone knows everyone," he said. "I go check on Irving, he shouldn't take a dip yet." Ivan walked away.

"You want to sit a little?" Selma asked, without opening her eyes.

"No, thank you."

"Sol is a fine man. A gentleman," Rita said, out of nowhere, also without opening her eyes.

"Don't start, Rita," Selma admonished.

"Start what? I tell the truth."

"Rita wants to find a wife for Sol. That's all," Irene added.

"A man forty-five years old should have a wife."

"He's only forty-three," Selma corrected.

"What's the difference between two years?"

Terry listened to them, amazed that they never opened their eyes while arguing.

"Rita's right, Selma. It's time."

"So, Terry, what do you think?" Rita asked her, turning to face her, but not opening her eyes.

"About what?"

"About Sol. Who else? You think I have Irving in mind?" The women all laughed.

"I'm just a customer. Actually, I'm from Wisconsin," she said, nervously.

"Wisconsin! How did he come to meet you?"

"He's giving me a tour -" she began.

"In that farshtinkeneh cab of his?" Rita asked, disgusted.

Terry said nothing.

"What's wrong with his cab all of a sudden?" Selma asked.

"A man like that shouldn't be driving a cab his whole life," Rita stated. Then she opened her eyes. Looking at Terry, she said, "Right, Terry?" as if she would understand.

"I'm not sure I understand."

"You will," she said, and closed her eyes again.

The other women paid her no attention. Then Natalie said something in Russian, and Rita answered her in Russian.

"She doesn't speak English," Rita explained to Terry. "Or else she says she wouldn't be so rude to speak in a foreign language. She wants me to ask you a question."

"Yes?"

"Are you Jewish?"

At first Terry bristled. This was rude beyond anything she had ever encountered. Knowing they were Sal's friends, she didn't want to insult them. "No, I'm not. Why do you ask?"

Natalie obviously understood Terry's answer. She got up, placed her reflector on the sand, and walked toward Terry. She stood very close, too close. Natalie's skin wasn't yet tanned or wrinkled and her eyes were an interesting hazel color. They turned up slightly, giving her an Oriental look. She was actually a lovely looking woman, even a bit exotic, clearly younger than the rest, and she spoke quite softly. Terry couldn't understand her words, but she understood the intent.

"She says you should know that Sol's first wife was not a good soul," Rita translated.

Terry said nothing. Natalie took Terry's gloved hand in her own and spoke again.

"She says that Sol is a lost soul who has lost also his faith in himself."

Terry and Natalie stood practically toe to toe on the blowing sand. Terry could hear the men arguing on the water's edge. She saw Sal walk across the sand towards Irving. She saw him take off his coat and hat and shoes, but she didn't move. It was as if she was in a spell and couldn't leave until Natalie dismissed her.

"She says you must be good to him because," Rita paused, waiting for Natalie to finish the sentence. "Because he has a gentle heart." Natalie was looking right into Terry's eyes, and yet Terry didn't feel uncomfortable. There was no judgment. Then Natalie turned and sat down again on her spot against the wall. Terry didn't bother with polite good-byes. She hurried away from the women and returned to the men.

As she approached, Ivan waved her back, and she waited as the men circled Sal. He was changing into his swim trunks. Then, the circle of men opened, and Sal and Irving stepped forward. Sal turned and motioned to her to come closer. He was stripped down to his swimsuit now, and suddenly the whole scene struck Terry as hilarious: the circle of men in heavy coats, skinny, old, wrinkled Irving in his Band-Aid-like swimsuit, the greasy-faced women staring closed-eyed at the sun. And Sal, so involved in it all that he couldn't even see the humor.

Hearing her laugh, Sal looked down, checking himself.

"It's not you," she said. "It's ... it's all of this!"

Sal looked around, but didn't see what was funny.

"It's freezing out, and you're standing here with another nearly naked guy old enough to be your grandfather, and you're going swimming!"

"Yeah, so?" he asked. But Terry had given up trying to explain. "Look, I gotta take Irving here for his dip, then we'll split," he said, in all seriousness.

Terry bit her lip, trying not to laugh. Sal looked down again, scrutinizing himself, sure it was something about him that was causing her laughter.

"You look fine," she said, to reassure him.

"Yeah?"

"Really," she said, seriously.

It made Sal a little self-conscious, and he turned away from her.

"Nu?" Irving called. "I'm waiting and waiting."

"All right, all right," Sal said, turned from Terry, and walked off with Irving.

Terry watched them retreat; the frail, pale old man in his bright red Speedo suit and the tall, muscular, olive-skinned man in his paisley swim trunks. "What about your cold?" she called out, but they were already too close to the water to hear her.

She stood with the men as they watched Sal and Irving plunge into the water. The men who had been in the water when they arrived were just coming out. They were dripping wet on the sand and drying off when Terry noticed some people walking on the boardwalk and pointing at them. Maybe these men really were crazy. And maybe Sal was also. Or maybe she was the one who was crazy to be roaming around Brooklyn with a "lost soul" who went swimming in the winter and who had a "gentle heart," whatever that meant.

―――――――――――――――――

"Is everything okay?" Terry asked, as they got back into the cab.

"Sure. Why?"

"Your beeper."

"Oh. Just Schmuli," he said, and turned the heat on.

"Your religious friend?"

"Yeah. Nothing important."

"Why don't you have a cell phone?" Terry asked.

"A beeper is a lot cheaper. And it keeps people from bugging me all day. With a beeper they know it has to be important enough for me to pull over and find a phone."

Terry didn't respond. Instead she asked, "Are you sure you don't want to go home and dry off properly? You'll get sick again."

"Nah. The heater's pretty strong," he said and turned up the fan. "Sorry I had to go off and leave you in the clutches of those guys," he said as he pushed the car seat all the way back, got on his knees on the seat, and bent his body so that his head was in front of the heat vent.

"They were very sweet. The women, on the other hand ...."

"The women? You met Selma and company?"

"Ivan insisted."

"Good old Ivan," he said, as he slowly rotated his head before the vent. "So, what did you think?"

"I think all that sun is destroying their skin."

"I mean besides that," he said, as he ran his fingers through his hair, tousling it.

"You really want to know?"

"Sure."

"They're rude and offensive."

"I mean besides *that*," he said again, turning around so that he could dry the other side of his head.

Terry laughed. "Besides that? What else is there?"

"I don't know. That's why I'm asking."

His face was turned away from her, so she couldn't read his expression.

"I don't think I'm following this conversation anymore."

"Did they say anything about me? They usually do."

"Usually? Do you often bring women to be interviewed by them?"

"That's not what I meant. They're always kvetching about me for some reason or other. They're like a whole committee of Jewish mothers."

"K-vetching?"

"Complaining."

"Well, *Natalie* wasn't k-vetching," she said, struggling with the word.

Sal stopped what he was doing, turned to face her, and sat up. "What did she say?"

"She said you were ...."

"Yeah?"

Terry hesitated. Natalie had said so many things, all quite strange. She probably shouldn't have mentioned her at all, but now that she had, she had to tell Sal something. The problem was that none of it was very flattering. "A lost soul."

"She really said that?" he asked, running his hands through his still wet hair and zipping up his jacket.

"Yes," Terry answered, stopping herself from asking everything she wanted to.

"You still wanna see Coney Island?" he asked, turning to face the steering wheel.

"Sure. Can we get a hot dog at Nathan's?"

"You and that fast food crap. But it's your tour."

"Sal, Nathan's is nationally famous. And you did promise me real native cooking."

"Yeah, yeah. But they're not exactly using Mother Handwerker's own recipe anymore -" Sal stopped as his beeper went off again. He glanced at it. "It's Joe. I better give him a call."

"Here, use my phone," Terry said, reaching into her purse.

"Nah, I'll find a pay phone."

"Don't be ridiculous!" she insisted, thrusting the phone at him.

Sal took it and phoned Joe. Terry was quiet as she observed him. Then she turned away and closed her eyes and listened to his voice. It soothed her. The deep tone, the soft, comforting words he spoke to his son.

"Yeah? Your stomach hurts?" he asked. "When did it start?" he continued, and she could just barely hear Bennie's small voice on the other end. It was like a lullaby, a gentle love song to his son who would never know what it meant not to have that melody in his life.

"Terry," he said, "I'm so sorry. Bennie doesn't feel well. Joe said his temperature's a little high, about a hundred or so, and his stomach hurts. I gotta go home and see what's up. But if it's not serious, maybe I can kiss it better and we can continue."

"No, no. Go take care of your son," she said, took the phone from Sal, pushed down the antenna, and shoved it back into her purse.

"It's just a slight fever. Kids get fevers like grown-ups get warts. No one knows what causes them or why they suddenly disappear."

"Oh, really?"

"Yeah. Babies get fevers when they teethe too, only doctors don't want to admit it 'cos they can't figure out why it should be. But every parent knows it. Sometimes they get diarrhea too."

"Who? The doctors?" she teased.

"I don't think this'll be serious," Sal said.

"Just drop me at a cab stand on your way home. I'll get back to the hotel by myself."

"Cab stand? In Brooklyn? No such animal. Let's check up on Bennie, and then we'll figure things out."

"Will you just go home and tend to your sick child, please? I can take care of myself."

Sal said nothing. He chewed on his lip and thrust his hand through his short hair, so Terry filled the silence. "You spent hours with me when you could have been with your family, and I appreciate it. Now you should be with your family," she said firmly. Still Sal said nothing. "What is it?" Terry asked.

"I love my family, but I do see them all the time, and I was kinda looking forward to a *whole day* of this."

"This?"

"You know. Showing you around Brooklyn," he said clumsily, fidgeting with his belt buckle.

Terry glanced at it.

"It's a Model T," he explained.

"I know."

"Sometimes I think it's tacky or corny."

"Then why do you wear it?"

"I only wear it on days when I *don't* think it's tacky or corny."

"I guess this is one of those days," she said, idly.

"Yep, I guess today is just one of those days," he said, feeling suddenly at a loss. It was like they had started some conversation long ago and just began it again yesterday when he picked her up at the airport. And now that he faced the prospect of her leaving, of maybe ending this conversation forever, it didn't feel right. In fact, it felt like they had just gotten started.

"If Bennie needs you, then -"

"Then believe me, I'll know it. Okay?"

Terry said nothing. Instead she just nodded.

"Well, I guess it's back to Park Slope," he said, and started the cab. "That is, if you can trust this 'lost soul' to get us there."

CHAPTER SEVEN
Ocean Parkway Northbound –

"So, when did you decide to become a bar mitzvah?" Terry asked, as they headed back to Park Slope and a car service. "I never heard of an adult doing that."

"I first got interested when my mom died fourteen years ago."

"And you've been studying for it ever since? I never realized Hebrew was that difficult!" she joked.

"Maybe I'm a slow learner," Sal said with a smile. "Anyway, it's not just Hebrew. It's learning some basic stuff about religion. My mom said her only regret in life was not giving her sons a Jewish education. She made me promise that if I ever had children I wouldn't make the same mistake. So I promised.

But after she died I realized I couldn't educate my kids if was ignorant myself, so .... "

"The autodidact at work," she teased.

"You're mocking me, huh?" he asked, also smiling.

"Would I do that?"

"I'd say the *potential* was definitely there," he smiled.

"You know, I have to admit that I was looking forward to an entire day of this, too." She smiled. "You're a nice guy, Sal, in spite of your tendency toward hostility."

Sal laughed. Then he said, "Look, Terry, we'll go in and check up on him. And if he's okay, we'll pick up where we left off."

"I'll feel terrible if he's really sick and we abandon him."

"Well, here's the thing: firstly, if he's really sick, I'll know it. Bennie gets fevers sometimes just because his favorite GI Joe action figure is lost -"

"I know, but -"

"Secondly, I think 'abandon' in this context is a little too strong a word."

"Maybe I'm just being overly protective."

"If you don't have kids yourself, it can be hard to judge -"

"My not having kids has nothing to do with my ability to know if a child needs his parent."

Sal almost answered, then stopped himself. He could tell she was suddenly angry. What did he say?

"You don't think my judgment would be good enough in a case like this?" she pushed.

"Put the boxing gloves down, will ya? I didn't mean anything. No one starts out knowing this stuff. We all learn as we go."

Terry took a deep breath and turned to Sal. "I want to tell you something, Sal. Something very personal about myself that I haven't told anyone else. I know we hardly know each other -"

Sal pulled the cab to the curb.

"What are you doing?" Terry asked.

"I don't know what you're gonna say, but I don't wanna be doing forty-five on Ocean Parkway when you say it."

Terry nodded silently. Sal parked the car under a skinny, naked tree and noticed a young woman with her baby in the stroller. He studied the woman for moment and could tell she was an immigrant. He rolled down his window.

"Mameleh, reyden English?" he called out to her in Yiddish.

The woman turned and eyed him suspiciously. Then she said, "Neyn."

They continued speaking in Yiddish, and Terry could tell that things were getting a little heated.

"What are you talking about?" she tried to interrupt.

Sal ignored her and continued his conversation with the woman.

"Sal, what's going on?"

"I told her to put a hat on the baby! It's below freezing with the wind chill!"

"What?"

"She's insane! She told me to mind my own business."

"So mind your own business."

"That kid'll get sick!"

As they were speaking the woman turned and walked away.

"Maybe she's not going far," Terry offered.

"So what?"

"Calm down. The baby will be fine. His face was all flushed. He's probably overdressed anyway."

Sal took a deep breath then signaled as if he were pulling out.

"Wait a minute. Why'd I pull over, anyway?" he asked. "Oh! Yeah! Okay. You were gonna tell me something," he said.

"Forget it," Terry said.

"No, no. I wanna hear. I just got distracted. Please."

"Well, I'll probably wind up regretting this. I'm really *not* a confessional personality." But before Sal could respond, she added, "The reason I came to New York this time was to go to the best A.I. clinic in the country," she said very quickly, as if to get it over with.

"Artificial Intelligence?"

Terry broke out laughing. "It's artificial all right, but it's not intelligence. It's artificial *insemination*."

Sal was struck silent. She came here to get pregnant? To go to a clinic? A woman as beautiful and smart as her?

"I just felt a need to share it with you. I don't know why. Maybe because I feel like we've known each other a long time, or maybe because you seem so comfortable being a parent."

"Thank you," he said, and immediately felt stupid.

"I hope I didn't make you uncomfortable. I really don't confide in people very much."

He was barely paying attention. "Why?" was all he could manage.

"Because most people can't be trusted."

"No, I mean why artificial insemination?"

"That's simple. I want a child."

"Yeah, I can understand that. I wanted Bennie real bad too."

"The difference is that you were lucky enough to be married at the time to a woman who also wanted a child."

"I wish."

"How do you mean?"

Sal sighed deeply. "I'd have to get personal to explain that."

"So?"

"Sometimes I get tired just thinking about it."

Terry looked at her watch. "Tell me on the way back to your house."

"I can't tell this story while I drive. So, after we go home and check on my febrile offspring, I will tell you my tale, and if, after that, you are still my friend, then, well, then.... "

Terry saved him. "I'm glad I've made a friend, Sal. I haven't done that since college."

"Well, you know what they say about being a grown-up."

"No, what do they say?" she asked.

"I have absolutely no idea."

CHAPTER EIGHT
Park Slope/President Street

"How long has it been hurting?" Sal asked Bennie as he sat down next to him on the couch where the little boy was lying, watching television. Joe was trying to get Bennie to eat some plain toast.

"For a while," Bennie said.

"Did you eat lunch?"

"Janet gave us lunch," Joe explained.

"The lady across the street?"

"Yeah, yeah. The children were playing, and she didn't want to send Bennie home, so she offered to make lunch. She made some curried chicken."

Sal looked suspiciously at his father. "Curried? Since when do you eat curried *anything*?"

"I can't try something new?" Joe protested.

Terry sat opposite Bennie, on an overstuffed armchair, and said nothing. She was glued to Bennie's large, sad eyes.

"Did Bennie eat the curried *anything*?" Sal asked.

"Yeah, I think so."

"Did you, Bennie?" Sal pushed.

"You mean that stuff with the funny smell? I only took one bite. Janet said I'll get used to it."

"It wasn't the food, Sal. No one else got sick," Joe explained.

"What else did he eat today?" Sal asked.

"He had a nice breakfast. Then he had a nice lunch."

"No snacks or treats or anything?" Sal persisted.

"Janet gave us ice cream," Bennie offered.

"Did you eat much?" Sal asked.

"Not too much," Bennie answered, but there was a hesitancy that Sal caught.

"How much is not too much?" he asked Bennie, then looked at his father.

Joe shrugged. "I wasn't paying attention."

"What were you doing? I mean, you stayed the whole time he was there?" Sal asked.

"She invited me. It wouldn't be nice to say no."

"Papa! It was the best ice cream I ever tasted. You liked it too, Grampa!"

"Mango ice cream," Joe said softly. "Wasn't bad."

"Well, that's one mystery solved," Sal said, and stood up.

"You think it's the ice cream?" Joe asked.

"Come on, Pop. The kid can't tolerate much dairy, and then he gloms down a buncha ice cream ... mango ice cream, no less! It's a wonder he isn't throwing up."

Bennie and Joe shot each other an awkward glance.

"Oh, don't tell me! He threw up?"

"Just a little, Papa."

"Pop, why did you let him eat so much of it?"

Joe looked so forlorn that Terry had to stop herself from coming to his defense.

"I said he could have a little, next thing I know he's throwing up."

"It's not his fault, Papa. Me and Courtney snuck some extra when they weren't looking. Anyway, I'm feeling a lot better now," he said and sat up. Then, to Terry, he asked, "Did you bring the Crazy Glue?"

"We didn't have time for -" Sal started.

"Sure. How could I forget?" Terry said and reached into her purse.

"When did -" Sal tried to ask.

"At Manny's," Terry explained.

Bennie jumped off the couch, ran up to his room, and returned with his broken toy, which he handed to Terry. "Now you can fix it right," he said.

Terry took the toy and led Bennie to the dining room table. "Get some newspaper or something to put under this so we don't ruin the table."

As they were working on the toy, Sal cornered Joe. "What's goin' on?" he asked.

"Don't get so excited. The children got a little carried away with the ice cream is all."

"You know he can't tolerate much dairy."

"Sal, I told you. I thought a little taste wouldn't hurt him. How should I know he would do this? He's only a child. Every child loves ice cream."

"Mango?"

"It's very good. You should try it."

Sal waved him off. Then he asked, "You think I need to stick around?"

"No, no! Go finish your tour. We'll be fine. We'll see you for supper."

CHAPTER NINE
Coney Island Aquarium

The aquarium was dim and quiet. Sal and Terry stood in front of the electric eel tank, reading the description.

"The next show is in ten minutes."

"Is it worth seeing?" Terry asked.

"Yeah, if you're about five years old. So, was Nathan's a let-down or what?" he asked.

"I wouldn't make it the highlight of your tour."

"Who said highlight? The real highlight is this way," he pointed, then led her down a darkened corridor lined with brightly lit fish tanks. "Are you ready to see something truly disgusting?"

"How can I resist?"

Sal escorted her to the end of the corridor and stopped.

"This thing is a Japanese Spider Crab," he said, and stepped out of her way.

Terry gasped as she stood before the huge tank with a crab that stood four feet tall with legs that must've been five feet long. "It's monstrous."

"It escaped from a Godzilla movie. Wanna see a little octopus?"

"How little?"

"Very little."

She followed him to the end of the corridor to a small tank.

"I don't see anything."

"There, behind the rock."

"It's very cute."

"It's Bennie's favorite," he said, then walked on, leading her to the exit. "The penguins are this way."

Terry reached into her purse and pulled out her half-empty bag of candy.

"You're gonna ruin your appetite."

"You want one?"

"Okay. But don't try to pawn the pink ones off on me again."

"I purged those a long time ago," she said as she reached in and plucked a piece of candy from the bag, then handed the bag to Sal. "I want to hear about you and Angela," she said, very casually, chewing her licorice.

They approached the penguin area and watched as the birds just stood around doing nothing. The wind blew up and the cold ocean spray stung.

Facing the penguins, Sal said, "They feed them later on, by the way. You wanna find out when?"

"No. Why did you marry her?"

"I was obsessed with her."

"Why?"

"She was gorgeous."

"How old were you?"

"I was eighteen and she was sixteen when we met. I was working for -"

"Give me a piece of candy," Terry interrupted. "I want to give the birds some."

"Are you crazy? It'll probably kill them!"

"No it won't. They'll probably take one sniff and leave it alone. They eat fish, not candy."

"Then what are you trying to do?"

"A little experiment," she said and reached for the bag in Sal's hands.

He clutched it to his chest. "No! Absolutely not!"

"Oh, come on," she said, and tried to wrest the bag away from him.

"What's wrong with you?" he asked, as he hid the bag behind his back. "See the sign? Can't you read?" he asked, outraged at her behavior.

"I'll make you a bet. I say they won't eat it."

"You're worse than Bennie!" he said, still holding the candy bag behind his back.

"Come on. I say they'll ignore it. They won't recognize it as food."

"What if they do? And they choke on it or something?"

"On a tiny piece of candy? They swallow whole fish!"

"What if they can't digest it?"

"Well, we know what will happen then, don't we? It will come out the other end, intact."

"What if it ruins their teeth?"

"They don't have *teeth*! They have beaks. They're birds!"

"You're nuts. Forget it."

"Be logical, Sal. If they're not meant to eat it, they won't."

"Yeah, like it really works that way."

"They're not like people. Humans are the only animals that eat things they shouldn't and eat when they're not hungry."

"Oh, yeah? What about dogs? I had a dog once, you couldn't even eat a Twinkie around him. You'd have to fight him for it!"

"That's because *humans* domesticated dogs and influenced their eating habits."

Sal shook his head with disbelief. "This always happens."

"What? People wanting to feed candy to the penguins?"

"No. I think someone is a normal, intelligent, *sane* person, and then wham! They pull something like this."

Terry laughed. "People probably feed these birds all kinds of garbage. If it killed them, they wouldn't still be here."

"Maybe they're not the same birds. How would you know? They all look the same."

"So you think the aquarium has a stock of penguins in the back somewhere and just replaces them every time one keels over from eating a piece of popcorn or a Popsicle or something?" she teased.

"Look, you asked about me and Angela. You wanna hear about it or not?"

"Oh all right. May *I* have a piece of candy, then?"

He looked at her suspiciously. "For *yourself*?"

She gave him a look.

"Okay. But I don't trust you, so open your mouth. I'll put it in myself," he said, and took a piece of candy from the bag. "Blue okay?"

Terry shrugged and opened her mouth as Sal put the candy inside.

"So, I was working for my uncle Paul, in construction. I was doing masonry, and I felt like a big shot. Angela dropped out of school and was working in her father's dry cleaning store. I started to hang around and made some moves on her. Every guy in the neighborhood wanted Angela."

"And what did Angela want?" she asked, when she was done chewing.

"I convinced her she wanted *me*. I also convinced her family, which counted for a lot back then."

"How did you do that?"

"You sure you wanna hear all this?"

"Why not?"

"I don't think I come out looking too good."

Terry laughed.

Sal stared at the penguins, thought for a moment, and said, "Do we have to stand out here freezing our gagoots, or can we go inside and get warm like the mammals God meant us to be?"

"Sure. Is there anything else worth seeing?"

"The whale tank is being repaired, so forget the belugas. I wonder where they put them. I wish I coulda brought Bennie here when they moved them. I bet that would've been a sight to see, huh?"

"So what else is there?" she asked, as he held the door for her.

"You wanna see fish or you wanna hear 'The Sal and Angela' story?"

They stepped inside, their eyes adjusting to the darkness.

"Can't we do both?"

"It's too distracting," he said and led her to a small bench at the end of the corridor. "Let's just sit down a minute."

They sat down and took off their coats. In the soft yellow light Sal noticed how lovely Terry looked. She had such fine eyelashes. Like a baby's. He watched her in profile, admiring their delicacy each time she blinked. Finally he snapped out of it. "See, the thing is, I was a cocky kid."

"Past tense noted."

"I thought if I could figure out what Angela wanted, I could provide it. Simple as that."

"And what did she want?"

"I knew she wanted someone who could take care of her. So I flashed a lot of money around. I was making nice money and I was living at home, so I had money to spend. I came to her house for dinner, I brought wine and flowers. Her mother loved me. Her father liked that I always picked her up at the door and stayed and made conversation. The knuckleheads she usually went out with couldn't even figure out that much. So, I guess, next to them I looked pretty good."

"Were they that bad?"

"They were jerks, but I was a smarter jerk."

"No one outsmarts adolescence."

"You sure you wanna hear this next part?"

"Does it get ugly?"

Sal laughed. "Nah. Just a little off-color, as they say."

"I'm a big girl. Give me another piece of candy."

"Will you stop with the candy already?"

"Just one more."

Sal plopped the whole bag in her lap. "See, Angela had a little bit of a reputation for putting out. But it turned out she never really went that far."

"And how did you manage to find that out?"

"I knew a guy who dated her for a while, and I managed to get it out of him. I decided I wanted to be her first, but I wasn't that experienced myself. Of course, I acted like I was."

"Fascinating," Terry said, chewing her candy.

"So I read up on it," he said.

"You what?" Terry asked, accidentally swallowing her candy and starting to choke.

"Are you okay?" Sal asked, as Terry coughed. She nodded. Finally she coughed up the licorice and took a deep breath.

"You *read up* on it?"

He was surprised by her surprise. "Yeah. So?"

"You mean, you read up on *sex*?"

"Yeah," he said, quizzically.

"You are some character."

"Why? How's a guy supposed to learn that stuff?"

"How do most guys learn?" she asked.

"They fumble around a lot. I wanted to skip that phase, so, I read up on it and learned a few things about ... you know, about pleasing a woman," he started, becoming embarrassed.

"And ...?" she prompted him.

"Ah, forget it. I can't tell you this."

"Why not?"

"I've never told this to anyone, and it's not making it any easier you being female."

"Okay. Let's forget I'm female. Pretend I'm Manny."

"I've got a better idea. Why don't *you* tell *me* about you and your ex."

"What do you want to know?"

"I wanna know about the guy you were engaged to."

"Charles."

"Yeah, Charles. Why didn't you marry him?"

"I wasn't in love with him."

"Then why did you get engaged?"

"I *thought* I was in love with him."

"Did *he* love *you*?"

"I thought so."

"You thought you loved him and you thought he loved you. But now you're telling me, not only didn't you love him, but you don't think he really loved you either."

"Right," she said, and dug into her candy bag.

"So, why did he want to marry you?"

"I was appropriate."

"Appropriate? What the hell does that mean?"

"Our fathers were partners. We grew up together. We both planned to make real estate our careers, and we both enjoyed the same things and wanted a family."

Sal paused to consider all this. He had a quizzical look on his face that made Terry laugh.

"You know what you look like now?" she asked.

"What?"

"Nipper, the RCA dog. You know, with his head slightly tilted to the side, trying to figure out what he's hearing." She imitated him, but he was too intent on her story to react.

"See, something doesn't add up here. You figured out that you really weren't in love with him and called it off. But did you realize he didn't love you too? Or -"

"No. I believed he *did* love me at the time, which is why I felt so damned guilty about it all."

Sal nodded his head and said nothing. They sat silently, watching families stroll by, dragging tired children along.

"Enough stalling," she announced, suddenly.

"Huh?"

"You said you had something to confide in me after we checked up on Bennie. Surely it wasn't that you were a dopey teenager."

"Oh, yeah. Well, it's not that great as confidences go. Not as good as your AI thing, anyway."

"You think mine is great?"

"It was the best secret I've heard in years."

"What was the *last* secret you heard?"

"That Josie the Peach was gay."

"Excuse me?"

"A good friend of mine. I'm gonna take you there after we leave here. But anyway, I kinda had that one figured out long before she told me."

"You're so clever?"

"Not clever enough. I never would have guessed *your* secret."

Terry said nothing. Sal sensed that she already regretted having told him.

"Anyway, I promise I'll tell you my story if you at least finish yours. When did you realize that Charles didn't love you?"

Terry paused, considering whether to tell, and if so, how much. The soft glow of the aquariums along the wall had a calm, lulling effect. "Well, this may sound strange, but I realized that it wasn't Charles I wanted, it was his mother."

"Get outta here."

"I'm serious. I had known Rose most of my life, and she had been the closest thing to a mother I'd ever had. I loved her very much. She had four sons and always wanted a daughter."

"A perfect match," Sal said.

Terry just nodded and stared absently into her candy bag. "I actually met Charles' wife a few years ago. She seemed so eager to please. It reminded me of myself back then. So glad to find someone who would love me. Or at least go through the motions."

"Do you think he loves her? Or is *he* going through the motions?"

"Who am I to tell?"

"I think, for some people, the motions are enough. Even preferable."

"Why preferable?" she asked.

"Safer," he said, and thrust his hand into the candy bag. "See, if marriage is an institution, then the motions are what matter," he said and popped a candy into his mouth. "Now you got me eating this crap."

"Oh, come on! It's not really an institution. It's all based on *emotion*," she insisted.

"Yeah, so? Selfishness is an emotion. So is fear."

"You're saying marriage is an institution based on selfishness and fear? This is from your own experience, no doubt," she said.

"From a lot of people's experiences."

Terry sighed, frustrated. "I don't know why *I'm* defending marriage to *you*. I couldn't care less."

"So, are you rich?" he asked, wanting to change the subject. "Manny said you are."

"Nice transition," she said. "By your standards I guess I am."

He made a face.

"Don't be insulted. Wealth is relative, and relative to the people I arrange loans for, I'm not considered wealthy."

"Okay then. What exactly do you do?"

"I buy and sell properties. Mostly commercial, some residential."

"Where do you do this?"

"All over the world. My father and his partner started this business forty years ago. When I graduated from college, I went into the business and they taught me everything I needed to know. I found I had a talent for it and … and that's it really."

"What about the stuff about arranging loans?"

"It's a service we offer. Actually, we started offering it about five years ago. It was my idea. We always have clients who want to buy property but need a loan. Sometimes it's difficult to arrange, especially if the client resides in one country and the property is in another country."

"And you get a cut?"

"Of course. It's a service charge."

"So, you never felt any passion for Charles?" Sal asked, suddenly.

"How long were you married to Angela?" Terry asked, instead of answering him.

"Sixteen years."

"That's a long time. Why would you break up after all that time together?"

"You know what I wish? I wish there was such a thing as a remote control for my life. That way, when I met Angela, I could have fast-forwarded my life and I could have avoided it all."

"All of it? What about Bennie?"

"Except for Bennie. But the rest.... "

They were silent for a moment.

"Ya know, Bennie used to think all these fish tanks were televisions," he said, gesturing toward the wall of tanks. "I used to crack up imagining a world where the only TV shows are about fish, twenty-four hours a day, every day. Now there're channels a lot like that."

Terry had been thinking. Then she said, "And you really feel that all sixteen years of your life with Angela were wasted?"

"Yep. Sometimes, when I picture myself during that time, I see this sad guy howling at the world. But if there was some kinda remote control for my life," he said, and made a clicking motion with a make-believe remote, "click, click, and click."

"But at least you wound up with Bennie. Most men don't get custody."

"Most men don't care enough. I cared."

"And Angela agreed?"

"That's where the real story comes in," he said, standing up and stretching his long legs. "But, like I told you, I don't come out looking so good."

"Because you fought for custody?"

"No, I mean ... I was stubborn and blind. When Angela started playing around, I didn't even know."

"You trusted her," she suggested, still seated and looking up at him.

"I was fooling myself." He sat down again. "Sometimes I worry that I could fool myself like that again. I wish I could fast-forward to about ten years from now and see if I do better. You ever think about getting married?"

"It's not in the cards."

"How can you be so sure?" he asked.

"I used to visit Rose sometimes when I was home from school, and I'd sit in her living room while she was ironing. She used to watch "Loretta Young Theater" all the time. And I'd watch with her. I can still remember being eight or nine years old and sitting on that scratchy couch and smelling the spray starch she used to use. And I remember how, at the end of each episode, Loretta and the leading man would fall into each other's arms, the music would swell, and they'd live happily ever after. Of course, this was always after the man had overcome enormous obstacles to get to the woman. And, at the end of each episode, Rose would sigh and say 'He *really* loved her.' Rose was a romantic. She believed love conquered all and that there was exactly one woman for each man and vice versa. I used to call Rose's notion of love 'The Really Love.' It didn't take long for me learn that it was all make-believe."

"Boy, and I thought *I* gave marriage a bad rap."

"It's something I've learned to come to terms with. Most people marry to avoid loneliness. They're running for shelter. The truth is, being alone is very natural and I won't fool myself into thinking otherwise," she said, and, as she began to stand up, placed her hand on his thigh. Did she give it a squeeze, or was Sal just imagining it? He felt a confusing combination of things, all of which he chose to ignore, and instead, stood up and looked for the exit sign, glowing softly at the end of the corridor.

"We gotta go. I want you to meet The Peach," Sal said.

CHAPTER TEN
Borough Park/The Peach

From the aquarium to D'Apeche's Italian Bakery in Borough Park took only fifteen minutes, but it was a very long fifteen minutes in which Sal and Terry said little. He got the feeling she was clamming up a little, maybe because she wasn't used to talking about herself. Was she sorry she told him so much?

He glanced at her peripherally. She was looking out the window, and he just wasn't sure what more to say. Her ideas about marriage were kinda sad. Not that his were better, but he felt he had a right. He had been there. She hadn't. Didn't everyone deserve at least the brief, fleeting belief that marriage *could* work?

He looked at her again. She was really such a serious person ... except for that stuff about feeding the penguins! And he liked her. Jeez. How long had it been since he'd liked a woman? Really liked spending time with her out of the bedroom?

They turned onto Thirteenth Avenue in Borough Park. Because it was a predominantly Hasidic Jewish neighborhood, it was quiet for the Sabbath. All the stores on the main shopping street were locked up, except for a handful of places owned by non-Jews. Even the Carvel shop had a sign in the window that read "We serve Kosher ice cream."

Sal pulled up to the bakery and parked the cab.

"Tomorrow you'd never get parking anywhere in this neighborhood," he said.

"Sunday?"

"The place is pretty much closed down on Saturdays. Sunday is their big shopping day.

"So this place is not Jewish?" she asked, indicating the bakery.

"D'Apeche's? This is the absolute quintessential *Italian* bakery. You gotta see the window. It's a work of art," he said, and got out. Terry did the same.

The window was crowded with row after row of gorgeous Italian pastries: fat éclairs oozing custard, baba au rums soaked through with so much rum there were small puddles in the bottom of the tray, crispy cannolis with white cream filling, and an entire shelf of gaudy marzipans.

"It's fabulous!" Terry exclaimed.

On the other side of the doorway was another window, this one for breads of all shapes. There were round braided breads, plump golden rolls, long, crusty Italian breads, and piles of pignoli cookies.

"I'll have to taste everything," Terry said.

"I think that can be arranged," Sal said, as he pushed against the bakery door, finding it wouldn't budge.

"They're closed," Terry said, pointing to the sign in the window.

Sal walked up to the door and peered inside. Sure enough it was dark and seemed empty. "Wait here," he said, and walked around to the side of the building. In a few minutes, he appeared inside at the front door with a short, rotund woman, who unlocked the door. Josie was about forty with no make-up and very little jewelry except for a small, delicate cross on a chain so thin it was practically buried in the folds of her neck.

"Come in, come in!" she ordered and held the door open for Terry.

Inside, Terry was embraced with the fragrance of fresh bread and sugar.

"Josie, this is Terry, my friend from Wisconsin. Terry, this is Josie the Peach!"

Josie pulled the door closed, locked it, dropped the key into her apron pocket, and thrust out her fat hand. Terry shook it and noticed that she had quite a lot of dark hair on her arm. Another look showed her that Josie's nose was slightly off-center.

"You ever been to Brooklyn before?" Josie asked.

"This is my first time," Terry answered.

"Ever eat pastries like this?" Josie asked.

"No. I can't say I have."

"I'll put together a nice box for you," she said, and walked behind the counter.

The Peach must've weighed two hundred pounds and couldn't be more than five four. Her brown hair hung limply to her shoulders.

"Listen, Sollie, I gotta run over to the hospital to see my dad, but you two can stay long as you want. I'm expecting Denise to call any minute, so if she does, tell her to call my cell."

"You sure?" Sal asked.

"Yeah, just lock up when you leave," Josie said as she began to tie up the cake box.

"Why are you tying it up?" Sal asked.

"Oh man, I don't know," she said, and dropped the string.

Sal walked up to her and pulled her toward him, head first. She complied, buried her head in his chest and sobbed.

Terry watched silently.

"So, what's with Dad?" Sal asked, finally.

"The doctor says we might have him 'til Easter," Josie said, looking at them, red-eyed. "I'll be happy if we have him another month."

"Go see him. I'll tell Denise to call you if she calls here."

"Crap, that's another mess. She wants us to move in together and -"

"And it's an old story."

"Yeah, but what about Joann?"

"You gotta tell Joann about you and Denise. It's been three years now. Don't you think she might have a little clue, anyway?"

Josie paused to consider, but only for a moment. "Nah. What kid suspects their mother's a dyke?"

"Joann's no dope, Jos. Just tell her, and then have Denise move in with you."

"With me *and* Joann?" her eyes widened.

"Well, yeah. Why not?"

"I don't feel right."

"She's nineteen, for God's sake! You think she doesn't know what goes on?"

"Yeah, but I don't have to underline it, cross the t's and dot the i's, do I?"

Sal threw up his hands.

"If you guys want some espresso, there's a fresh pot," Josie said.

"You selling it now?" Sal asked, not seeing a machine.

"No way. Too much hassle. I got the machine in the back, just for us. The cannolis are fresh too," she added, as she yanked off her apron, threw it on a chair, and headed for the back door.

Sal locked the door behind her and turned around. He found the espresso machine and poured them each a demitasse. Then he brought over the box of pastries that Josie prepared and put it on a small table. Terry came over and sat down. Sal handed her the cup and the box.

"Help yourself to as many as you want," he said.

"She sounds ashamed of being gay," Terry said as she plucked a fat canola from the box.

"What do you expect? She's a Catholic-school girl, plus, she's kept it a secret so long I don't think she knows how to come out."

"Was she ever married?"

"Sure. To Joann's father, Vinnie. He put her through hell when she came out. Threatened to take Joann away from her."

"And Joann never found out her mother was gay?"

"Vinnie didn't want her to know. He thought if she found out, then she would suddenly decide to go gay herself."

"That's ridiculous."

"That's Vinnie. Anyway, he made Josie swear not to tell Joann she was gay until Joann was at least eighteen."

"But now she can."

"Yeah, but she can't."

"And she won't let her lover move in because her daughter is still living at home?"

"Yeah, pretty much."

"Maybe she's using her daughter as an excuse not to commit to this woman."

"Another county heard from," he said, blandly, ignoring her. Then he said, "Josie is family. When her dad goes …" he started, but stopped himself. To continue would only bring him to tears. Truth was he probably should have gone to the hospital with her. "The Peach is such a great kid. My mom used to say there's someone for everyone. Lucky for her she's gay though."

"Why do you say that?" she asked, and sipped her espresso.

"It would be harder for her to find someone if she was straight."

"You mean, you think women don't care about physical appearances as much as men do?"

"They don't. Everyone knows that."

"Oh, really?"

He laughed. "You don't think I'm right?"

"Women want good-looking men as much as men want good-looking women. Of course, men don't like to believe that," she said and nibbled the cannoli, getting powdered sugar all over her lips and the tip of her nose.

"But you don't think women forgive more with men's looks than men do with women?"

"I only know that sex is very important to men, and yet, at the same time, they often play a game with themselves that it's not." She paused to continue eating her pastry.

"That, you gotta explain."

"Okay," she said, putting down the pastry. "A man I dated always used to say that sex was 'just recreation.' At the same time he went to incredible lengths to get me into bed. I imagine he did the same with most women. One day, when he used this 'just recreation' line on me I told him I found the word insulting. But he thought I meant the word 'recreation.'"

"So?"

"I meant the word 'just.'"

"Oh, heavy duty!" he teased.

"Don't you see my point?"

Sal laughed. "Semantics. You knew what he meant."

"Of course I did! He meant that he didn't want any emotional entanglements with me. But to try to minimize the importance of the sex by saying it was 'just' anything was a lie. Not that he was lying to me, naturally, because *I* understood quite clearly how important this particular form of recreation was to him. He was lying to *himself.*"

"You're over-complicating it. He was just warm for your form."

"You're missing my point. I'm not surprised," she said, picking up her cannoli and jutting her tongue inside the shell to get at the hidden cream filling.

"Why? Because I'm a Neanderthal like that guy? Okay, I confess. I've probably used the expression 'just sex' myself on occasion. Does that mean my knuckles scrape the ground when I walk?" he asked, and examined his fist.

"My point is," she started, "there's nothing 'just' about sex. For a man or a woman. Whether it's recreational or emotional."

Sal started to answer her, but stopped himself. Suddenly he became aware that he was getting aroused. Was it the sex talk? Was it her tongue jabbing away at her pastry? Was it the dim late afternoon light that partly shrouded her face? Or how delicious the whole place smelled and how she looked with that sugar all over her face?

"So, which is it?" Sal asked.

"Excuse me?" she asked.

"For you? Is it recreational or emotional? I gotta know."

Before she could answer, Sal stood up, walked around the little table, knelt down in front of her so they were eye to eye, and kissed her.

Terry scrambled to put down the cannoli, missed the table, and was startled as it hit the floor with a splat. She attempted to turn and look for it, but Sal held her face in his hands and began to cover it with small kisses, licking the powdered sugar from her lips.

At first, he could feel her surprise and even resistance, her body tense, her lips, her mouth merely allowing his mouth to kiss hers. But, slowly, he could feel her relax into his kiss, and then, she was kissing him back, leaning into him, almost throwing him off balance. Her unexpected response brought a surge of excitement Sal hadn't felt in years.

He stood up and gently lifted Terry up out of her chair, as he pulled her closer and continued to kiss her. Then he slowly inched them toward the long stainless steel counter Josie used to roll out her dough, pushed aside the rolling pins, dough cutters, bags of flour and sugar, and leaned Terry up against it.

He could feel her kisses becoming more urgent, her tongue, sweet with cannoli cream and warm from the coffee, exploring his lips, then darting inside his mouth, making his desire intensify. He placed his hand on her breast. The pink cashmere was soft and warm, driving him to reach for her body underneath it. He ran his hand up under the sweater, under the bra, to feel her breast in his palm, like a promise, like a fruit. The nipple tightened to his touch.

"Let me just put in my diaphragm," she whispered and slipped away from him, heading for the tiny bathroom.

Sal could feel the heat rise in his face. He was flushed with excitement, desire and confusion. She was using birth control even though she was going to be artificially inseminated?

"That has got to be the smallest bathroom I have ever been in," Terry said with a smile, as she came toward him. But instantly she realized something was wrong. "If this is your 'come hither' look, you'd better keep practicing," she joked.

"Why'd you put in your diaphragm?"

"Because it's my most fertile time and -"

"Let me get this straight. You came to New York to get pregnant and you took your diaphragm along?"

Terry stood still, stunned by the turn of events.

"I didn't exactly *take it along*. I carry it in my purse like my *wallet* or my planner."

Sal said nothing. There were a hundred things going through his mind, any one of which might just burst out of his mouth.

"I hope you aren't upset that I carry it with me. I really don't use it much -"

"I thought you wanted to have a baby."

"I do."

"Then why the diaphragm?"

"Why the diaphragm?" she repeated stupidly, taken off-guard.

"Yeah."

"Well," she began, thoughtfully, "because I want to make love with you and -"

"I know it isn't exactly high tech, but making love works pretty well for making babies," he said, hearing himself becoming strident and angry. "I've got state of the art equipment with a proven track record," he added, trying too hard to make a joke, to convince her he wasn't upset. He could tell she was thinking about what to say. She always did. But now it made him mad as hell.

Why was he so angry and she so calm?

"Deciding to have sex isn't the same as deciding to have a child together, Sal. Is that what you're proposing?"

"I'm not *proposing* anything! This isn't a negotiation, and a baby isn't a deal! Jesus, Terry! *You* want a kid and I want *another* kid and you came all the way here to get pregnant and we hit it off and all, and we're attracted to each other too, and you put in a diaphragm! I don't get it."

"You mean you can't see that there's a difference between having sex with an attractive, intelligent stranger and deciding to link our lives together, essentially to get married? I think you can. But maybe you have another agenda."

"Why do you talk like this is some kinda business deal? I don't have an agenda, damn it! I have a ..." he grappled for the word and found himself losing steam. "I don't know what the hell I have. A hope, maybe. A desire ... for a family. Excuse me if I got carried away and mistook a fling for the beginning of a relationship."

"I'm sorry. I really am. But I just can't have a child with a man I hardly know," she said, as she walked up and down the kitchen, trying to look preoccupied. She picked a pastry off a full tray and nibbled it.

"Yeah, I see your point. It's much better to have a child with a man you *don't know at all*."

"It has its advantages."

"Please," he held up his hand. "Whatever you do, don't start listing them."

"And anyway, why are you so willing to have a child with a woman *you* barely know?"

"Nine months is enough time to get to know someone."

Terry couldn't control her nervous laughter. This was just too ridiculous.

"And what happens after nine months if you realize you were wrong about me? Do we have a custody battle?"

A custody battle. Why did his relationships with women always come down to custody battles?

Terry was straightening out her hair and her blouse. Then she Headed for the door.

"Where are you going?"

"To have sex with a turkey baster that doesn't expect me to play house afterward," she said and walked out of the bakery.

Sal hesitated and then ran after her.

"Hey! Terry!" he shouted.

She stopped and turned, saying nothing.

"What's your last name?" Sal asked.

"Are you out of your damned mind?" she shouted back.

"We both know I'm gonna call you later and apologize but I gotta know your last name if I'm gonna ask for you when I call the hotel."

She sighed, her shoulders drooping, and walked back toward him.

"Then why don't you just apologize now?"

"Because that's not how it works."

"How what works?"

"Fighting. I told you there're rules. And there's a rule that says apologies come later."

She smiled weakly. "Look, Sal, I had a lovely day. Let's not have our parting words be angry ones." She looked at him a moment longer, added, "I hope Bennie is okay," then crossed the street, heading for the car service.

Sal just stood there and watched her walk off, not knowing what the hell to do. Then, she stopped and turned. "The name's McManus!" she called out, and kept walking.

He licked the remains of powdered sugar from his lips and went back inside to lock up.

CHAPTER ELEVEN
Park Slope/President Street

Sal jumped into the shower, rinsed off the salt and pollution from the Atlantic, and decided he really should go to the hospital and see old man D'Apeche. It would be tough, though. He would have to console Josie while trying not to bust out bawling himself. Since his mother's death from emphysema all those years ago, Sal had managed to avoid hospitals. During the two years that his mother was dying, he had had his fill. Luckily, Joe had been pretty healthy, and Bennie had never had an emergency. Still, he knew he had to go now.

It was four o'clock and the house was incredibly quiet when Sal walked out of the bathroom with a towel around his waist. He shaved again, combed his hair, put on clean clothes, and considered his day with Terry. It had all been going great until the bakery. What the hell had made him think that he could jump her bones like that? What had gotten into him? Was he that horny? That needy? Was *she*? She sure was eager. For a beautiful woman it was strange. Hell, it didn't even matter now. Now she was gone. Still, he knew he would call her, and he knew she knew, too. So he would. But not now. He was still too confused by what had happened back there. Now he would visit the old man, and then he would see what was up with Bennie for tonight. He had promised the kid Godzilla, after all.

At six-thirty, when Sal got back home, Joe and Bennie were eating supper at the dining room table. The TV was going full blast.

"So, where's your lady friend?" Joe asked. "I made some nice soup and salad and - "

"She's not coming. But everything smells great. I'm starved," he said and walked into the living room, picked up Bennie, and sat down on the couch with the child on his lap.

"What about the movie?" Bennie asked.

"Got it all ready," Sal said. "And how was your day?"

Bennie shrugged. Sal could see that the boy was too involved with his TV show to make conversation.

"Sal, come on inside for a minute, okay?" Joe called out from the kitchen.

Sal gently nudged Bennie off his lap and stood up. He walked into the kitchen. "Pop, if you're gonna bug me about Terry and why she didn't come for dinner ..."

Joe waved him off. "Have you thought about the letter? What are you gonna do?" Joe asked as he stirred his escarole soup.

"There isn't much I *can* do. Larry says it looks like I'll finally have to fight it out in court with her."

"Jesus, Mary and, Joseph," Joe whispered. "Doesn't he say anything that can help you?"

"He said, and I quote, 'If you could get a job that paid even seventy-five thou a year, and get married to a respectable woman by the time the court date rolls around, then you'll have a good chance.'"

Joe wiped his brow with the back of his hand. The soup was steaming, but Sal could tell Joe's sweat wasn't because of the soup.

"Pop ..." Sal began, feeling a need to comfort his father. If they lost custody of Bennie, how the hell would the old man survive? He didn't even want to think about his own life. His own loss.

"Let's pray to God the judge sees how good we're doing with him," Joe said.

"Yeah, Pop, let's," Sal said and sat at the kitchen table, as Joe ladled some soup into a bowl and then brought it to Sal.

"Why is she doing this *now*?" Joe asked, as he sat down next to his son.

"Why does she *say* she's doing it? Or why do I *think* she's doing it?"

Joe just sighed. Sal continued. "I think she wants to screw me over, that's why. She knows how important Bennie is to me. He's all I have, really. And she can't stand to think I'm happy."

"But she has two of her own now," Joe reminded him.

"Yep. She sure does. Two bouncing beauties that don't look anything like her Italian family from Brooklyn. I'll tell ya something, Pop. If she wins this thing, she's gonna be sorry. You know why? 'Cos there's no way in hell she's gonna pass Bennie boy off as a WASP."

Joe took a tissue from the box on the table and blew into it. He was crying. Sal took his hand and squeezed it. "It's not over yet," he said. "I came up with something last time, maybe I will again." And he blew gently on his soup to cool it off.

"Teresa McManus, please," Sal said to the hotel operator. And then he waited. He knew he had to apologize, but after that he had no idea what to say. "Terry? It's Sal. I called to apologize."

"What a surprise."

"No, I really mean it. I know I was flippant about it earlier, but that's not because I don't mean it."

"I don't doubt your sincerity."

"You don't?"

"Why would I? You're a straight shooter. You say what's on your mind."

"For better or worse, huh?" he said, knowing this wasn't going too well.

"Look, I think I must've seemed pretty desperate yesterday, in the bakery," she said.

"Desperation can be very attractive in a woman," he joked.

"I'd like to finish our tour tomorrow, if you can make the time."

"Sure. Sure I can."

"But I need some ground rules this time."

"Hands to myself, I promise."

"Is that what you think I'm getting at?"

"Now *there's* a question with no right answer."

"Let's not get personal this time…in *any* way. All right?"

Sal was hurt. He had enjoyed all the banter, the stories of each other's lives. But apparently *she* was regretting it.

"Okay?" she asked.

"It's your call," he said abruptly.

"Good. Pick me up at ten, no earlier. I'll leave it to you to plan the itinerary," she said and hung up.

That night, while Sal undressed, he found himself wondering about her. But not only about the sex. Sex was the easy part. Now he was starting to wonder what it would be like to really get to know her. To live with her. To have a woman's things all over the bedroom again – the things he missed so painfully when Angela moved out, but that he hadn't thought about in years. Now all those ghost-objects seemed to fill his bedroom again, the objects of everyday life with a woman: the jumble of make-up, brushes, barrettes, and bobby pins on the dresser, flannel nightgowns and torn stockings strewn on the chair, the long lost high heel hiding under the night-table, the slight scent on her side of the bed. If all those things came crowding back into his life, could he ever survive their loss again?

CHAPTER TWELVE
Crown Heights

He picked her up at ten, as she'd requested, but he didn't have much of an "itinerary" in mind. His heart wasn't in it anymore. He had promised Schmuli he would have lunch with him and his family on Sunday, and didn't want to cancel because of Terry. Why sacrifice any more of his time for her? She was a tough, bitter lady with no excuses. Never married. No kids. Plenty of money. What the hell did she have to be so unhappy about, anyway?

"This is Crown Heights," Sal explained as they turned onto Carroll Street. "The row of houses Schmuli lives in is kinda unique. When they were built, in the early nineteen hundreds, they were supposed to be luxurious, even though they're only about seventeen feet wide. But still, they're walking distance to the museum."

"Which museum?"

"The Brooklyn Museum."

"I didn't know Brooklyn had its own museum."

"Oh, yeah. If it was nice out, I'd take you to the Botanical Gardens right next to the museum."

They got out of the cab and walked up the steps to Schmuli's house. Sal knocked. Reba answered the door.

"Sollie!" she said, smiling from ear to ear. She was a thin, pale woman in her thirties, wearing a long, shapeless dress, an apron, and a kerchief on her head.

"Reba, this is my friend Terry."

"Nice to meet you," Reba said.

"Nice to meet you, too," Terry answered.

Then Reba stepped back to allow them to enter. "I haven't been out yet. Not too cold," she said, and turned to come inside.

"Enough with the bullshit! Come in already!" a booming man's voice called out. And then Schmuli emerged from the hallway with his arms extended. He wore the traditional black pants and white shirt of the Orthodox Jews, with a yarmulke on his scraggly black hair. Schmuli grabbed Sal and hugged him tightly. They were about the same height but Schmuli appeared bigger because he was heavy.

"Terry, I want you meet the youngest old Jewish man in history, Schmuli Goldberg."

Terry smiled. "It's a pleasure," she said as she put out her hand. But Schmuli didn't return the gesture. Sal noticed it and explained softly, "He's not allowed to touch a woman who isn't his wife," Sal said.

"Come eat. You'll meet the whole family," Schmuli said as he led them down the hallway to the dining room.

They entered a large oak-paneled dining room with dark brocade curtains and a large foldable clothes-drying rack in one corner. There were diapers and baby clothes drying, along with the shirts and skirts of older children. The table was filled with people, the room loud with talk and laughter.

"Just squeeze in here next to Motke," Schmuli said as he moved the young boy's chair.

"Hey, Motke, how's it going?" Sal asked.

"Okay. But I'm not eating the gefilte fish."

"Why not?" Sal asked, as he sat down.

"It looks like a dead whale," Motke answered.

Terry laughed. "What is it?" she asked.

"It's a fish dish," Sal explained.

"Just be glad she didn't make petcha!" a little girl called out.

"Ugh!" Motke exclaimed.

"Motke! Enough!" Reba called from the kitchen. "Just because *you* don't like it doesn't mean everyone else has to hear all about it."

"What's petcha?" Terry asked.

"It's snot in a jar," Motke shouted.

Sal and Motke broke into laughter while Reba scowled.

"Something smells wonderful," Terry noted.

"*Everything* smells wonderful!" Schmuli added. "A wonderful Sunday brunch with my oldest friend in the world. Let me introduce Terry to everyone," he began, from the head of the table. "Starting on your left is

Zeyda, Reba's father, then Sarah, my oldest girl, next to her is Chana, my youngest girl, and then Rachel, my middle girl. Then there's Chaim, and Avi, who just became a bar mitzvah, and this is Reba, who you met," he said as he turned himself to face her. "And this is our baby, Yankeleh, who won't be the baby for much longer, right, Yankeleh?" he said as he reached over and pinched the toddler's juice-stained cheeks. "And Motke, Motke is my little monkey. That's everyone. Now we eat."

The children erupted into noise and laughter as food was passed around the table.

"You're pregnant again, Reba?" Sal asked.

"This is news?" she answered as she fed Yankeleh.

"You have a big, beautiful family," Terry commented, as she surveyed the children. They were all dark-haired like their parents, and most had Schmuli's green eyes and dark lashes. Only little Yankeleh was fair-haired.

"Thank you," Reba said. Then to Sal she commented, "I like your friend already."

Suddenly a small, high-pitched voice called out "Help!" from the other room. Terry alone was startled.

"That's Ted, our parrot. He's not so good in the language department," Schmuli explained.

"Why does he say 'help'?" Terry asked.

"Some wise guy must have thought it was funny to teach him that," Schmuli said. "The sad thing is whoever it was also must have neglected him because when we got him he was in bad shape."

"He had almost no feathers," Motke explained.

"How awful!" Terry said.

"With a bird like that, you have to pay attention. They like company. If they're ignored, they get a little meshugah and start to develop bad habits … like plucking out their own feathers."

Terry grimaced.

"My teacher said parrots are very social," Avi spoke up.

"All living things need companionship," Reba said, as she fed the baby.

"When we got him he was practically naked," Avi added.

"But he looks great now. After lunch you'll go in the living room and see for yourself," Schmuli said.

"How did you get him?" she asked.

"The man who owned him brought him to the pet shop where my friend works. This guy bought the bird at Woolworth's."

"Woolworth? They sell birds there?" Terry asked.

"They sell everything there!" Schmuli exclaimed. "My whole house when I was growing up was furnished in early Woolworth. Curtains, cushions, the yarn my mother used to knit our clothes, the fabric she sewed with. She had plants from Woolworth all over the house. You remember what she used to say, Sollie? She would only buy plants from Woolworth because she figured if they could survive there they could survive anywhere."

"She was right," Sal added.

"Yeah, she was. But not when it comes to the 'Living Gift'."

"The living *what*?" Terry asked.

"The Living Gift. That's what the sign in the Woolworth pet department used to say."

"That poor bird," Terry said.

"My friend at the pet shop begged me to take the bird. He figured with a family as big as mine, how could Ted ever be lonely?"

"Help!" Ted called from the next room.

"Why don't you teach him to say something else?"

"Why? You think we didn't try?"

"He won't," Sarah explained. "We've all tried. He seems to like Mama best, but even for her he won't say anything else."

"Maybe in time he will," Terry suggested.

"Maybe this, maybe that. It's a year already he says only 'Help!' If it makes him happy to say one word, so what? So, how's the tour going? See anything interesting?" Schmuli asked Terry, changing the subject.

"Does Zeyda need help?" Reba asked her husband before Terry could answer Schmuli's question.

Schmuli looked at the old man, sitting directly across from him at the other end of the table. He was quiet and moved slowly but seemed to be able to feed himself.

"Change seats with me," Sal said to Terry. "That way I can keep an eye on him."

Terry got up and switched seats with Sal so that he was now seated next to Zeyda.

'So,' Schmuli persisted.

"So far you're the most interesting thing I've seen," Terry joked.

"See, Sollie? If you would have put me on your tour in the first place, maybe you would still be in business."

"You did enough for us," Sal said.

"Well, we all tried," Schmuli said.

"This is delicious," Terry commented on her food. "What's in it?"

"A little of this, a little of that," Reba answered.

Suddenly, Zeyda dropped the bread he was using to dip into his soup. Sal retrieved it and handed it to him, which got the old man's attention. He took in Sal's face for a long moment and then broke into a grin.

"How are you, Mr. Greenspan?" Sal asked.

"Sollie," he said, finally able to recall the name.

"Yeah, that's me."

"You're a good boy," he said, as if Sal were another one of the children at the table.

"He should only know," Schmuli chimed in.

"He *was* a good boy," Reba insisted. "If not for him, who knows where *you'd* be by now." Then she bent down to pick up yet another thing Yankeleh had tossed over the side of his high chair. "Oy, Yankeleh, I have no strength left from you."

"So what did you think of Avi's bar mitzvah?" Schmuli asked Sal. "Was that something?"

"Again with the bar mitzvah?" Reba mocked. "It was four months ago. We talked all about it. What's left to say?"

"Terry doesn't know about it, what's so terrible if we describe it to her?"

"Not again, Papa," Avi chimed in for the first time. Terry and Sal could see that the boy was embarrassed.

"Everyone who visits has to hear about the bar mitzvah," Sarah added, shyly.

"He's the proud father. That's what it's all about, right Schmuli?" Sal came to his friend's defense. Then he turned to Sarah. "One day, when you have children, you'll understand," he said. The girl blushed deeply and didn't respond.

"So Terry, tell me, where are *you* from?" Reba asked.

Sal noticed Zeyda having trouble finding his napkin. He had placed it on his lap and forgotten. Sal found another one and handed it to him.

"Wisconsin," Terry answered.

"Quick, Chaim, what's the capital of Wisconsin?" Schmuli asked suddenly. "He's in a geography contest at school," he explained to Sal and Terry.

"Madison," the boy answered immediately.

"You're being rude, Daddy," Sarah scolded.

"Excuse me. What were you saying, Terry?"

"I was born and raised in Racine."

"How many brothers and sisters do you have?" Motke asked.

"None. I was an only child."

"You want some of mine?" he joked. And with that Sal reached across Terry and tried to tickle the boy, who was the same age as Bennie. But Motke slid his chair back quickly enough to get out of the way.

"Motke! We have company!" Reba scolded. "What can I do with him?" she asked, shaking her head. "He's a whole comedian."

"All the great comedians are Jewish," Schmuli said, as he popped the last piece of bread into his mouth.

"But not all great Jews have to be comedians," Reba said, this time more seriously to Motke.

But the boy was oblivious. It was obvious to Terry that he adored Sal and also adored all the attention his antics brought him.

"No brothers or sisters, huh? That's unusual," Schmuli said.

"Not where I come from," Terry said.

"Are your parents alive?" Schmuli asked.

"My mother died when I was two. My father raised me alone until I was seven, then I went to boarding school. At seventeen I graduated and went to college for four years. Then I went into my father's real estate business."

Sal could tell that she was offering all this information preemptively. But it didn't work. The questions kept coming.

"Real estate," Schmuli said, nodding his head. "That's a good business."

"Yes, it is. My father was very good at what he did, and he taught me the business. He died two years ago," she said, unemotionally.

"So, do you have *any* family?" Reba asked. And for some reason, all the children were suddenly quiet.

Sal started to regret bringing her here. Even though it was his idea, and Schmuli was glad to have her join them, now it seemed totally inappropriate. They were grilling her.

But Terry handled herself beautifully. "I have two aunts. One on my father's side, one on my mother's side. A couple of cousins. Of course, it's not like this," she said with a smile. And Sal felt himself sigh with relief. "So," Terry continued, "how did you two meet?" she asked. Sal realized she was letting them know that this was the end of the story of her life, and he was impressed at how she handled it.

"Reba and I grew up together," Schmuli said. "Or did you mean me and Sollie?"

"Me and Schmuli grew up together too," Sal said. "Until he was about fifteen. Then he moved away, close to where Reba's family lived."

"Away! You say it like he moved to another country," Reba remarked.

"In Brooklyn, if you leave the neighborhood, it might as well be another country," Schmuli said.

"It was only twenty-five blocks to Borough Park," Reba explained to Terry. "And then, when I was eighteen and Schmuli was twenty-one, we got to know each other better and that was that," Reba said with a smile. Through Reba's thick glasses, Terry could see that she had pretty blue eyes.

"Help!" Ted called out.

"Were you always religious?" Terry asked.

"*My* family wasn't that religious," Schmuli said. "Reba's was. You want the woman, you play by the rules," Schmuli shrugged.

"Schmuli!" Reba exclaimed. "Don't talk about Halacha like it's a game!"

"I didn't mean it that way," he apologized. "Anyway, before I met Reba, when I lived on Sixty-fifth Street with Sollie, I was a little wild."

"You were, Papa? What did you do?" Motke asked.

"Nothing so interesting," Reba said, mildly disgusted.

"Like what?" Chaim asked. At ten he was mature for his age, and large too. Although only two years separated him from Motke, it seemed like much more to Sal.

"He would light firecrackers and watch people jump when they went off," Sal said. "And he liked to play on the roof of the apartment building we lived in."

"You lived in the same building?" Sarah asked.

"Yeah, I lived on the ground floor and your dad lived on the fifth floor," Sal explained. "There were no elevators, and he hated to walk up and down the steps."

"Was he fat like now?" Motke asked.

Schmuli laughed, but Reba scolded the boy.

"He was a little thinner, but not much," Sal said. "The stairwells were very wide and straight with long, wooden banisters, so your father would slide down them."

"Remember when I actually broke one, Sollie? And you had to promise not to tell?"

"Everyone knew it was you."

"What else did he do?" Motke begged.

"Look what you started," Reba said to Sal.

"He squirted his water gun out the window at people passing by."

"If not for Sollie, I would have done much worse, believe me," Schmuli added.

"What else, Sollie?" Motke asked. "What else?"

"Should I tell about Halloween?" Sal asked.

Schmuli looked at Reba for the answer.

"You had Halloween?" Rachel asked, shocked. She had said nothing throughout the meal, but the thought of her father celebrating the secular holiday of Halloween brought her out of her silence.

"You're as bad as the kids," Reba said to Sal.

"I didn't know better back then," Schmuli explained. Then he stood up and headed to the bathroom, only to return and sit back down. "Sarah's in there," he explained. Then, to Sal, he said, "So? Tell the story already!"

"I'll wait," Sal said.

"For what?" Schmuli asked.

"For you to go to the bathroom."

"Why?"

"I can't take the pressure," Sal said, sheepishly.

"*I* have to go to the bathroom, and *you* can't take the pressure?"

"It's just that I'll start the story, but you'll be more interested in when the bathroom is empty. Then, just when I'm about to tell - "

With that Sarah left the bathroom and Schmuli jumped up.

"See? What did I tell you?" Sal said.

"You're a meshuginah!" Schmuli shouted as he closed the bathroom door. They could all hear him through the door: "*He* feels pressure!"

Sal glanced around the table to see if anyone would sympathize. He caught Terry's eye but all he got was a confused stare.

Schmuli returned to the table and faced Sal. "You feel better now I went?"

"Okay, okay," Sal said. "Am I telling the Halloween story or not?"

The kids all shouted for him to continue.

"Well, your father was dressed as a robber and went out trick-or-treating. You know what that is, right?" he asked.

"Sure! That's when you go to people's doors and they give you candy!" Motke volunteered. It didn't surprise Sal that the little boy knew all about it even though he had never done it.

"So he knocked on one door and a very old lady answered, and remember, your dad was pretty big even when he was eleven. The old lady didn't realize it was Halloween and screamed and started to hit him and made a whole commotion."

The children all broke into laughter. Reba wiped Yankeleh's dirty face and swept him out of the high chair. "Time for his nap," she said, as she left the room.

"Help!" Ted yelled.

"So what happened?" Motke asked.

"So I came running, but I was dressed as a bum myself and the lady thought I was also going to hurt her, so she slammed the door and called the police!"

Sal could see that Terry was enjoying the story as much as the kids were. "And the policeman actually came and calmed down the woman and told us to go home. He said we were too old to go trick-or-treating anymore."

"And we were only eleven!" Schmuli added.

"Yeah, but we were pretty big for eleven."

"See Avi, I told you, it's not always so good to be big," Schmuli said to his son, who was small for his age.

Reba came back into the room without Yankel.

"So fast?" Schmuli asked.

"He was exhausted," she explained as she sat down. "Me too," she added.

"So what else?" Terry egged him on.

"Okay, okay. That's enough," Sal said, trying to stop it before it started.

But Schmuli ignored him. "He hates dirty butter."

"Excuse me?" Terry asked.

"Ah, come on. No one likes dirty butter," Sal pleaded.

"I don't get it," Terry said.

"Once I made the mistake of putting out the butter without scraping off the crumbs from the toast, and Mr. Martha Stewart here wouldn't eat it," Reba explained.

Terry turned to Sal and gave him a puzzled look.

"So? Would *you* eat it?" he asked her.

"I think I probably already have, many times. Who cares about some toast crumbs?"

"There. You see?" Reba said emphatically. "Now, where are you two heading next?"

Terry looked to Sal for an answer.

"I was thinking of taking her to the F train stop at Smith and Ninth Street."

Reba made a face. "A subway stop?"

"Yeah! The one outside, way up there. You've been there, Schmuli. Don't you remember the view?"

"I was there?" he asked.

"This man has a mind like a sieve. We were there together when we were teenagers," Sal reminded him.

"During the Jurassic Period?" Motke teased.

"Help!" called Ted.

"Well, I've always liked it. It's the highest elevated line in the entire New York system, and it's got a panoramic view."

"What's that?" asked Motke.

"It's when you can see all around you, for miles and miles, with nothing in the way. You can see the Statue of Liberty, the bridges, a lot of Manhattan, and then you can see the Verrazano Bridge, Staten Island, and parts of New Jersey. I mean, if you like that kind of thing."

"I think it would be interesting," Terry said.

"*You* never took *me* there," Reba teased Schmuli.

"Who could take you anywhere with all those brothers of yours!"

Reba and Schmuli teased each other for a while as Sal listened. He felt good just being there. Angela had always refused to visit Schmuli and Reba because she found their orthodoxy ridiculous and their children too messy and too noisy. It was difficult, during their marriage, to visit as much as he would have liked to. Though he was sure they understood why he didn't come, he always felt bad about it. Since his divorce six years ago, he visited more often, and Bennie and Motke played together. Sometimes Reba even watched Bennie for him in a pinch, though Sal didn't like to ask her. With seven of her own, and another on the way, the last thing she needed was another wise-ass eight-year-old.

"Sollie, I have some canned tomatoes for your father. Come, I'll give them to you," she said.

Sal stood up and followed her to the small pantry off the dining room. She rummaged through the Mason jars and boxes as she spoke.

"So, you're giving her the tour?" she whispered.

"Yeah."

"How did she hear of you all the way from Wisconsin?"

"She happened to get her hands on an old brochure."

"Happened to? Nothing just *happens*. There's a reason."

"Coincidence, that's all."

"She's beautiful, Sollie. And rich."

"How do you know she's rich?"

"An only child. Her father sent her to boarding school. He made money in real estate, now it's all hers."

"She lives in Wisconsin, Reba."

"What's in Wisconsin? Cows are in Wisconsin."

"Her business is there."

"There's plenty of real estate in Brooklyn, too."

Sal laughed. "You're like a real old Jewish yenta."

"And you're acting like an old man. You don't even go out anymore."

"What is this? Did you and Joe write this script together or something?"

"Your seventy-year-old father acts younger than you," she stated. "At least he keeps his eyes open."

"What the hell does that mean?"

"It means that sometimes you're like ... like that stupid bird with one word that no one can get through to," she said, pointing in the general direction of the living room.

"Help! Help!" Sal called, using a tiny, squeaky voice.

Reba reached her arm all the way back into the pantry and rummaged around. "I wonder if I actually used that last jar," she said to herself. "Sollie, listen to me. This woman is for you, I can tell."

"Yeah, how?"

"The way she looks at you. A woman can tell with another woman."

Sal felt himself get embarrassed. And Reba saw it.

"I know you as long as I know Schmuli; I think I can talk to you like this."

"Come off it, Reba. I know her maybe twenty-four hours."

"Why do you think she came here? To meet your friends."

"She came because she has nothing better to do."

"A beautiful, wealthy woman has nothing better to do in all of New York City than eat lunch with a whole mishpocha of Orthodox Jews she never met?" she asked, tilting her head in disbelief.

"Well, I made it sound interesting."

"So? She could have said no, no?"

"Look, she's not interested in a long-term relationship."

"What woman her age isn't interested in marriage?" she persisted.

"And even if she was, why would she want me?"

"Because you're handsome and sincere and you have something she needs."

"What the hell do I have that a woman like her could possibly need?"

"You have a big heart." She handed him the jar of tomatoes. "And now you also have a jar of tomatoes," she teased. "Tell Joe they'll keep awhile," she said, and left him standing in the pantry, a little confused, as she walked back into the dining room. As he started to follow her, his beeper went off. It was Joe. Probably nothing. The usual request to pick up something on the way home.

"I gotta make a phone call, then we'll be outta here," he told Terry, who was still at the table talking to Schmuli and his family.

"Take your time," she said, obviously feeling very relaxed.

Sal went upstairs where it was quieter, to Reba and Schmuli's bedroom, to use the phone. The room was a wreck. Clean laundry was strewn all over the bed, waiting to be folded and put away. The blankets were on the floor. The walls were bare except for the jumble of photos of the children over the bureau, which was old and stained. Still, it was the heart of the family and Sal enjoyed being there. He sat on the edge of the bed, picked up the phone, and dialed.

"Yeah, Pop, what's up?" he asked, when Joe answered.

"Sweetheart, Angela called," he said, without beating around the bush.

Sal said nothing. He could hear the laughter of Schmuli's kids all the way downstairs, even through the door.

"Yeah, so?"

"It's not so bad. She just says when she gets into town next week she wants to see Bennie and have him spend some time with her twins - they should get to know each other a little bit."

Sal said nothing. Anger and sadness washed over him at the same time.

"Okay, Sweetheart?" Joe asked, tenderly.

"Yeah, okay."

"Everything is all right?"

"Yeah, sure. I'm at Schmuli's."

"How's Terry?" Joe asked.

"She's here too."

"Maybe you can bring her back here for supper. I'm having some people over anyway."

"'People?' Since when do you know 'people'?"

"If you tell me she's coming, I'll make it special. You call me and tell me, okay?"

"I don't think so, Pop."

"You take her to Schmuli's for lunch, but you won't bring her to your own home for supper? You're ashamed of me?"

"Come on, Pop."

"She's a very nice lady. Bring her here for supper," he said, this time more firmly.

Sal sighed. "Okay, okay. I gotta go."

"Don't worry too much, Sweetheart, about Angela. Maybe it would be good for Bennie to meet his brothers."

"Yeah," he said. "I'll call you later." He hung up.

'His *brothers*', Sal thought, and just the words choked him up. They weren't really his brothers. They were twin strangers and he would be damned if he was going to facilitate a relationship. It had been a long, long time since he'd cried over Angela. A long time since he'd felt that sorrowful, sinking feeling starting to come over him, and he wasn't going to start again now. Instead, he took a deep breath to calm himself, and opened the door. The voices and the laughter from downstairs felt like a warm breeze.

He could hear Terry's familiar chuckle, and it made him smile. He felt like he had known that laugh for a long time. Jeez. The last thing he needed was to fall in love with some woman who lived in Wisconsin and wasn't interested in a long-term relationship and who had given up on marriage before she even started. Still, Reba's words were interesting to think about. Maybe Terry really dug him, more than only physically. Maybe he was being blind. He sat on the bed and thought about it. About what he felt. About why he'd even brought Terry here to begin with. Because he knew she'd enjoy them. Because he knew they'd like her. Because, let's face it, he wanted to see how she'd fit in with his friends and wanted to show her an example of a great family.

He stood up quickly and headed down the steps to get Terry and get going.

"Sollie! Sollie! Come! Terry's talking to Ted!" Motke shouted as Sal came to the bottom of the steps.

"What's goin' on?" he asked, jolted out of his thoughts.

"It's a miracle!" Schmuli said.

The whole family was in the small living room with Terry, standing next to Ted's large cage. He walked over to her.

"What's up?"

"Ted decided to say something new for a change, that's all," Terry explained.

"She discovered the magic word to make Ted talk!" Avi said.

"Oh, yeah?" Sal asked, breaking into a smile. "And what is it?"

"I just walked over to him and whispered, very softly: 'Help!', and as soon as I did, he said 'Ted,'" Terry explained.

"He knows his name!" Motke shouted.

"He doesn't know anything!" Reba said.

"He likes Terry!" Motke said.

"Maybe he'll say something else. Talk to him, Terry," Schmuli asked.

"Let me try!" Motke said, sticking his face close to the cage bars. "Help! Help!" he yelled at the bird. But the bird just blinked.

"Enough, Motke. Let Terry try again," Schmuli ordered.

Terry had no choice. Sal considered rescuing her from all this, but decided not to. He was pretty sure she could get herself out of it if she wanted to. And he was enjoying himself.

She bent down, and instead of sticking her face close to the bars as Motke had done, she moved back a bit. Then, when everyone was quiet, she gently said 'Help!' and, immediately, the bird said 'Ted!' The children exploded into applause and laughter. Terry shushed them. Then she said to the bird, 'Ted,' and the bird said 'Jerk face,' which only got the children more excited.

"We're going to regret this," Reba said. "Who knows what other words they taught him. Better he should stay quiet."

"No! Make him talk some more," Motke demanded.

Terry looked at Reba. Reba shrugged.

"Jerk face," Terry said to Ted.

"Fart," said Ted.

"That's enough!" Reba said, this time seriously.

"We wait a whole year for the little stinker to talk, and when he does, what does he say? He curses us!" Schmuli said, laughing.

"Some miracle," Reba commented. "You know what miracle I'd like to see?" she asked. "A bird that helps with the housework!"

Schmuli laughed, and walked over to Reba. "Now come eat dessert," he said to them all.

"We're gonna split," Sal said. "We have a lot more to see before dark."

"Oh, come on! A little dessert first!" Schmuli thundered.

But Sal wouldn't relent.

"Stubborn as a mule, this one," Schmuli said, patting Sal on the back. He turned to Terry. "Thank you for coming, and thank you also for teaching my bird to talk dirty," he said, teasing her.

Terry laughed. "Any time."

"So long, Reba!" Sal called out.

She came back into the living room. "You have the tomatoes? Here, let me put them in a bag."

"Don't bother."

"They'll break rolling around that cab of yours."

"I'll be sure they don't," he said. "Thanks again."

"Send my love to Joe and Bennie," she said.

"I will," he answered, and they turned to leave.

"Remember what we talked about!" Reba shouted as they closed the door.

As they walked down the front steps, Sal said, "How the hell'd you get that crazy bird to talk?"

"I guess we must speak the same language," Terry said, as she put on her sunglasses and headed down the street to the cab.

CHAPTER THIRTEEN
Smith & Ninth Street Elevated

"This snow probably won't even make it to the ground," Sal said. "Down there I bet they don't even know it's snowing," he observed.

They were standing on the elevated train platform, eighty-eight feet above the street. Brooklyn spread out below them, the neighborhoods forming a patchwork of grids made up of short streets and long avenues. The sun broke through the clouds and lit up the panorama so that Sal could point out the Verrazano Bridge in the distance, linking Staten Island with New Jersey, and even the parts of New Jersey west of the Hudson.

Terry stood against the wall, looking down on the street below. Sal was right. The snow seemed to simply dissolve mid-air. Yet, where they were, it was like a small magical snow shower, shimmering in the sunlight.

"Come sit down and warm up," he said.

"One moment," she said. "Where's the best place to put this?" she asked him, taking one of Manny's flyers from her purse.

Sal shook his head with disbelief. "Why don't you just shower them down on the general public? They'll think it's a ticker-tape parade."

"Come on," Terry demanded.

"Try stapling it to the wooden part of the wall here," he said.

Terry stapled down the flyer and then sat down on the cold cement bench.

"Here, sit on this," he said, as he opened his backpack and took out a warm woolen lap blanket.

Terry stood up, and Sal folded the blanket lengthwise. Then he placed it on the bench and they both sat down.

"That'll keep our butts warm. And I brought you a hat, too," he added and plopped it on her head. Then he fished around in his pack and came out with a brown paper bag, greasy with oil. He pulled out a cannoli and handed it to her.

"What a nice surprise. Thank you," Terry said, and took the pastry. "Wow! It's so heavy! I don't recall it being so heavy yesterday."

"Yesterday you were distracted," he said and pulled a small thermos from his pack along with two paper coffee cups.

"You're very prepared, I see."

"It's part of the tour. Even says so in the brochure."

Terry took a steaming cup of coffee from Sal.

"Sorry I don't have your milk, but I do have some sugar packets."

"Black is fine," she said and smiled. He had remembered how she liked her coffee.

"You sure? I can go right downstairs and buy a pint."

"All the way down there? All *eighty-eight feet*?" she asked, gently mocking him. But he didn't seem to pick up on it.

"Why not? You gotta enjoy your coffee."

Terry smiled. "Everything's just fine," she said. "Let's just sit awhile. What are these little green things?" she asked.

"Where?" Sal asked, looking around.

Terry started to laugh. "Here!" she said, pointing to her cannoli.

"Oh. Those are chopped pistachio nuts," Sal said. "I refused to eat them when I was a kid. They looked too weird. Now Bennie does the same thing. You think taste is inherited?" he asked.

"Could be. My father and I both loved cantaloupe."

"Everyone loves cantaloupe. What's not to love?"

"I had a nanny once who didn't like cantaloupe."

"You had a nanny?" he asked, as he drank his coffee and ate his pastry.

"Several. Until I was seven. What's that called?" she asked, indicating Sal's pastry.

"Sfogiatella. Also called lobster tail. Doesn't look like it to me, but what the hell. It's great. You want a bite?" he offered.

"That's okay," she said.

"No, I insist. You gotta taste it," he said, as he handed her the napkin-wrapped pastry.

Terry took a small bite, and handed it back to him.

"You didn't get any filling," he said, and refused to take it back.

Terry took it again, this time taking a larger bite.

Sal looked at her expectantly. "Good, huh?"

She nodded as she chewed.

"You like it better than the cannoli?"

Again she nodded, this time enthusiastically.

"Let's switch," he said, and took the cannoli from her hand. "I like all of them."

A train emerged from the tunnel and made its way up the platform.

"These people are going to think we're nuts," Terry said, as the train doors opened. "Having a picnic on a train platform in winter."

"Us? We're nothing compared to what most of these people probably see every day, living in New York. One time, no kidding, I was walking down the street near where I live and a guy walked past me and said something. I thought he was saying hello to me, so I turned to him and said 'Oh, hello,' and you know what he did?"

Terry shrugged, as she nibbled the pastry.

"He shouted, 'I'm not talking to you, I'm talking to *him!*'"

"Who?"

"A spoon."

"Excuse me?"

"He was carrying a spoon and having a little chat with it when I so rudely interrupted," Sal said, deadpan.

Terry gave him a look of disbelief.

"I swear to God," Sal said. "He was talking to a spoon. But it was obviously a spoon he knew pretty well, so it was okay."

"You're pulling my leg."

"How come no one believes me when I tell them this stuff?"

The platform was empty again. The noises from the street far below drifted up, mostly car and truck horns. The snow spun in the strong wind currents, circling them, never quite landing.

"Should we get on the train and go somewhere?" Terry asked.

"Nah. It'll just take us into Manhattan."

"So, isn't there *anything* in Manhattan worth seeing?"

"All cities lose their novelty after awhile, remember?" he teased.

"Quite a memory."

"I'm a good listener. It's just that when I'm not listening I'm usually talking."

Terry smiled and continued to eat her pastry. "So, I take it you've never lived anywhere else?"

"Never. And I don't plan to."

"And why is that?"

"This is where I was born and raised. It's what I know. It's where my friends are, where my home is." Then he added, "Where do you live? I mean, you have a house?"

"An apartment."

"Not a house?"

"No. What's the point?"

"A house is … it's just more stable. You know, more permanent. A co-op doesn't have the same feel."

"It's not a co-op."

"A condo?"

"No. I rent."

"Get outta here! You're in real estate and you're telling me you don't even own anything yourself? Now *you're* pulling *my* leg."

"I'm serious," she said, patting her mouth with the napkin and starting her coffee.

"But why?"

"Because I move around a lot. And a house is a big responsibility."

Sal couldn't believe it. "I busted my butt to buy my house. And Joe helped me because he knew how important it was for a family to have a house."

"But I'm not a family."

"But didn't you grow up in a house? Most people, they grow up in a house, they can't ever live in an apartment."

"But we weren't a family, even when I was growing up."

Sal remembered her saying that her mother had died when she was two.

"Even one parent and one child are a family. When Joe's gone, me and Bennie will still be a family," he insisted.

"That's you and Bennie," she said.

"Yeah, you said you went away to school real young," he stated.

"*Went* away isn't exactly correct. Was *sent away*, is more like it. And, once I was away, my father sold the house and bought another one. And, when that one brought a good price, he sold it and bought another one. He saw houses as properties. He lived in them only until he could sell them. He could never resist a good price."

"What about once you came home?"

"I never really did. Not permanently. I stayed away until I was seventeen, then I graduated and went to college. I visited on holidays when I was younger, but eventually, I didn't bother. You know how most people have all their belongings, all their memorabilia, in their parents' attic or basement until they're settled?"

"Yeah."

"Well, I was the opposite. I kept everything I cared about with me at all times. When I was older, I rented storage space."

Sal shook his head. "That's pretty shitty," he said, feeling bad for her.

"I've learned to come to terms with it."

"How? I mean, don't you ever have any regrets?"

Terry smiled. "Of course I do. But you grow up, you learn to take responsibility for your own life, and not to waste time fighting for things you can never have."

She said it with finality, indicating to Sal that she wasn't much into talking about it anymore. Still, *he* wanted to talk about it. As if, somehow, he might be able to help if he only had more information.

"So, your father was some kinda bastard, huh?"

Terry's eyes widened. Sal started to apologize, but she cut him off.

"My father *wasn't* a bastard. He was never deliberately mean. He never hurt me. He just wasn't there for me. And he didn't know better. He was a cold, distant man, raised by cold, distant people. From what I've been told, my mother was just the opposite. Had she lived, I've always believed she would have warmed him up over time. I imagine sometimes that happens in good relationships. People learn to change just by living with another person that they love. You were married for sixteen years. Didn't you find that to be true with you and Angela?"

"Angela changed all right. But I don't think I did, not much. I mean, she wanted me to, but I didn't. I don't know. Maybe I resisted on purpose. Maybe I didn't trust her motives."

"Why not?"

"Because even though she was probably right about me being able to make something better of myself, her *reasons* for wanting me to stunk."

"How do you mean?"

"It wasn't really for my benefit that she wanted me to do better. It was for her."

"It seems to me it would have been better for both of you. And for your son."

"Yeah, but Angela didn't really want a kid, anyway. That was my idea."

"Really? She didn't want children?"

"Nope."

"Is that why you waited so long to have Bennie? I was wondering, he's eight, and you're divorced six years, and you were married sixteen years …"

"I can do the math."

"Sorry."

"Look, I've often wished to God we had Bennie after we were *married* two years, not two years before we split up. But it didn't happen that way. Bottom line is I have a beautiful, healthy son."

Terry was quiet.

"I think I've come to terms with it, as you would say. Some days I'm not so sure, though."

"What do you mean?" she asked.

"Some days the regret is so big, it's like a living, breathing *creature*."

"But it's only a matter of a few years' difference," she said.

"I don't mean the timing of when we had Bennie. I mean the entire marriage," he said and stood up suddenly. "See that building over there?"

"Yes?"

"That's the Williamsburg Bank Building. Once upon a time it was the tallest building in Brooklyn."

Terry stayed seated and watched as Sal stood gazing out over Brooklyn: over his entire world, his past, and most likely, his entire future. The snow came down harder, no longer just spinning in the air but actually landing on the platform, the tracks, and on him.

"You didn't wear a hat, but you made *me* wear one?" she said.

"I never wear them. They make my head itch." He could tell she was going to make a comment. "You have different hair than me. People with straight hair like yours don't seem to have that problem. Am I right?"

"I guess I never thought about it before."

"Well, once you think about it you'll see what I mean," he said softly. He was just making idle chatter, and he knew it. He was keeping his distance. Even though she looked so lovely wrapped in her parka with the snow on her fine lashes and on her nose. Even though he felt surer with each moment that they somehow belonged together. Even though she was unlike anyone he had ever met in his whole life, and at the same time she was like someone he had known forever.

"It's getting kind of cold. Maybe we should move on," Terry said, standing up. "Where to next?" she asked.

Sal looked at his watch. It was a little after three. Terry caught the gesture, as he knew she would.

"I'm sorry. I shouldn't have assumed -"

"No, no. I didn't mean anything. It's just that I really don't have anything else planned."

And she just stood there. So still. A blank expression. Like a child suddenly realizing that she's lost, trying to muster her courage. Just stood there with the snow falling on her hat, her hair, her face. She wiped her nose with her gloved hand. He walked over to her, not intending anything, not thinking, not really, and took that hand in his. He took off the glove and kissed the palm and then placed that palm flat against his cheek, his cold cheek, and felt the warmth of her hand. And still she just stood there. So he kissed her cheek, then her nose, then her mouth. And she didn't really respond to his kiss, but she didn't resist either. She let him. That was it. She just let him, and he could feel her willingness but not her desire, not like yesterday.

"Come on, I'll take you back," he said, and handed her her glove.

Terry took a deep breath and looked out over the rooftops. "It's a long way down," she said softly, as they headed for the stairs.

CHAPTER FOURTEEN
West Side Highway

He couldn't think of a thing to say. Not a single thing to ease the tension between them now. And she wasn't helping much. They were approaching the Brooklyn Bridge when Terry said, "You didn't have to take me all the way back. I could've taken a taxi or the train."

"Nah. It's no problem. Not much traffic on a Sunday afternoon, anyway."

"Does it ever scare you, driving around this city all the time?"

"I'm always worried, if that's what you mean. What would happen to Bennie if I was out of the picture?"

"He *does* have a mother," she said.

"Theoretically."

"Has she no interest in him at all?"

"Who knows what her interest is anymore. All I know is she never wanted him to begin with."

Terry said nothing, but Sal could practically feel the question forming, so he continued. "Not only did I have to agree to divorce her after the baby was born, I had to agree not to touch any of her money. Her lousy twenty-five grand that we were supposed to use to buy a house. And then she had the balls to try to get custody of Bennie anyway. But that was *after* she took up with James C. Wakefield the Third and had a weapon to use to get my kid away from me."

"What are you talking about?"

"Look, this is a whole story. And I thought you said you didn't want to get personal today."

"Well, since the tour is over ...." she began.

"Oh, I get it. Since you never have to see me again, it's okay if I spill my guts, make a fool of myself, and then disappear."

"I'm sorry. It's just that I'm curious. You keep saying that Angela didn't want a child, yet you had Bennie. Then you say she decided she wanted to keep Bennie, but you managed to get custody. You have to admit it's a cliffhanger."

"Why is it I can't get mad at you and stay mad?" he asked.

"Because -"

"That was rhetorical, Ter," he teased. "Actually, I knew it was all done between me and Angela two years before we actually ended it. I knew it was hopeless. But I still wanted a kid."

"You thought that would keep her?"

Sal held his tongue, knowing he would snap at her. Then he breathed deeply and said, too calmly, "Nooo. I didn't think it would *keep* her. Nothing could keep her."

"Then why get her pregnant?"

"You think I wanted her barefoot and pregnant, huh? Well, she accused me of the same asinine thing. It hurt me when *she* said it because I thought she would have known me better after all those years. But why would *you* think that?"

"Is that also rhetorical?"

"No, I mean it. You think I'm that kind of guy?"

"Every kind of guy, every kind of *person* will do things when they want something badly enough. You said you were obsessed with Angela. Maybe having a baby seemed like a way to keep the family together."

"I told you, it was over between me and Angela by then. But I knew I wanted a child. I remember it really crystallized for me one very specific moment in autumn when I was having lunch in Abington Square Park in the West Village. I was watching all these little kids and their mothers in the playground. It was the winter-end of autumn when it's already cold and the kids' cheeks are all red as apples. Me and Angela were having a really bad time. I think we both knew it was over. I watched those kids and I remember thinking, if I had only had a kid with her, it would have made it all worthwhile. All those wasted years," he said sadly, remembering. "And I regretted that my mother would never know a child of mine. And Joe wasn't getting any younger, either. So that night I hit her with it. I knew she'd refuse. She said, 'I don't want a kid. I want a divorce.' I wasn't surprised. But I wasn't ready to give up. I suggested we have a kid and *then* a divorce. She thought I was nuts. I don't blame her. But she must've thought it over and figured out a way to make it work for her, because the next night, after work, she laid down her terms. She'd get pregnant and have the baby, and then I would agree to divorce her and not ask for any of her money. It wasn't much. Her father had left it to her when he died. So, I agreed. She'd get her freedom and her money, and I'd get the baby."

"She was willing to give him up?" Terry asked, incredulously.

"Yep. For twenty-five thousand bucks."

They had made it across the bridge quickly, and Sal was driving across Canal Street as they continued talking.

"Bennie was a beautiful, healthy baby. We decided she would stay home with him awhile before going back to work and take some computer courses. Then it seemed like she really started to care about Bennie. And I was glad. I hoped we could be a family. I wanted to combine her money and some money Joe had promised me, and buy a house. Maybe I'd try going back to school again or something. But I was fooling myself. She wasn't staying home to tend to Bennie. Or to try to make it work with me, either."

"What happened?" Terry asked.

"What I didn't know was that she had been having an affair for several years on-again off-again. Then, I think when Bennie was about a year old, they got back together."

"And you had no idea?"

"Here and there I wondered. But, it was like, I didn't really want to think about it, even when she stopped sleeping with me."

"And you didn't guess?"

"She was very careful, and I was working a lot. We hardly saw each other. When she was home with him I didn't know what she did with her time. Then she lost all the pregnancy weight and was working out and looked great and I was taking courses and..." he stopped.

Terry said nothing, but to Sal she looked somewhat pained just hearing this.

"You sure you want to hear this?"

Terry nodded.

"Then she told me she wanted a divorce after all, and that she was gonna marry James. I guess I wasn't that surprised. What surprised me was that she wanted custody of Bennie. By then he was about eighteen months old. There was no way in hell I was gonna let her get him. It wasn't that she really wanted him, either. It was that she wanted to bust my chops."

"Why?"

"She was mad at me."

"For what?"

"For everything that was wrong with her life, and she was using Bennie to get at me. That's when I realized that Bennie was gonna keep me tied to Angela for the rest of my life. I would never be free of her, even after we were divorced. And it gave me this sick feeling. Like it was just the beginning of her using him to get at me. He was a pawn to her. I couldn't let that happen. I had to free both of us from her completely. Forever."

"So you had a custody battle?"

"No. My lawyer told me I couldn't let it come to a custody battle because she would have won hands down."

"Why?"

"Why? Because she had something I didn't: James C. Wakefield the Third. Once she was married to him, she could tell the judge she'd be a full-time mom. They'd be able to give him everything: life in a nice, safe suburb, private schools, you get the picture. If he lived with me, he'd be home with an old man all day while I went out and drove a cab on the streets of New York City. Who would you pick to raise a kid?"

Terry nodded.

"The truth is she hated being home with him. When he was a year old, she went back to work anyway and left him with a sitter. I hated that. Man, how I hated that! He wasn't a real person to her. She didn't really *know* him. Didn't pay attention. Didn't take him to the park or anything. Even Joe saw it. So he started to spend some time with Bennie to make up for it. 'Angela's for Angela,' he used to say. And I was a jerk. If I had known about good old James.... "

"So what did you do?"

"I asked the lawyer about joint custody, and he said I didn't need a lawyer, I needed a miracle worker. And then, it was like a miracle actually happened. Because Angela had told me she and Jimmy boy were gonna move to California where Jimmy was becoming a partner at a very posh law firm. Seems the firm he was with here in New York passed him up. They were both really excited about it. Angela always wanted to move out West, and Lover Boy's family was all from Nevada, anyway."

"But why was that good for you? If she had taken Bennie with them -"

"Yeah, but they couldn't. Not if we had joint custody."

"But you just said you didn't think you'd get joint custody."

"I know. But one day it dawned on me that it wasn't only me and Angela waging this mean little war. There was another player. And he probably knew very little about this stuff because Angela was probably smart enough not to bother him much about her kid. So I called James C. Wakefield the Third, man to man, and asked to meet with him. And he agreed."

Terry sighed deeply.

"You okay? I told you it was a whole story."

"I'm fine. Go on."

"We had drinks in this really swanky bar at The Waldorf. You know the kind of place, suits with suspenders and wingtips, cigars, Scotch, aged steaks. You walk through the door, you're in a time tunnel and it's the nineteen-fifties: no one's ever heard of the Surgeon General or cholesterol."

"What was he like?"

"Big, blonde, and bland. Opened his mouth and I fell asleep. One of these guys, he's talking and not saying anything. The ceiling fan made more interesting noises than he did."

"What did you say to him?"

"We made some small talk, sports, stuff like that. The guy was low-keyed, not really the asshole I'd anticipated, even though he stole my wife. He spoke about Angela like she was the Virgin Mother. But he didn't talk about Bennie, which was good. I made a big damned deal about his new partnership and moving out West. And he ran on about how glad he was to be able to go back out there. His big, blonde rich family and all ...."

"And ...?"

"Finally I said, 'Look, Jim, no hard feelings over Angela, okay? Me and her weren't right together from the start. But now there's a little kid involved, now it's complicated. I love my son. He's all I got, and all I care about in this whole world. Do you know how joint custody works?' I asked him. And he said he thought he did. It was where they got Bennie half the year and I got him half the year. I could tell he really didn't know much. That he hadn't been following the whole lousy fight between me and Angela. 'Well, that's not all of it,' I told him. 'You know, either one of us can demand that the other one not move beyond a certain distance of where we're living right now.'"

Terry's eyes lit up. "I get it."

"Yeah, so did he. He was a smart guy. But just in case, I made sure. I said 'Listen, Jim, I don't want this to become a custody battle because I'll demand joint custody and also demand that Angela stay within fifty miles of Brooklyn. If I do that, Angela will have to make a choice between you and Bennie. Now, I don't want to make trouble between you two, believe me. I just want custody of my son.'"

"How did he react?"

"He was hard to read. But I could tell he wasn't real sure who Angela would choose if she had to. And that made him worried. But I knew. Poor Bennie," Sal shook his head. "He had about as much chance as a one-legged man in an ass-kicking contest."

"Did he get angry?"

"Why would he? He knew how much I loved my son. And he knew I was giving him a way out. You think an up-and-coming hotshot lawyer like him wanted to be saddled with some noisy little brat that wasn't even his?"

"I guess."

"He saw what was what. 'Maybe I should talk to her,' he said. 'I think that would be a good idea,' I said."

Terry pulled her pack of cigarettes out of her purse and reached back in for matches.

"You're not gonna smoke that, are you?" he said, noticing that her hand was shaking.

"I need a cigarette."

He reached over, yanked the cigarette out of her mouth, broke it in half, and tossed it out the window without saying a word. She reached back into her purse and pulled out another cigarette and held it in her hand, protecting it from him.

"So you convinced James to convince Angela to give up Bennie," she said, putting the cigarette in her mouth.

"Yeah. But boy did I sweat it out. I mean, I figured this guy probably had about a dozen lawyer friends he could ask who would tell him how full of shit I was. That I'd be laughed right out of court. But I was banking on the fact that he didn't care enough about Bennie to bother fighting for him. And I was right." He stopped to watch her light up. "Screw it. You wanna smoke, smoke. What the hell do I care?"

"So Angela actually agreed," she stated, and took a deep drag of the cigarette.

"Angela never wanted Bennie to begin with. Angela was for Angela, and James was for Angela. Who was gonna be for Bennie? Me," he said, pointing to himself. "Me and Joe. *We* were for Bennie."

Terry had a strange expression on her face. Like she was trying to figure out something, and she was sucking so hard on the cigarette he thought she'd swallow it.

"It was the scariest thing I ever did in my life, and I never thought it would work."

They were heading north on the West Side Highway. The late afternoon sun was going down, drowning the huge apartment buildings in sunlight.

"You know," Sal continued, "I actually dreamed about him before he was born. I had his name picked out, and when I heard his heartbeat for the first time, inside her, I cried. And you know what she asked the doctor? His loving mother? She asked if it was too late to have an abortion!"

"Maybe she was just punishing you. She never would have done it," she said.

"I was never sure. Every day I went to work I was in a sweat that I'd come home and it would all be over. She threatened to do it. Often. Until she was in her fourth month I worried every day that she would do it. She tortured me with it."

Terry took one last draw on her cigarette, then crushed it out in the ashtray. Sal could tell she was upset.

"I told you it wasn't pretty."

But Terry said nothing.

"Hey, you okay?" he asked.

She nodded.

"Well, we're almost there," Sal said. Her silence was spooky. "I'm sorry if I upset you."

"I'm fine," Terry said. And it was all she said.

CHAPTER FIFTEEN
Marriott Marquis/45th & Broadway

Sal pulled up to the hotel to let Terry out.

"Sal," she said, "come up and at least have a drink with me. A goodbye drink," she added, before unlocking the door to get out.

He hesitated. Why bother? Why get his emotions in an uproar, get turned on to her again, and then have her go get pregnant tomorrow, hop on a plane, and go home. But it was as if she could hear his thoughts.

"You have to admit we've formed something of a friendship these past three days, don't you?"

"Yeah, but," he started. But what? But it wasn't enough. And at the same time the whole thing was impossible.

"Just come up and have a five-dollar-thimble-full of Ginger Ale," she smiled.

"Okay, okay. I'll pull into the parking lot," he said and left her waiting for him at the entrance.

They took the elevator to the eighth floor lobby, then another elevator to the twentieth floor, to her suite.

"You know, I thought these rooms would be much fancier for the price."

"You're paying for location. If you want to sleep on Broadway, you pay."

"I don't know about that. I just saw about a dozen guys sleeping out on Broadway for free," he said, checking out the bedroom adjoining the living room. "A whole suite, huh?"

"Why not be comfortable? So, what will it be?" she asked, taking off her coat. "Scotch? Wine? Some pop?"

"Got any beer?" he asked, and tossed his coat on the sofa.

"Sorry. I only have what came with the room."

Sal walked over to the kitchenette and opened the small fridge. Then he nosed around in the cabinets.

"See anything you want? If not, I'll call room service."

"That'll take a coupla hours, I bet."

"They're actually quite prompt."

"I'll have a scotch on the rocks, and I'll munch these pretzels if you don't mind."

"Help yourself. I'll fix your drink."

Sal scooped some pretzels into his hand and roamed the room. From the large windows he could see into a room across from theirs.

"Now *there's* something you don't see every day," Sal said. "Two clowns having an argument."

"Clowns? How do you know they're clowns?"

"It's that or they're psychotic."

Terry brought him his drink and looked out the window. Sure enough, the couple across the way were dressed in clown costumes, gesticulating angrily at each other.

"Maybe they're just rehearsing," Terry offered.

"I don't think so. Unless the universal symbol for 'Up Yours' is part of their act."

Terry burst out laughing.

"Is there a clown convention here or something?"

"I think I would have noticed."

"Maybe it's clown college graduation," Sal suggested.

"Clown college?"

"Sure. They exist," he said and took a drink of his scotch.

Terry sipped her white wine. "I believe you. I suppose even being a clown takes training."

Sal moved away from the window and sat down at the small round table. Terry turned on the radio and settled on a classical station. Then she sat at the table with him.

"You mind if I ask why you got so upset back there? When I was telling you about Angela?"

"I wasn't upset," she stated and stood up to get her cigarettes.

"Yeah, well, you don't owe me any explanations or anything," he said as he gulped the last of his drink, put it down on the coaster, and stood up to leave.

Terry looked genuinely surprised and also somewhat crestfallen. But she tried to joke it off. "Since when are you so easily put off?"

"I think I just ran out of conversation, is all," he said and picked up his coat. When he turned around, Terry took hold of his arm.

"I don't want you to go, but I can't think of one damned reason why you should stay."

"Repeat after me," Sal said. "Sal, I want you to stay."

Terry smiled and dabbed at her eyes with the bar napkin she had been using to hold her drink. She finally put down the cigarette without lighting it. "I was upset back there ...." she started, and paused to prevent the tears she felt coming, "because I realized that no one has ever fought for me the way you fought for Bennie. Not in my entire life. Not my father, that's for sure. Not Charles. Or Rose. And yet here, with you and your family and friends, everyone is fighting for something or...some*one*. You and Joe fought for Bennie. Denise is fighting for Josie, Josie's fighting to protect her child, and to keep her father alive for just a few more weeks. Even Manny, eccentric as he is, is fighting to keep your friendship! Why Sal? Can you tell me?" she finally sobbed. "Why didn't anyone ever fight for me?"

Sal's own tears were very sudden, from out of nowhere. Not like being sad and feeling them welling up. These were like cartoon tears, suddenly springing from his eyes, then falling onto his cheeks. He wiped them away with the back of his hand and dropped his coat to the floor. He pulled Terry to him and wrapped her tightly against him. He could feel her convulse with each sob.

"*I'm* fighting for you, Ter," he said, and he kissed the top of her head.

CHAPTER SIXTEEN
Marriott Marquis/Room 2010

"I haven't cried in years," Terry said, in-between sobs.

"I have that effect on women," Sal joked.

She laughed a small, almost sad laugh. Then she looked up at him, took his head in her two hands, brought him to her, and kissed him.

They kissed for a long time, at least it seemed to be. He considered moving them into the bedroom, but thought better of it. Let her make the decisions. Let her call the shots. He didn't want another disaster. And this might be his last chance with her.

"I want to make love with you," she whispered.

"I was starting to get that impression."

"You autodidacts are all alike." And she disappeared into the bedroom, leaving Sal standing there, not sure what to do. Did she want a minute to change, to put in her diaphragm?

"You'll have to be very well endowed if you're planning to make love to me from out there," she called out, finally.

He walked into the bedroom and sat down next to her on the enormous bed. "You know, making fun of a guy isn't most women's idea of foreplay."

"You're being awfully coy," she said seriously.

He took her hand in his and squeezed it. "Terry, if this is gonna be our first and last time, then let's not, okay? It's just too sad. If I make love to you now knowing I'll never see you again, I'll be concentrating on every detail, trying to memorize how fine your eyelashes are, and what a light, delicate amber your eyes are. And I'll be.... "

"I don't want you to be sad, Sal. Maybe this doesn't have to be our last time. Maybe we can work something out," she said softly, looking so intensely at him that he had to look away for a moment. Because if he met her gaze, that sincerity, he would fall apart for sure.

He leaned forward, put his head in his hands, and from the safety of the small darkness he had created for himself said, "Are you saying maybe we could be a couple? Or are you saying more like maybe you'll drop in and visit me next time you come back East?"

Terry gently tugged at him, forcing him to sit back up and face her. She held his hand again. "I'm saying it's a small, personal miracle that we found each other. That from the first moments in your cab on Friday I felt like I had known you forever and could tell you anything. It's a small miracle that I could feel this for anyone, but, maybe, maybe not for you? Maybe since you've had more intimate relationships than I have ...."

"Shhh," he said and kissed her. "It's a miracle for me, too," he whispered, and started to unbutton her silk blouse. It was so good to let go, to let himself feel everything he felt for her without having to hold back. He ignored the small voice of doubt and kissed her breasts gently, lingering, feeling their warmth and softness. She was so lovely. So womanly, all of her proportions just worked so well.

Terry stood up and undid her slacks, then slid them off. Her plain white cotton panties made him smile. A rich lady could wear silk and lace, but she wore cotton. And he loved them and loved how they looked on her, and he loved how her thighs swelled slightly and the gentle curve of her belly, not flat, not muscular, but soft and slightly rounded. She had an almost old-fashioned body, not chubby, but a bit fleshy, and he was so delighted he had to grab her.

"You're so beautiful," he said, lying her down and kissing her belly. "I feel like Magellan exploring a brand new land."

"Can I make one request, Senhor Magellan?" she asked.

"Bring back spices?"

"No," she laughed. "Take off all your clothes and lie down beside me."

Sal did as she asked. Once he was completely nude and lying next to her, she sat up and ran her hands along his chest, his thighs, his calves. She said nothing, just explored his body with her hands, slowly explored every part of him. Her gentle, loving touch aroused him. Her breasts grazed against him as she leaned over and kissed his mouth. He brought his arm around her and pulled her on top of him, had to feel her entire body on his, against him, feeling her warmth and taking in all of her subtle scents that reminded him of the earth itself, of the hot dusty earth and sweet lily-of-the-valley. He wanted it to last a long time, this embrace, this one-ness, this miracle of passion he had found, and in finding, knew what he had been missing his whole life.

CHAPTER SEVENTEEN
Marriott Marquis/Room 2010

"You know, the last woman I dated was so dumb that when I ordered three-bean salad she said, and I quote, 'Three beans? Are you on a diet or something?'"

Terry laughed. She was lying on her back with the covers pulled up to her chin. Sal turned on his side and gently pulled her to him. Terry ran her hands through Sal's hair, petting him and stroking him. "Why do you think *we* work so well? We're from such different backgrounds."

Sal thought about this as he ran his hand over her cheek and allowed his fingertips to trace along her nose and across her lips. "It's like you said, it's a small miracle."

"At our age, too."

"Our age?"

"We're not kids anymore, Sal."

"I know. But please don't say 'better late than never.'"

"I wasn't-"

"It's just that it makes whatever's good seem like second best because it didn't happen some other time, preferably before now. But years ago, even if we had met, we never would have gotten together, right?"

"Probably."

Sal took a deep breath.

"What is it?" Terry asked.

"I think some things in life are best when they happen later on. I wish people would just leave out the *'than never'*, you know? Just *'better late.'*"

Terry turned on her back again. She stared silently at the ceiling. They could both hear the alarm clock's tiny click as it moved from second to second. They could hear every little noise in the corridor.

Sal leaned on his elbow and faced her. "Remember I told you I was usually hostile with really good-looking women?"

"How could I forget?"

"Just so you know, I don't feel hostile anymore."

Suddenly they heard loud noises in the corridor, a variety of noises, difficult to discern.

"What the hell is that?" Sal asked.

Terry listened attentively. "Sounds like a gaggle of clowns." Then she added, "What *do* you call a group of clowns, anyway?"

"A giggle?" Sal suggested. Terry chuckled.

"Do you think it's symbolic that after we made love for the first time we are surrounded by clowns?" she asked.

"Well, I don't know about you, but I'm used to it," Sal joked.

"You're surrounded by *nice* clowns," Terry corrected.

"Sometimes my life feels like a circus, anyway. Or maybe more like a boxing match."

"There's been a lot of conflict."

"Yeah, and now I've gotta go another round with Angela."

Terry sat up and wrapped her arms around Sal. He turned towards her, and they embraced. The light in the room had shifted from dim to dark as evening fell, and they sat quietly in the darkness.

Sal looked at her, at the outline of her face in the darkness. "How can someone as beautiful and smart and funny and talented not be married by now? I just don't get it."

"What did you mean about going another round with Angela?"

"When she comes this week. I told you, didn't I?" He could feel her body stiffen slightly. "I thought I did. She's coming here with her whole crew."

"For what reason?"

"The custody battle, remember?"

Terry reached for the lamp on the night table and turned it on. "I thought you said you won that one years ago," she said, confused.

"I did. But apparently that was only round one. Now she wants to go at it again. I'm having lunch with her tomorrow."

"I don't understand. She hasn't lived with Bennie since he was two years old, and now she wants him back?"

"Let me explain: she hasn't lived with Bennie since he was two years old, and now she wants him back."

"Why didn't you tell me?"

"I thought I did. I mean, I told you some of it, I just didn't get around ―"

"What's your plan this time?"

"I don't have one. I'm just gonna have to let it go to court and see what happens. I don't have any bargaining chips, and good old Jimmy isn't gonna be a push-over like he was last time."

"Why is that?"

"I'm not sure. But I can tell this time they're in it together."

"What does your lawyer say?"

"He says I have a great case. All I have to do is get a better job, put a couple hundred thousand in the bank, and get married to a woman who will stay home with my kid." And as soon as he said it, the look on Terry's face made his heart jump. She stood up suddenly and tightened the sheet around herself.

"Ter! I was joking."

"What did the lawyer *really* say, Sal?" she demanded.

"Okay, okay. He *did* say if I were married and had more money I'd have a better chance."

"A better chance? Is that what I am then?"

"What are you talking about?" he asked, his panic rising. He could see where this was going.

"How dare you!" Terry accused. She became very calm and very quiet. Sal had never known anyone who got angry like that, and it scared the hell out of him.

"What?" was all he could manage, as he approached her.

Terry held up her hand to stop him from getting any closer. "Let me spell it out: your attempt to have unprotected sex with me yesterday was no spontaneous act of passion. That's why you got so huffy with me. And there I was thinking you were in love with me! And now I *have* had unprotected sex with you!" she cried, as the realization hit her. "Oh my God!" She ran into the bathroom and locked the door. He could hear her sobs.

"Terry ... I didn't know. I thought you were wearing the diaphragm. Why didn't you tell me? I didn't -"

"This was just a way to snag a rich wife! You knew I had money the day you met me at the airport. You knew I would like your family and friends, that's why you dragged me to meet them."

"Dragged you? You practically forced your way into my house. Not to mention invited yourself to dinner."

"You tried to manipulate me the way you did Angela. You think if you lose this custody battle with her that you'll take this baby from me!"

Sal banged on the door. "Who the hell are you to make a statement like that? You think I could just replace Bennie with another kid? That's because you never loved anyone, never wanted anyone the way I want Bennie." He could feel his temples throbbing with anger and took a deep breath to calm himself. How did they wind up screaming on opposite sides of a door?

"I'll tell you what I wanted!" she shouted from inside the bathroom. "I wanted a home, not some damned piece of real estate. I wanted a mother, a father, and a family. And I want a child."

"Well, maybe you should stop *wanting* and start fighting for it. You want someone to fight for *you*? Fighting means getting mean and messy sometimes, that's why you don't bother. You'd rather 'come to terms with it' instead. A nice little trick: if you can't get what you want, convince yourself it's not worth having. Well, screw that! I'm not proud of how things happened, but at least I fought for what I wanted, and no matter what happens I've had eight incredible years with my son. You quit before you even get started." And finally he was running out of steam. He felt ridiculous screaming at a bathroom door and went back and sat down on the bed. It was still warm, and Terry's clothing and underwear were scattered everywhere. He picked up her silk blouse and ran it absently between his fingers. There was no sound from the bathroom.

Sal rested and waited for his heart to stop pounding. Then he started to collect his clothes and stepped into his pants. He heard Terry emerge from the bathroom. Her eyes were red, her nose runny.

"I didn't leave Charles at the altar because I was quitting. I left him because he was wrong for me. We were wrong for *each other*," she explained calmly, still hugging the sheet close to herself.

"You left him at the altar? You didn't tell me that," he said, shocked, and zipped his pants. "How could you?"

"What should I have done? Married him and then divorced him?"

"You mean you let everyone show up and you had the priest there -"

"The minister."

"Whatever. You got all those people together and you crapped out on them?"

"Crapped out on *them*? It wasn't about them. It was about *me*!"

"It was about letting people down! It was about giving up! That's what it was about."

"How do you know what it was about? You weren't there! You didn't even know me!"

"What happened? Did you 'come to terms' with something at the last minute?"

"You're damned right I did! And thank God I realized it before I walked down that aisle only to find myself sixteen years later in a loveless marriage, betrayed, broke, and fighting for the right to keep my own child."

Sal couldn't believe what he was hearing. What kind of person does something like that? He laced up his shoes, threw on his shirt and coat, and walked out of the bedroom. As he approached the front door to leave, Terry called out, "Do us both a favor this time, and don't call later to apologize."

He pulled the door closed behind him and headed for the elevator.

CHAPTER EIGHTEEN
Park Slope/President Street

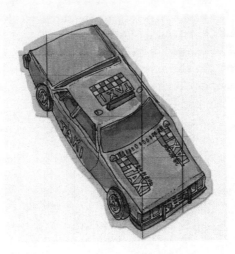

As soon as he opened his front door, Sal knew something was up. There were too many voices. Bennie came running up to him.

"Papa! Everyone's waiting! Where were you? Where's your beeper?" he asked, patting Sal's waistband.

Sal reached down and realized the beeper was gone. He'd probably left it at the hotel. "Who's waiting? What's going on?" he asked, as he maneuvered himself around Bennie and went inside. He draped his coat over the rocker as Joe came walking up to him. They were standing at the entrance to the dining room.

Joe stood quietly, realizing Terry wasn't there and somehow knowing she wasn't about to walk in the door.

Sal heard the voices in the kitchen. "What's up?" he asked Joe.

"I told you I was inviting a few people over, remember?"

"For dinner?"

"You think they're waiting for a trim?" Joe joked.

Sal pushed his hand through his hair and thought a moment. He didn't feel like socializing. Maybe he could get out of it.

"Come in and say hello, at least," Joe said, knowing that something was wrong, but not sure what.

"Who's in there?" Sal asked,

"Josie and Manny and my friend Frankie."

Sal was confused. The assortment of people just didn't make sense. Frankie was Joe's oldest friend in the world. Why the hell would he invite him and two of Sal's friends also? With that, a woman wearing an apron walked toward them.

"Hello. I'm Janet," she said, and held her hand out to Sal.

He reached for her hand mindlessly, trying to figure out who she was. Then it hit him. The new family from across the street. "Nice to meet you," he said.

"You're tall, like your father. Handsome too," she said and smiled. She was a lovely looking black woman, about sixty or so, with barely a wrinkle on her face. She had the whitest, straightest teeth Sal had ever seen, and she was obviously very at home in his house.

"Janet is helping with the cooking," Joe explained. "Come inside and sit down. You want a little wine?" he asked Sal.

Sal said nothing as he followed Janet and Joe into the kitchen.

The small television on the counter was on. When he walked into the room, everyone turned away from it to face Sal.

"Well, well, it's the prodigal son," Josie joked, as she stood up and gave Sal a peck on the cheek. "You trying to be fashionably late all of a sudden or what?" she asked and sat back down.

"I lost track of time."

"Where's Terry?" Manny asked.

"Yeah, wasn't she supposed to come with you?" Josie added.

Joe poured some red wine into a small Mason jar for Sal, since all of the wine glasses were being used, and put it down in front of him. They had all been drinking for a while before he got there, and their wine glasses were all over the table. Janet dropped some spaghetti into the large pot and stirred it.

"How ya doing, Frankie?" Sal said, realizing that he hadn't bothered to formally acknowledge the old man.

Frankie nodded. "Mezz a mezz," he said, gesturing with his hand.

"You know, I got a coupla calls off those flyers Terry put up for me," Manny said.

"Yeah? Who called?" Sal asked.

"One guy from Borough Park said he might want to buy them in bulk and could I sell him quantity?"

"You're gonna be a distributor now?"

"Maybe. The guy who's doing it now knows nothing."

Sal let it drop. He didn't have the energy to argue with Manny about yet another money making scheme.

"Listen, Brother-Of-Mine," Josie began, "I'm not real good at making nice, so I'm just gonna come out and ask you, what the hell happened to your lady friend?"

Sal sipped his wine and ignored her. What the hell was he supposed to say to them? He didn't know himself what happened. One minute they were talking about how great they were together, the next minute Terry was accusing him of some pretty shitty things.

"He'll explain when he's had something to eat," Joe said, protectively. Sal appreciated the gesture.

"You know, you don't look so good," Josie said, scrutinizing him. "Denise would say your gills are starting to look a little green."

"How's *she* doing?" Sal asked, changing the subject.

"Well, I'll tell ya the truth," she said, "she gave me an ultimatum."

"Yeah?"

"She said if we don't move in together within a month, she's leaving me."

"But she knows the sitch with Joann," Sal offered.

"She thinks I'm deliberately not telling Joann in order to keep her away."

Sal didn't say anything. Then he remembered what Terry said. "Well, Terry thinks you might be doing the same thing. So that makes two of them."

"*Terry* thinks?" Josie asked, shocked. "What are you, her agent?"

"Don't get your bowels in an uproar. We were talking about the whole thing with Joann, and she said it was just *possible* you might have some doubts about Denise, and that -"

"Jeez! She's some kinda witch or something," Josie said, still shocked.

"Don't be insulted," Sal said.

"Who's insulted? Me and Denise had this whole long talk, and, you know, she was right. So we made a plan."

"What's the plan?" Joe asked, as he set the table.

"You gonna have a wedding?" Manny asked.

"Something like that. But not just yet."

"You're married?" Frankie asked Josie.

"No more I'm not," she answered.

Frankie looked confused. He didn't know Josie very well and hadn't seen her in a long time. "You have a daughter, right?"

"Yeah. I think you met her once, a long time ago," Josie said, trying to help the old man remember. He was only a few years older than Joe, but his mind wasn't so sharp.

The doorbell rang. Janet put down her wooden spoon and headed out of the kitchen.

"Congratulations!" Schmuli's voice thundered as he walked through the front door carrying flowers and champagne.

Janet shot him a look.

"What? I said something wrong?" he asked her.

Janet shushed him and grabbed the flowers. They walked into the kitchen together.

"Schmuli, how are you?" Joe asked, as he gave the big man a hug.

"Ah, Giuseppe!" Schmuli said. "And how are you, Mr. Foglia," Schmuli asked Frankie. But Frankie was obviously unsure of who he was. "Sam Goldberg. Sollie's friend," he explained.

"Oh! Sure, sure. Now I remember. From Bensonhurst."

"Absolutely. From Bensonhurst!"

"Who were you congratulating?" Sal asked Schmuli, noticing Janet putting the champagne in the fridge and the flowers in a vase.

Schmuli was stumped and wasn't much good at hiding it.

"I told him about me and Denise," Josie jumped in.

"When?" Sal asked.

"Earlier. I happened to bump into him."

"Yeah, she told me all about it," Schmuli ad libbed. But Sal could see that something was up.

"About what?" Sal asked Schmuli, knowing he didn't know anything.

Schmuli looked at Josie for help.

"About me and Denise moving in together," she said quickly and got up. "You guys need any help?" she asked Joe.

"Yeah, go get me some forks from that drawer," he said, pointing at the silverware drawer.

"So *that's* what all this is about?" Sal asked Josie. "A celebration for you and Denise?"

"Yeah, yeah," Joe said and bumped into Josie who dropped the forks. Joe bent down to help pick them up.

"Sit, sit. I've got them," Josie ordered him.

"Grandma, when is dessert?" Courtney said, as she padded into the kitchen. She was a tall, barefoot seven-year-old wearing denim overalls.

"Come in here and be properly introduced," Janet told the child.

Courtney walked in shyly and let her grandmother introduce her to Sal. Sal smiled and shook her small hand. "Good to meet ya," he said.

"Thank you," she said.

"Where are your socks?" Janet scolded. "You go right now and put them on and don't come back until I call you for supper, hear? You know you have to eat your supper before dessert," she said, firmly.

Courtney walked out and headed back upstairs to play with Bennie.

"That's my granddaughter, Courtney," Janet said to Sal.

"I figured."

Janet dried her hands on her apron and went back to the stove.

"So where's Terry?" Schmuli asked Sal, as he sat down next to him.

"He's taking the fifth," Josie said.

"What? Something's wrong?" Schmuli asked, looking around the table, waiting for an answer. But nobody spoke.

Sal broke the silence. "So, if we're having a celebration for Josie and Denise, where's Denise?" he challenged.

"She's coming a little later. She got stuck at work," Josie said quickly.

Suddenly Sal stood up. He downed the remains of his wine and walked out of the kitchen, into the living room, and sat down in a rocker facing the fireplace.

Josie put the forks on the table, picked up her wine glass, and followed Sal.

"What's the story, Bro? Where's your friend?" she asked and sat down on the couch, facing him.

"Where's *your* friend?" Sal asked.

"I told you, she'll be here."

"Bullshit," he said, unemotionally.

Josie didn't answer. She fidgeted with her cross and sipped her wine. "Terry went home early?" she asked.

"What's the big deal about Terry, huh? It's not enough that I'm here?"

"Yeah, you're the life of the party. Now, tell me what's goin' on."

"She's back at the hotel."

"Why?"

"Because that's where she's staying, that's why."

"Screw off."

"Bringing her back for dinner was tentative, anyway."

"You two were pretty tight when I saw yiz yesterday."

"That was yesterday."

Josie stood up. "If I wanted to pull teeth, I woulda become a dentist," she said, and put her empty glass on the mantel.

"Just sit down and shut up, okay? I didn't expect a whole Shriner's convention when I came home. I need to think about a few things."

Josie didn't sit down, but she did keep quiet.

"You think I was wrong in taking Bennie away from Angela?" he blurted out.

"Whaddya mean 'taking away'?"

"I mean, fighting her for custody."

"That selfish bitch! You're still thinking about that?"

"Think of the lifestyle, will ya? Maybe Angela will be better to him now she's got her own kids."

"And maybe I just needed to meet the right man, huh?" she teased. Sal was quiet. "Sal, Angela's been gone a long time now. Not that you shoulda ever married her."

"All right, all right. That's old stuff by now."

"Can I ask you a question?" Josie asked, leaning toward Sal.

"Yeah?"

"Was Terry making a play for you?"

"Yeah, I think. Well, maybe not exactly."

"What the hell happened?"

"Everything was going fine. She invited me back to the hotel and we talked, and ...."

"And?"

"And it was so incredible, Peachy. I thought I was in love with her. But who the hell knows? I haven't felt much for a woman in years, you know?"

"I know."

"I know you know," he said and sipped his wine. "Then I mentioned that Angela was coming and I was gonna have another battle with her, and Terry flipped out."

"Why? I don't get it."

"Think about it from her point of view. She thinks I'm only interested in her so I can get married to a rich lady and win the custody battle."

Josie's eyes lit up. "Hey! Great idea!"

"Quit it, will ya?"

"She serious?"

"Hell yes."

"But, how does she feel about you?"

"She said it was a 'small, personal miracle' that we just met and felt like old friends."

Janet had walked quietly into the room. "Supper is ready," she announced, then went upstairs to fetch the children.

"Look, I gotta tell you something," Josie began, and sat down on the couch, leaning toward Sal. "I know this is shitty timing, but this whole dinner thing isn't really about me and Denise." She paused. She could tell by his blank look that he had no idea. "It's about Joe and Janet," she said quietly, not meeting his eyes.

"Janet?" he asked.

"Yeah. They're pretty tight. You really didn't know?"

"He never even introduced us."

"He was afraid. He's so worried about you."

Sal jumped up.

"Hold on a minute, will ya?" Josie grabbed his arm. "They've been seeing each other for six months now. He was waiting for you to find someone for yourself. But he doesn't have that much time to play with, you know?"

Sal sighed deeply and walked back into the kitchen.

As soon as Joe saw him, he could tell that his son knew. They walked toward each other.

"Congratulations, Pop," Sal said, as he embraced the old man and patted him on the back. "I wish you all the best." Janet and the children had walked into the kitchen. Sal turned to Janet and gave her a hug also. She started to cry.

"You're already so special to me, you know that? I feel like I know you so well," she said and stepped back to wipe her eyes.

"Well, bring out the champagne. This is a celebration, isn't it?" Sal said.

But Joe had sat down and was crying into his apron. Josie was holding his hand and petting it. Manny was serving up the spaghetti as Schmuli noticed that Janet didn't look well. "Sit down," he said and pulled up a chair for her.

"Why's everyone crying? This is supposed to be a happy occasion!" Sal said, unconvincingly.

The two children had come into the kitchen and were puzzled.

"Sit! Sit and eat!" Schmuli ordered them.

"Why's Grandpa crying?" Bennie asked, and walked over to Joe.

"It's just that I'm so happy," Joe said to the child, as Bennie patted the old man's head.

"Because of the wedding?" Bennie asked.

So, even Bennie knew. Everyone knew except Sal. Even Terry seemed to guess. And that was only after knowing Joe a few minutes.

"Who's getting married?" Frankie asked.

"Joseph and I are getting married," Janet explained.

"And me and Denise are moving in together," Josie told him.

Frankie nodded, then looked confused.

"Okay, okay. The macaroni's getting cold," Manny announced, once he was done serving.

"So, when's the wedding?" Frankie asked.

"We don't have a date yet," Janet offered. "We'll have to sit down and discuss it. As a *family*," she added, looking at Sal, as if for his approval.

He nodded. "Hey, it's up to you guys. You wanna have it here?" Sal asked.

Joe and Janet looked at each other. "You feel okay about it?" Joe asked, timidly.

"Sure! I'll do the cooking for the reception."

"Oh, no! We'll do the cooking ourselves!" Janet offered.

"Yeah, I heard about your famous roti," Sal said.

"You did?" Janet asked.

"Yeah, Bennie can't stop talking about it."

"You think Terry would come back for the wedding?" Joe asked.

Sal reached for the wine and poured himself another glass. His stomach already felt lousy, so why not? "I wouldn't count on it," he said.

"Listen, Blood. I gotta talk to her about this Pet Day stuff. You planning to see her again before she goes back?"

"When *is* she going back?" Schmuli spoke up.

"I have no idea," Sal said, and clammed up, even though everyone was staring at him.

"That's too bad," Schmuli said. "The kids have a lot of plans for her and that meshegeh bird of mine."

"Enough, already!" Sal said, standing up and banging his palm on the table. The wine glasses shook. "I only know her ..." he looked at the kitchen clock. It was seven. "Forty-eight hours! Okay? I don't know when she's going back."

Everyone was still until, finally, Schmuli bent over his plate of spaghetti and started eating. Then everyone else did the same. But Sal couldn't. He was too upset. He sat back down and ran his hand through his hair.

They all ate in silence, even the children, who didn't know what was going on but knew Sal was angry at something. Finally Joe spoke up.

"So when are you and Denise setting a date?" he asked Josie.

"One thing at a time, okay, Pop?" she said, as she ate her food. "Let's see if we can stand living together first."

"What's to stand? You know her a long time."

"Yeah, I know. We been through this, believe me," she said and kept eating her spaghetti.

"Maybe we'll have a double wedding," Joe offered, with a small, playful smile.

"Now we just have to get someone for Sollie, and we'll make it a triple play!" Schmuli said, and immediately wished he hadn't.

Sal stood up slowly, looking like someone who'd just had the breath knocked out of him. He started to walk out of the kitchen, then turned to face them all. "Terry was right. You're all just running for shelter. Well, let me tell you something. Sometimes it's lonelier inside than outside," he said. He walked into the living room, picked his coat up off the back of the rocking chair, and left the house.

CHAPTER NINETEEN
Park Slope/Snooky's Bar and Grill

Sal zipped his coat all the way up to his neck. It was colder now that the sun had gone down. He walked to the corner, to Seventh Avenue, and turned. He didn't know where he was going. Hadn't intended to leave in the first place. Still, it felt good to be alone with his thoughts.

The Avenue was bustling with people looking for a restaurant for dinner, or shopping, or dragging sleepy children home from shopping. Sal loved all the activity of evening, especially watching the families. He knew how their lives went. How they planned their days around the kids. How they had to get things done while the kids napped. He loved all the details of everyday life as a family and had tried to maintain them all after Angela had left. Not that she'd been any good at the details when she was there. If only he had known that about her before he married her. But, the truth was, he hadn't known her at all. Of course, that hadn't stopped him back then from wanting her, wanting her so badly he did everything he could to get her and from being so damned proud of himself when he succeeded. Talk about learning a lesson. What was it that Terry had said that morning? Learning the *right* lesson.

He continued up the street and stopped in front of Snooky's Bar and Grill. He was considering getting a drink when he heard Manny calling his name.

"Wait up!" Manny called as he slowed his run to a walk.

Sal wasn't in the mood for company.

"Where you goin'?" Manny asked breathlessly, as he approached.

"I have no idea. But wherever it is, I'm going alone."

"Whaddya mean?"

"I need time to think, okay?"

"Sure," he said, still trying to catch his breath. Manny wasn't in the habit of running after anyone or anything. "Sure. Let's go inside and have a beer," he suggested, nodding toward the bar.

"Where I come from, 'alone' translates to the singular."

Manny linked his arm with Sal's and started toward the door of the bar. Sal tried to wrest his arm away, but it was no use. Manny wouldn't let go.

"I'll pay," Manny said as he opened the large glass door with his right hand while maneuvering Sal inside with his left arm.

The few people at the bar checked them out when they came inside. Sal was used to the looks they got when he and Manny were together, but this time people seemed more alarmed than usual. They were trying to figure out if Sal was in any real trouble, and, also no doubt, if *they* were.

Manny released Sal, and they both took a seat at the bar. Everyone turned back to their drinks, but the bartender was keeping an eye on them.

"Why can't you leave me alone for just once?" Sal begged.

"Because you're dangerous alone."

"To who? To you?"

"To yourself."

"Yeah, how?"

The bartender came over and took their order. He didn't seem entirely satisfied that they weren't there to make trouble.

"I don't know what happened with Terry, and I'm not gonna ask, either. But I'm willing to bet whatever it was, *you* screwed it up."

Sal didn't answer. He was watching the television perched high on a shelf above the bar. The news was on. Disasterville all over the place.

"Okay. What are you betting? A pack of Sen Sen?"

Manny stood up to reach into his rear pants pocket, and the bartender, who had been watching them from a distance, must've assumed he was reaching for a gun because he dropped down behind the bar and put his arms over his head. Manny didn't notice, but Sal did.

"You're scaring the shit outta the bartender over there," he said, casually.

Manny retrieved his wallet and sat down again. He slapped a twenty dollar bill on the counter. The bartender peeked out from behind his hands and determined that it was safe to get up. The other customers were too involved in themselves to even notice.

"Twenty bucks says it's your fault."

"*What's* my fault?"

"The break-up with Terry."

Sal shook his head. The bartender brought their beer and waited for payment. Sal handed him the twenty that Manny had put down. "He's big, but harmless," Sal reassured the man. Then, to Manny, he said, "There's no break-up. There has to be a relationship for there to be a break-up."

"Listen, Blood, I wanna call her myself about this business deal, okay? So if you don't intend to see her again, at least give me her number."

"I don't have her number."

"Where's she staying?" he asked, and drank his beer. Then he looked around for something to eat. "No pretzels or nothing?"

"They never put anything out in this place."

"Yo! Bartender!" Manny called.

The bartender walked over, still a bit cautious.

"How about some pretzels or something?" Manny said.

"I don't keep any," he said. "But if you want -"

"Just ignore him," Sal said to the bartender. The man nodded and walked away. "Don't embarrass me anymore, okay? It's bad enough you dragged me in here like some kinda little kid."

Neither of them noticed when the door opened and Schmuli and Josie walked in. They came up to the bar and stood behind Sal and Manny.

Sal spun around. "What the hell is this?"

"Whatever happened with you and Terry, you should go apologize," Schmuli insisted.

"*I* should apologize? Do you know what *she* said to *me*?"

"Whatever it was, you deserved it," Josie said. "Now come on."

Manny stood up, walked behind Sal, who was still seated, and slipped his arms under Sal's armpits. As he tugged on Sal, trying to force him to get up, Sal simply yielded. "Leave me go, will ya?" he said as he pushed Manny away. "We'll talk about this outside."

Sal headed for the door, with the three others behind him.

"My car is parked a block away," Josie said, once outside. "Now, you listen up, Brother-Of-Mine," Josie started, pointing her finger at him. "I'm gonna drive you into the city, and along the way you're gonna tell us what happened. Then, when we get to her hotel, you're gonna tell Terry 'I'm sorry for being such a big-time jerk and not bringing you home to dinner like I said I would.'"

"I never promised that. *She* invited herself."

"Yeah, well, that's not the story I got from Pop," she said and poked his shoulder.

"Cut it out!"

"She's a nice woman. Pretty. Intelligent," Schmuli began. "Did he tell you she got my meshuginah bird to talk?" he asked them.

"Ted? Ted's talking now?" Josie asked.

"Well, not exactly *talking*. Let's just say she expanded his vocabulary."

"You gotta go get her and bring her back for dinner, like you promised," Manny said, matter-of-factly.

"I never promised! Okay? *Joe* invited her, not me. I don't even remember telling Joe anything either way."

"Then why was Joe expecting both of you, huh?" Josie asked.

"Because Joe has a stick up his butt about me getting married to whoever he can pawn me off on."

Manny, Josie, and Schmuli looked at each other, trying to decide what to do next. Finally, Josie spoke up. "So what if he does? He's your father."

Sal ignored her and started to walk away from them but they all fell into step with him. Manny shoved his hands into his pockets as he walked. Schmuli stayed silent, not knowing what to say or do. It was Josie who took control.

"Sollie, listen to me. It's not right, what you did. Whatever happened between you two, you *did* tell Joe you were gonna bring her back. And he wanted her there when he made his announcement."

"It's too late now," Sal said as he continued walking.

They walked with him.

"Where we goin'?" Manny asked.

"I don't know where you're all going. But I'm gonna get the cab and take off. You Mouseketeers can find another beach blanket bingo."

They came to President Street and turned. Sal headed for the cab with all three of them still in tow.

"I can't remember the last time the four of us were together like this," Schmuli said, as he raced along behind Sal.

"Last September at Joe's seventieth birthday," Sal said.

"No, I don't mean at an event. I mean like this, hanging out on the street."

Sal stopped and turned. Schmuli and Manny nearly knocked him down as they tried to come to a stop after walking quickly.

"When did we four ever hang out together? Huh?" Sal challenged.

"When we were kids," Schmuli explained, and searched all their faces, feeling a little confused.

"When we were kids your parents didn't want you hanging around with an Italian girl, remember?" Josie reminded him.

"How'd you know about that?" Schmuli asked her.

"Everyone knew about that. They didn't want you getting mixed up with a shiksa. They had nothing to worry about, believe me. You weren't my type."

"I'd probably have to be built very different to be your type," Schmuli teased.

"I mean when I was into men. Sollie here, he was more my type," she said. "If we four hung out together when we were kids, we woulda scared the hell outta everyone," Josie said. "A buncha over-sized mutts like yous with a fat lady as a sidekick."

"You weren't fat when you were younger," Sal reminded her.

"I got fat to punish Vinnie," Josie said, casually.

"Great plan, Peachie," Manny said, and gave her the high- five. She returned the gesture, with her usual self-mocking expression.

"We didn't hang together back then, and we're not starting now, either," Sal said, and continued to walk towards his cab.

Josie rushed past him, ran up the street a little, and blocked the driver's door of the cab.

"I'm not getting outta the way until you hear me out," she said.

Sal crossed his arms across his chest and said nothing. Josie motioned with her head for the other two to disappear. Schmuli and Manny walked to the nearest stoop and sat down.

"I love you like a brother. You believe that?"

"Don't start," he said.

"Do you?" she demanded.

"Okay. Yeah. I do."

"You been better to me than my whole family ever was. You loved me no matter what. Straight or gay, single or married to a dope, you stood by me. Anytime I needed you, you were there for me. During all that crazy shit with Joann and the drugs, who came and stayed with us? When Vinnie broke my nose and I threw him out, who took me to the hospital and gave me the strength to go through with the divorce?"

"You're writing my epitaph?"

"You're digging your *own* grave here," she said softly, her tone changing.

"Why's everyone acting like Terry's the only woman left in the whole world? Like she's my last chance. Is it just because Joe's getting married and you think I need someone to replace him?" he asked.

"Didn't you say it was a miracle you two met?"

"*She* said that."

"Uh huh. And you don't agree?"

He paused. Did he agree?

"See? You don't even know what you think. You're like, on auto-pilot. What are you so scared of? You can't possibly be as scared shitless as I was when I threw Vinnie out. Or when I thought I lost my only kid to drugs. That's *scary* stuff. What you got now is the good stuff."

"I'm scared I'm gonna make another wrong decision about a woman, okay?" he blurted out. "I know me and Terry got along real well. And I enjoyed it all. But she's so, so.... "

"Yeah?"

"So perfect. You saw how beautiful she is."

"So? Beautiful people don't deserve to be loved too?"

Sal paused. He'd never thought of it that way. The truth was, as beautiful, smart, and wealthy as Terry was, she really never was loved right.

"The way I see it, people like Terry probably attract all kinds of users.

"She said her fiancé wanted to marry her because she was 'appropriate.'"

"Jeez. How sad. Don't you think that's sad?" she asked.

"Yeah. I wish I could slug the sucker."

"She married him?"

"She left him at the altar."

"Shit, that's what I shoulda done with Vinnie. And you shoulda done with Angela. Me and you can take lessons from this broad."

"And her mom died when she was only two, and her dad sent her away when she was still just a little kid. Seven-years-old, Josie. Seven year olds still have their baby teeth. How could he do that? I'd like to punch his lights out, too," Sal said.

"You wanna beat up on everyone she knows?"

"They didn't deserve her."

"Do *you*?" she asked suddenly, looking him squarely in the eye.

Schmuli and Manny had gotten restless and were approaching the cab.

"My butt's numb from that step," Manny said. "I gotta get in the car and warm up."

Sal opened the cab and they all got in, him and Josie in the front, the other two in the back. Josie moved her seat all the way up to make room. Still, it was a tight squeeze.

"What the hell are you getting in for, anyway?" Sal asked.

"It's getting cold out there," Manny complained.

"Then go home!"

"*You* already ruined Joe's party by leaving, now you want *us* to abandon him too?" Josie asked.

"I didn't know it was a party. He said he was inviting '*people.*'"

"So what the hell are we?" Manny asked.

"You're the friggin' Mod Squad," Sal answered, and suddenly they all started laughing, including Sal. "One Kike, one Dyke, one Godzilla."

"One black, one white, one blonde," Schmuli corrected.

"Like blonde was a separate race," Manny commented.

"I had a crush on Link," Josie admitted.

"I bet that went over big in your house," Sal said.

"You think I ever told anyone I liked a black guy? Speaking of black guys, Manny, you got anything to eat on you? Any candy or anything?" Josie asked.

"Nope," he answered.

"Him and that damned candy," Sal said. "He got me and Terry eating it all day yesterday. Why didn't you give us nuts or something? You know I love those macadamia nuts."

"Are you crazy? They cost like fifty dollars for a tiny jar!" Manny said.

"Why are they so expensive?" asked Schmuli.

"Tariffs," Josie said.

"From where? Where do macadamia nuts come from?" Sal asked.

"From Macadamia," Josie said seriously.

"Get outta here," Manny said. "There is no Macadamia. You're thinking of Macedonia. And there's no such thing as nuts from Macedonia. You want me to sell macadamia nuts, fine. Take out a second mortgage on your house, and I'll make a down payment on some," Manny said.

The group all laughed. Sal said "Why don't you sell other things? Like cake or something."

"So, cake's better than candy?" Manny asked.

"Cake is more *mature* than candy," Sal explained.

"What the hell are you talkin' about?" Josie demanded.

"Have you ever been invited to someone's house for coffee and *candy*? No. Coffee is an adult drink, and cake is an adult food by association. And then there's *coffee cake* ...."

"You're insane, Brother-Of-Mine," Josie laughed. "What in the world can this Terry broad see in you? I mean, aside from the cute butt."

"What happened there, anyway?" Manny asked.

"Yeah, Sollie, you two seemed pretty comfortable at my house before. And Reba's crazy about her."

Sal knew he couldn't put them off much longer. And, now that he had calmed down and had them all gathered together in his cab, he suddenly felt like telling them. Since he had somehow managed to have Terry meet all of them in only two days, they were probably owed an explanation.

"Look, let's go back and party with Pop, and later I'll fill you in, okay?"

CHAPTER TWENTY
Park Slope/President Street

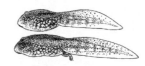

At eleven o'clock everyone left except Josie. Joe was walking Janet home. Sal took Josie into the living room. They were drinking the remains of the wine, and Sal lit a fire in the old fireplace.

"Jos, there's just one thing I didn't tell you guys."

"What's up?"

"Well, I told you me and Terry made love, right?"

"Yep."

"Well, she wasn't using anything, and I wasn't using anything, and -"

"You had unprotected sex? With a stranger?"

"I'm not worried about disease. She's not promiscuous or anything-"

"Shit, Sollie! How do you -"

"Will you shut up and let me finish?" Josie did as he asked. "Here's the real story: she came to New York to get pregnant. To get artificially inseminated. And this is her fertile time. And we had sex. Unprotected sex."

Josie swallowed her wine so hard Sal could hear her gulp.

"I know, I know," he said, holding up his hand as if to prevent her from speaking. "It was stupid. But I really thought she had her diaphragm in. I mean, she made it very clear she didn't want to have a baby with me."

"Have a baby with you? She hardly knows you!"

"I know. But -"

"Something doesn't make sense here, Sollie. Why the hell were you two even *discussing* having a baby? You meet a stranger at the airport for a tour and start talking about having a baby together?"

"Listen, Jos, we're two adults, we're single, I have a great kid and I want another one, she never had a kid and is here specifically to get pregnant ...."

"So you decided you would do the honors?"

"I considered it."

"That, I believe. What I can't believe is that *she* considered it."

"Me neither. And that's the problem. She did, I mean, she more than considered it. She might be pregnant right now ... with my kid!"

"Holy shit."

"And she's royally pissed off at me too, and her appointment at the clinic is tomorrow."

"But if she's already pregnant with your kid, why would she go through with it?"

"Because she doesn't know for sure, and she's not gonna fly home and wait and see and then come back. And maybe she's hoping she isn't pregnant now and will get pregnant tomorrow. I don't know. Maybe she'll do it just to be able to *not* know for sure either way," he said and ran his hand through his hair.

"That's stupid. You ever hear of something called a paternity test?"

"That's if she ever wanted to do it. I couldn't force her."

"Why not? If a guy suspects a kid is his, he could hire a lawyer."

"Here we go again. What the hell is it with me and custody battles?"

"Like flies on shit."

"Thanks loads."

"Forget the baby stuff for a minute, okay? Do you love her?"

Sal was standing near the fireplace and sat down on the couch near Josie. He drank his wine and thought about the question.

"I can't stop thinking about her. And even though I'm pissed off about her leaving some guy standing at the altar -"

"And how do you think she feels about you?" Josie interrupted, placing her empty wine glass on the end table.

"Well, that's another story. She's really down on marriage."

"But how does she feel about *you*?"

"I don't know. I think she's confused. Me too."

"And she thinks you're using her."

"Yeah. There's that."

"Well, my man, I'm stumped. I mean you really check-mated yourself this time."

"Think so?"

"Yeah. But, hey, it isn't the first time."

"That's encouraging."

"You know what you gotta do, don't you? You gotta stop her."

"How can I possibly -"

"I guess calling her - ?"

"She told me not to bother."

"Well, how many clinics like that can there possibly be in New York?"

"Who the hell knows? And I don't have the time to try to find her, anyway. I'm meeting with Angela tomorrow."

"Maybe *I* can try ... or Manny, or both of us."

"Forget it, kid. It sounds like a screwball comedy with a stupid ending."

"So? What else is there?"

Sal shrugged. "I guess I gotta let her do what she's gonna do. I have to get into the ring with the mother of a child I know for *sure* is mine. I can't also go a round with a woman who might be the mother of a child that might be mine. I just can't fight a war on two fronts."

CHAPTER TWENTY-ONE
The Plaza Hotel/Palm Court

At one o'clock Sal parked his cab in a parking deck on East 57th Street and walked into the Plaza Hotel. It had been years since he'd actually been inside, though he had dropped people there countless times. The red carpet on the steps always made him smile. It was a stupid little touch, but people liked it; people like Angela, who liked to feel important. Of course she was staying at the Plaza. God forbid she should stay someplace modest.

She had said to meet him at the Palm Court. He walked over and scouted the tables. No doubt she would have gotten there first to be sure to get the table she wanted. The maitre d' approached him and asked if he needed help. When he explained that he was waiting for someone, the pale, thin man smiled falsely and said, "I believe your party is already seated. Please follow me."

He was led to a small table in the corner, nestled between two potted palms as large as Bennie's room. There sat Angela, dressed to kill in a honey-colored silk suit. In spite of himself, Sal felt his breath catch. She was gorgeous.

And now she had the money and connections to learn how to dress to heighten her looks. Her hair, her beautiful dark hair that she used to wear shoulder-length, had been cut into a shorter, almost geometrical style. She probably thought it was more sophisticated. But she was too thin. Her collarbones jutted out, and her cheekbones looked like they could slice meat. And yet, it made her eyes look even larger and more luminous. Not a trace left of the working class Italian girl from Brooklyn.

She looked up and smiled, and he knew he was seeing the person she had always wanted to be. The person she had wanted *him* to help her become. A beautiful woman in a thousand-dollar suit with a four-hundred-dollar hair-do lunching at the Plaza ... with her ex-husband, the *cabby*. A host of lousy feelings flooded him, all of which he had to ignore.

"Good to see you," she said and held out her hand. Sal almost expected white gloves. He held back taking her hand, though. She ignored it. "I see time has been good to you. Have you eaten?"

"Yeah. You know. I eat early."

"Same old routine, huh?"

"Old dogs, I guess ...."

The waiter came by and asked for their orders. Angela asked for the smoked salmon plate with goat cheese. Sal ordered a coffee.

"How's your father?" Angela asked.

"Joe's getting married."

"How wonderful!"

"Yeah, he's very happy about it."

"And you're not?"

"I didn't say that."

"Who's he marrying? Anyone I know?"

"Nah. A woman and her granddaughter moved in last year -"

"Her *granddaughter*?"

"The mother died, apparently."

Angela just nodded.

Sal's coffee arrived with a small flourish that he found bothersome. All the accoutrements were unnecessary. He took his coffee black, anyway.

"How does Bennie feel about it?"

"He loves it. He's been playing with the granddaughter for months. They're like brother and sister."

"Really? Do they look alike also?" she joked.

"Hardly. They're a black family."

Angela's eyes opened wide. "Joe is marrying a black woman?"

"Yeah. So?"

"So, I'm surprised."

"She's a wonderful, beautiful, smart woman. He's lucky to get her."

"Did I say otherwise?"

"You didn't have to. Some things never change."

"You still think I'm a racist?"

"You never liked Manny."

"I never thought you really did, either," she said. "He was your protection."

Sal smiled. The Bitch lurked right below the surface. Thankfully, Angela was letting her emerge. It would be easier to do battle with The Bitch than The Angel.

"We're half-breeds. That's why you dislike us both."

"That's convenient for you, isn't it? To blame me for everything?" Angela said. But before Sal could answer, she added, "But I don't see that it's gotten you too far."

Sal decided not to engage her. He was there for one reason.

"So tell me, why have you suddenly decided you just have to have Bennie back now?"

"I'm sure there's no explanation I can give that will satisfy you, so I'm not going to bother. I want to see him, Sal. Preferably this week, but if not, then next month when I return from France."

"Forget it," Sal said, staring her down.

"So you're still punishing me for leaving," she stated. "But what are you punishing Bennie for?"

"Nice try," Sal answered and drank his coffee.

Angela clearly saw that there was no room to negotiate. "Jim says to say hello. He wondered how your tour business was going."

"It's gone."

"What happened?"

"Why does he care?"

"He recently invested in a venture capital company, and they're looking for the next 'big thing.' With the population aging and having more discretionary income, travel is going to boom. There's always interest in Brooklyn, and nostalgia only gets bigger and with some professional PR -"

"So this is a business lunch?"

"It could be," she said, and nibbled her salmon.

What a pro. It was like she was born to this life. He could barely remember her behind her father's dry cleaning counter. A time when showing up at her door with a three-dollar bunch of daisies impressed her.

"But it would take a real full-time commitment to make it work. You couldn't drive the cab also," she added, too casually.

"What are you getting at?" he asked, though he saw it coming. He just had to hear how she would put it.

"If Jim's company decided to invest in your company, they would be willing to pay you a full salary for a few years as you grew the company. That way you could give it your full-time attention. And, with no other distractions in your life, the odds are -"

"I like how you reduced my son to a 'distraction.'"

"*All* children are distractions, Sal. You have to admit that."

"Distractions from what, exactly? Manicures and massages?" But before she could answer or protest, he continued. "If you want to know the truth, the only reason I even agreed to meet you today was to try to get an answer to my question: Why are you doing this to me? Revenge?"

She took a deep breath as if to steady herself, and for the first time Sal could see a sign of weakness. "I knew you'd think that. I swear to God I knew it. And I knew there was nothing I could say or do that would convince you otherwise."

"So, what is it then? Guilt? After all these years?"

"I've regretted what I did for years now. I'll tell you the truth, Sal, but you're not going to like it. I just don't want Bennie poisoned by your self-defeatism. Remember when he was tested for pre-school? What did they say his IQ was? One fifteen or something?"

"One twenty-five."

"He needs a more stimulating environment. We can offer him that. And private schools. We can take him traveling too. He'll grow up seeing what else there is in life. *His* world doesn't have to be limited by the Brooklyn-Queens Expressway and the Gowanus Canal," she said, and nibbled some more.

Her voice was calm, her tone serious, and it worried Sal. Because he could fight a vengeful person, but not one who was starting to make sense.

"Look," she began, pointing her fork at him. "Why would I want revenge, anyway? *I* left *you*! Remember? *I'm* the one who married the rich guy! I'm the one who lives in California with a summer home in the south of France. The truth, Sal? I feel *pity*. Because I'd bet this diamond ring that your IQ is even higher than Bennie's. But I can't rescue *you*. I tried, and you just wore me out. But I *can* rescue my son. And I'm gonna do it, Sal. It's only a question of where, *in* court or out. So, you decide," she said, and opened her purse. She fished out a piece of notepaper and a pen and wrote something. Then she handed it to him. "This is the phone number of our room here, and this is Jim's parents' number in Beverly Hills, in California -"

"I know where Beverly Hills is," he said, refusing to take the note.

"We'll be checking in with them while we're away, so if you have anything to communicate, leave a message with them," she said, and slid the paper toward him. "Think about it. Bennie's life doesn't have to be so provincial."

"'Provincial?' What have you been reading, <u>Thirty Days To A Better Vocabulary</u>?"

"I may not have your vocabulary, but you know what I *do* have? A five-hundred-dollar-an-hour lawyer. What do *you* have?"

Sal slammed his fist on the paper, shaking the entire table. Angela snatched her hand away. The noise startled the other patrons, and they all turned to stare. Angela was embarrassed.

"I have Bennie," he said, crumpling up the small note and tossing it onto Angela's plate.

CHAPTER TWENTY-TWO
Brooklyn Heights/St. George Hotel

Sal went from the Plaza directly to the gym at the St. George Hotel in Brooklyn Heights. His friend Larry was also his attorney and he worked out there just about every day. If Larry couldn't be reached at his office, the best bet was the gym. Not that there was much more Larry could possibly tell him that he hadn't already. But Sal needed to know what to expect.

The young woman at the desk let him in when he said he was looking for someone, and soon enough he spotted Larry at the Nautilus equipment.

"Hey, buddy, good to see you! Though it doesn't bode well if you're chasing me down like this."

"How ya been, Lar?"

"How are *you*? That's the question," he asked, but didn't stop lifting the weights. "How come you never joined?" he grunted. "Didn't you say you were thinking about it awhile ago?"

"Yeah, I was. But I'd rather just work out at home. I spend enough time away from the house as it is," Sal answered. "Look, Lar, let me ask you something," Sal began. "What can Angela do if I don't give in and let her have custody of Bennie?"

"I told you already. She can take you to court and let the judge decide," Larry answered, struggling with the arm weights, pressing them together.

"And how do you think the judge *would* decide ... honestly?"

"I already told you that also, Sal," he panted. "There's significant money there. And motherhood is a very tough thing to beat."

"Even though I've been raising him?"

"How old's Bennie now?"

"Eight."

"Angela was there for the first two years, right? Gone for a while -"

"Gone for six years, Lar."

"Okay, six years and now she's back. So what?" he panted as he squeezed the weights together in front of his chest. His temples throbbed. "He's got ten years before he goes to college. The judge is going to consider that," he said and kept pressing. "He's going to look at what Angela can offer him, the schooling and the contacts." Larry caught Sal's expression. "You asked me to be honest, right?"

"So if I get notice from Angela, then I have to appear in court, right? What do you think that will cost me?"

"Aw, Sal, I don't know. Don't put me on the spot, okay? I told you, if you want we'll work on a retainer instead of an hourly. You'll save a few bucks that way."

"You ever handle a custody case before?"

"Yeah, sure," he grunted. "A long time ago."

"How long?"

"Oh, probably ten or fifteen years."

"Did you win?"

"I think so. I don't remember."

"I bet the parents remember."

"What are you trying to do? Alienate the only hope you have by insulting me?" Larry asked, and stopped pressing. He looked directly at Sal.

"Who says you're the only hope?" Sal raised his voice.

"Did I ever tell you what a pain in the ass you are when you're belligerent?"

"I'm thinking maybe of representing myself, if you want to know the truth."

Larry snickered. "Big mistake," he said and stood up. He removed the key from the weights and moved it lower down on the stack. "Pressing almost a hundred now," he said and sat down again.

"Maybe the judge will take pity on me," Sal said.

"You want the judge to *feel bad* for you? Are you crazy? You want him to look at you and see a working class slob driving a cab, living with his old father, too poor to afford counsel? Or you want him to see a winner, on top of the world?"

Sal saw his point. Only, now his plan was ruined. He had decided that representing himself was the best way to go for many reasons. Now what?

Larry paused before pressing again and leaned on the arm rests. "You don't have to use me if you don't want to, no hard feelings. But whatever you do, do not, I repeat *do not* enter that courtroom without an attorney."

"Who's the best attorney you know for this kind of thing?" Sal asked, suddenly getting an idea.

"You mean an ace family lawyer?"

"Yeah. Someone who does this a lot. Someone well known in their profession."

"I know the guy you want but there are no guarantees he'll take your case."

"Why not? My money's green."

"It's not about the money with this guy. He's on a mission or something."

"I don't get it."

"You ever hear of the 'Children's Defense Fund of New York?'"

"Sure."

"Well the guy who started it, who still runs it, in fact, is the guy I have in mind. He's still a practicing attorney, and if *he* takes your case then it's a shoe-in."

"What's his name?"

"Let me call him first. It'll give you a better shot. Only thing is, even if he does take you on, I doubt he's going to give you any breaks on the money."

"Let me worry about that," Sal said. "So how are *your* kids?" he finally asked.

"Still living with their mother."

"Don't you miss them?"

"I see them a lot."

"But it's not the same."

"I'm used to it. I like the freedom, actually. I go out a lot."

"Yeah? Where do you meet women?"

"Right here!" Larry exclaimed. "It's great. They're all dressed in these skimpy leotards, so you know what they look like before -"

"I get the picture," Sal said.

"You should let me get you a date, and we'll double sometime."

"Maybe when all this is over. Let me know when it's okay for me to call that guy, will ya? And let me know when you want to get together for some basketball."

"You got it, buddy," Larry said, and continued to lift his weights.

CHAPTER TWENTY-THREE
Brooklyn Heights/Clark Street

At least he wasn't thinking about Terry too much. Where she was at this very minute, doing what. At least he had a plan now. A plan that might actually allow him to keep his son. And with Janet and Courtney moving in they could rearrange the house, give Joe and Janet the top floor that no one used anyway, give Courtney Joe's room. He liked the idea of a full house and another child. And once he won this custody battle, it would be over forever.

Sal found a pay phone and called home. He missed his beeper. Felt out of touch. If Joe or Bennie needed him, what could they do? He'd have to get another one quick. There was no way he was going to call Terry and ask for his old one back. Christ, there was no way he was going to call her, period.

"Josie's been looking for you," Joe told him when he called.

"What'd she say?"

"She didn't explain. Just, she's looking for you. How did it go with Angela?" Joe asked.

"No surprises."

Joe was quiet a minute. He said, "Did you ask her what I told you to?"

"No Pop, I didn't."

"Why not?"

"Because it wouldn't have worked anyway, that's why."

"It was worth a try. Anything is worth a try."

"I know you think Angela still cares about you Pop, and maybe she does. But she's not about to give up her kid for you."

Again Joe paused. "We were very close for a while. If you said it right, if you told her it would hurt an old man -"

"Pop, I know. But it wasn't the right thing to say, somehow. She's very determined. She thinks we're bad for Bennie."

"Bad for him? How?"

Sal was starting to get cold standing outside. "I'll explain later. Is Josie at the bakery?"

"Sure, sure. Try her there. Are you working?"

"For a little while. I'll be home for supper, though."

"Is it okay if Janet and Courtney come for supper?"

"She's your fiancée, for God's sake! You don't have to ask my permission."

"Maybe tonight when you calm down, we can talk some more about my marriage."

"Sure, Pop. After Bennie's asleep." He hung up and dialed Josie at the store, but Joann answered and said Josie was at the hospital. Her father had taken a bad turn, and Josie had hoped Sal could meet her there. At this rate, he might as well forget working. He'd pick up a new beeper after visiting old man D'Apeche and head home and then call Larry and nag him about that contact.

"Hey, Sal, that you?"

He turned away from the phone and found himself staring at Roxy Ramos, his old girlfriend.

"Roxanne Sylvia Ramos! What the hell are you doing here? Seeing how the other half lives?"

"*I* live here now, big shot," she smiled, leaning toward him and planting a kiss on his cheek. Sal could smell that familiar perfume. "My fiancé lives right over there," she pointed, "in those apartments. And I'm living with him."

"Not bad for a Puerto Rican girl from Coney Island," he joked.

"Pretty swanky place. The doorman likes me 'cos I speak Spanish, and we gossip about the tenants."

Roxy Ramos. How long had it been? At least three years since they broke up. Truth was he didn't think about her much, except her body, which was still incredible. She was the exact opposite of every current standard of beauty: she was short and very voluptuous with large breasts and hips, yet she was gorgeous. Her skin was a light beige with a few small freckles under her eyes, which were almond shaped and dark brown. Her lips used to be considered too large, but lately it seemed women were paying to have lips as full as Roxy's.

"How's Hector?" he asked.

"Can you believe? He's thirteen already! And, ooh, is he handsome! All the girls call him up all the time. He's staying with my mom."

"How is *she*?" Sal asked. He had always like Roxy's mom. In fact, he liked her more than her daughter because she was smart and funny. Unfortunately, even though Roxy was younger than him, her mother was still fifteen years older than him.

"Oh, she's great. She asks about you a lot, you know?"

"Yeah? After all this time?"

"Oh, sure. She had great plans for us."

Sal felt awkward. It was he who had initiated their break-up, and it hurt Roxy at the time, though she didn't seem any worse for it now.

"My new boyfriend's a CPA."

"Really? Where did you meet him?"

"Right here at the gym! It's a real hang-out now," she explained.

"So I hear," he said, running out of conversation and remembering how easy it was to get bored with her.

"So, what about you? You married yet?" she asked, and tilted her head flirtatiously.

"Me? Nah!"

"Why not? You're eligible," she laughed, and thrust out her hand, showing Sal her diamond ring. "It's real."

"I figured."

"Let's go get a coffee or something. We'll catch up."

"I really can't. I have to pay a sick call."

"Joe?"

"No, no. He's fine. He's getting married too, in fact."

"He's a great old guy. You're pretty great too, you know," she said. "Hey, I'm not exactly married ... *yet*. We could still fool around," she said, meeting his eyes. One thing about Roxy - she loved sex and wasn't shy about it.

"Oh, wow, Roxy. I don't think so -"

She held up her left hand and pointed to her ring finger. "Once *this* finger has a ring on it, forget it, baby. But until then ...." Those were her private rules for fidelity. Sal just laughed.

"Okay, okay. But you were always the best, muchacho. I still think about us together, you know. The way we -"

"What about the CPA? He any good?"

Roxy burst out laughing. It was a loud, unrestrained laugh, like everything else about her, and people turned to look. "You think CPAs are boring in bed, huh?"

"I thought that's what the initials stood for: Can't Possibly Arouse."

Roxy laughed again and took Sal's hand and stroked it in hers. Her hand was warm and soft, reminding him of her body and the incredible times they'd shared in bed. Breaking up hadn't been easy, and he'd come very close to proposing to her a few times after especially passionate love-making.

"You saving yourself for someone special, huh?" she asked.

And she was right. He couldn't even imagine himself with her now, in spite of the great memories. He had spent only one night with Terry, and she wasn't even speaking to him, and yet it was her he wanted.

"You're special," he said, and kissed her cheek. "But I don't think it would be right. Who knows where it would lead."

"It ain't leading anywheres, believe me. I'm over you, lover-boy. My fiancé and I are like this," she said, and intertwined her two fingers. "But I understand. Hey, it's gettin' cold out here. I gotta run," she said and leaned toward him. Sal leaned in, expecting another kiss on the cheek. Instead, she took his head in her two small hands and held it so she could kiss his lips. He felt her tongue brush against his lips, and then she took a gentle bite as well. "Adios, muchacho," she said, and walked inside the St. George. Sal stood there a little dumbfounded. He *was* saving himself for someone special, whether he wanted to or not.

CHAPTER TWENTY-FOUR
Flat Iron Bldg /Law Offices of Armstrong & Birnbaum

"So, Mr. Iorio, you're anticipating a custody battle."

"I'm gonna be served any day now."

"What makes you say that?" he asked, drumming a pencil against his huge, blindingly shiny mahogany desk.

"My ex already gave me the news. Either I hand over the kid or we go to court."

"And you're sure she intends to follow through on that threat?"

"I'm positive."

William Armstrong paused and swiveled a bit in his fancy chair which was large enough to fit two and a half of him. He was a tall, slight man with a lot of gray hair.

"Okay, then. Let me give you my standard orientation. This consultation is gratis. Once I evaluate your case, if I decide to take it, there will be a flat rate and I will ask for a retainer. Ballpark is usually in the ten - to twenty-thousand-dollar range with a thousand-dollar retainer." Armstrong waited for Sal's reaction.

Sal grimaced.

"Does that concern you?" Armstrong asked.

"Of course it concerns me. I'm a working person. But it's not an obstacle," he added, afraid to let on that he had no idea at all where he'd get that kind of money.

"Okay, then. Secondly, I don't know what you know about me or my history, but let me fill you in. I've been an attorney for twenty-five years, the last fifteen in Family Court. I specialize in custody cases, and I usually win. There's no secret to my success. I put my clients through a rigorous, sometimes painful screening process before I agree to take them on. So, thirdly, you will have to agree to this process."

"You mean you're gonna ask me some questions?"

"*Many* questions. And you must answer me absolutely honestly every time. If I neglect to ask you something, and you don't "remember" to mention it, and I find out about it later on, I reserve the right to walk away from the case. It's your responsibility to brief me completely. If, after our intake, I believe we have a case, I will take you on. If not, I will tell you so. I think you can understand that at this point in my career the remuneration is a very small part of my motivation."

"Then what *is*?" Sal had to ask even though he already knew about Armstrong's cause. But the guy was making him crazy. What a jerk.

Armstrong paused again, swiveled again, and tapped his pencil. "Mr. Iorio, the only basis on which I decide to take a case is my belief that my client is the best guardian for the child in question. So, fourthly, I must caution you that just because you are a potential client doesn't mean I will decide that you are, in fact, best for your child. If that is what I conclude, I would hope that you wouldn't take it personally and that we could part amicably." Armstrong finished, tapped, and looked at Sal.

What could he say? Mr. Personality had him charmed. "Okay."

"Do you have an hour right now? We can cover just about everything in that time."

Sal glanced at his watch. It was almost three. Joe was home and Bennie would get home soon. At four Bennie had his Tuesday saxophone lesson, and Sal wanted to be home by five so they could all eat dinner together.

"Yeah, sure. The sooner the better. I wanted to thank you, also, for seeing me on such short notice."

"That's quite all right. Would you care for a glass of water or some coffee before we begin?"

"Sure. Coffee would be great. Thanks." He was starting to relax a little now. Maybe this guy would be okay even if he was doing the Popsicle imitation: frozen solid with a stick up his ass.

The secretary brought the tray of coffee and served them both. Armstrong brought out a legal pad and pen and a micro-recorder. He snapped in a tiny cassette and pressed RECORD.

"How old is your son?" he began.

"Bennie's eight."

"And how old are you, Mr. Iorio?"

"I'm forty-three."

"Were you married to Bennie's mother when he was born?"

"Yeah. We were married for sixteen years. We divorced when Bennie was two."

"You waited a long time to have a child."

"Yes, we did."

Seeing that Sal wasn't forthcoming, Armstrong persisted.

"Why is that?"

"Angela, my ex, wasn't really into having a kid. Our marriage was floundering, and when I suggested having a kid she refused. She said she wanted a divorce. So, we talked about it and -"

"Excuse me a moment. You wanted a child. She wanted a *divorce*?"

"She agreed to get pregnant and let me keep the child if I agreed to divorce her after she gave birth and not make any claims on her money."

"How much money are we talking about?"

"About twenty-five thousand dollars."

Armstrong looked surprised. Sal could see his eyebrows raise, as if he were thinking 'is that all?' So he added, "See, Angela came from a lousy family. They were always scrambling. So that was a lot of money to her at the time."

"And now it isn't?"

Sal laughed. "Now she's married to a multimillionaire! That's why she thinks she can get Bennie now."

"Did you ever sign any agreement with your ex-wife stating these terms?"

"No."

"Yet you honored the verbal agreement and never asked for any of her money?"

"Yes."

"Even after she told you she wanted the child?"

Sal had to think for a minute. The truth was he never even considered asking for any of Angela's money. Even after she decided to fight him for Bennie. "No."

"Did you go to court for custody, Mr. Iorio?"

"No. My lawyer advised me not to."

"So how did you resolve this issue with your ex-wife?"

Sal explained the entire story of how he decided to talk to Jim and how it worked. Once or twice he could tell Armstrong registered surprise, though it was subtle. The man was obviously very good at hiding his emotions.

"Let me get the time frame straight. You lived together for two years after the child's birth in spite of the fact that your ex-wife had stated that she wanted a divorce after the child was born."

"Yeah. See, she had quit her old job and was taking classes so she could get a better job. I was working and supporting her during that time. But I didn't know she was having an affair with this rich guy -"

"His name?"

"James C. Wakefield, the third."

"How long was that affair going on?"

"I can't be sure. But I think she had to be seeing him *before* she got pregnant. I don't know if they broke up or not, but I suspect they did and that's why she agreed to the pregnancy in the first place. 'Cos once she lost *him*, she had no reason not to get pregnant. Then, I think, when Bennie was about eighteen months old, I think she started up with him again."

"Were you having sexual relations with your wife?"

"Well, we *did* have Bennie -"

"I understand that, Mr. Iorio." Deadpan.

"No. After she got pregnant it was hands off. And then after he was born, she wouldn't even let me see her undress."

During the entire conversation, Armstrong wrote. He seemed to be able to write without looking down at his pad. He would look at Sal and keep writing. It was uncanny.

"Okay, then. Angela finally moved out and you legally divorced?"

"Yes."

"And you raised your son alone?"

"Oh, no. My father, Joe, lived with us. Still does. He's always taken care of Bennie while I worked."

"How old is your father?"

"Just past seventy."

"Does he have an income?"

"He retired a few years ago. He was a barber. He saved a few pennies for retirement, but it's not much."

"Is he in good health?"

"Sure. He's even planning to get married soon."

"Congratulations. I imagine he'll move out?"

"Nah. They'll probably move in with us."

"By 'they,' you mean your father and his fiancée?"

"And his fiancée's granddaughter."

"How does your son relate to this woman and her child?"

"They're like family already. The kids are like siblings. Fight like siblings too."

Armstrong nodded. But Sal couldn't guess where this was leading. For the good or bad. Still, he had to tell the man what he needed to know.

"How old is the fiancée?"

"Let's see, Janet's about fifty-eight."

"Does she work?"

"I don't think so."

"You will have to find out. Is she in good health?"

"I think so. Maybe some arthritis."

"Again, you will have to find out."

"Why is she so important?"

"Having a capable, healthy woman home full-time for your son can only help your case, Mr. Iorio. But if there are any mitigating factors, we must know in advance. After all, your son will most likely be spending quite a bit of time with this woman. And your ex-wife's attorneys, if they are any good, will certainly go to the trouble to find out everything they can about her. And they will also be comparing her to the child's natural mother."

"I see," he said. Whoever thought Janet would be so important to his future with his son!

"So you and your father have been raising your son for six years now. How much child support has your ex-wife been contributing?" he asked.

"Child support? Are you kidding me?"

"She doesn't contribute?" he asked, genuinely surprised.

"No!"

"And why is that?"

"Why is that? Because I ... I never asked for it."

Armstrong didn't seem entirely convinced.

"Her husband is a multimillionaire, yet you never asked the child's mother to contribute anything?"

Sal realized just how amazing this must have sounded, but, until this very moment, it really never had occurred to him to ask Angela for anything.

"Look. As far as I was, *am* concerned, the less I have to do with her the better."

"So you never asked and she never volunteered any financial support?" he said, this time just to verify.

"Exactly."

"Have you any idea what her husband is worth? Ballpark?"

"Sure. According to Angela, exactly thirteen point thirty-three million dollars. But she also makes sure to let me know that 'In our circles that isn't considered a lot of money.'"

"Thirteen point thirty-three million dollars is a lot of money in *any* circle, Mr. Iorio," Armstrong said. "Aside from child support, has she ever contributed in other ways, say by paying any medical expenses, or summer camp, or new school clothes?"

"Never."

"How about gifts for the child, for his birthday?"

"Never."

"Christmas?"

"Never."

Sal could tell Armstrong was incredulous. And yet, somehow, Sal wasn't. Not only because he was used to it, but because he had never ever considered Angela a real parent anyway. He expected nothing. He got nothing. It all worked out.

"Have you ever had any problems with your son? Behavioral or medical?" Armstrong moved on.

"None."

"No visits to the emergency room for an injury or illness?"

"Nope. Thank God."

Armstrong nodded slowly, as if he didn't quite believe it.

"You probably should think about that one, Mr. Iorio. In case you've forgotten. Check in with your father also. What hospital would you use if the child did have an emergency?"

"Methodist. In Brooklyn."

"We will need to run a check on their emergency room records for the last six years."

"Why? I told you he's never been there."

"Because your ex-wife's attorneys will immediately look for any evidence that you might have abused or neglected your son."

"For Christ sakes. I can't believe she would sink that low."

"I understand. Has he had any caretakers except your father?"

"Only here and there when we both had to go out."

"Can you give me a list of those people and their phone numbers?"

"They were just some local teenagers. Some aren't even living on the block anymore."

"Do the best you can," he said, then paused and tapped. "Are you romantically involved with anyone right now, Mr. Iorio?"

"No," Sal snapped. Of course, Armstrong caught it. Again the eyebrows went up. "There's a woman I met recently who I like. I mean, I thought I loved her, but, anyway, she's of no consequence to this case."

"How long have you known her?"

"Since Friday."

"This *past* Friday?" Armstrong asked, puzzled.

"Yeah, why?"

"Today is only Tuesday, Mr. Iorio. You met this woman and thought you loved her and broke up with her all in only a span of four or five days?"

If you think that's unbelievable … Sal thought. "Yes, I wound up spending all day Saturday and Sunday with her. So we got to know each other pretty well, and we hit it off and -"

"Did your son meet her?"

"Sure. She met my family and some of my friends."

Armstrong sighed deeply. Sal became alarmed.

"What's the big deal?"

"When single parents bring home their dates before the relationship is serious, it doesn't look good. One might suspect that other women have been brought home. Perhaps many other women. It implies poor judgment on the parent's part. Are you planning to see this woman again, pursue a relationship?"

Sal squirmed. Armstrong watched.

"Look, ask anyone. I hardly go out. My father's always on me to go out more. I do nothing but work and come home and watch friggin' Godzilla movies with Bennie. That's my whole goddamned life. Oh, yeah, and once a week I have a Hebrew lesson. That's my really wild night out, so I would conceal that from the judge if I were you. The women I have gone out with, none was for more than one date. Except about three years ago I was serious for a while, and, yes, she did know Bennie and I knew her family too. But there hasn't been a parade of women through my house, that's for sure."

"What do you do for a living, Mr. Iorio?" Armstrong asked.

"I drive a cab."

"Any college?"

"No."

"What high school did you graduate from?"

"I didn't."

Now Armstrong stopped and put down his pencil. "Are you telling me you dropped out?"

"I got my GED. I tried college for a semester, but then my mom got sick and I was bored anyway so -"

"So you've been driving a cab for how many years now?"

"Let's see. I tried starting a business with a friend a few years ago, but it fell apart."

"What was the nature of the business?"

"We gave tours of Brooklyn. Mostly to out-of-towners, but sometimes to New Yorkers."

"It sounds lucrative. But you say it didn't work out?"

"Nope. We didn't really have the cash, and my partner, Manny, is a little over the edge."

"Do you have health benefits and a pension, Mr. Iorio?"

"Yep. Sure do."

"And is this the line of work you intend to stay with until you retire?"

Sal was silenced. He felt, in fact, like he had been punched in the gut. Until he *retired*? Holy crap. Who thought about retirement? Of all the questions, this was the one he couldn't answer. Didn't want to answer. Like he was signing his own fate or something. Until he retired. Hell, that was only about twenty years! He only had twenty years to turn his life around and then retire!

"Mr. Iorio?" Armstrong prodded. He could see that Sal was struggling with something. "Do you have any plans at all to change careers?"

He took a deep breath to regain his composure. "I suppose not," he said softly.

"I see," said Armstrong, and kept writing. He was so damned hard to read. "Okay, then. If you would answer these next few questions with a yes or no, that would be preferable."

Sal nodded.

"Have you ever, to your knowledge, gotten anyone pregnant?"

"Well, Bennie wasn't exactly the Immaculate Conception ..."

"I meant other than your ex-wife."

"No," he said decisively. He didn't actually *know* if he had gotten Terry pregnant. He only suspected.

"Have you ever had unprotected sex with a woman?"

Sal actually blushed. "Oh, hell," he said.

"I'll take that as a yes," and he kept writing.

"Why does it matter anyway?" he asked.

"If there is any chance that you fathered a child that you had no knowledge of, that child could surface at any time. Any incident of unprotected sex could have led to conception that you didn't know about. I know it seems ridiculously remote, but believe me, it has happened to clients of mine."

Sal wasn't in a position to doubt it. Not with Terry walking around possibly pregnant with his child. By now she had probably gone to her clinic and he wasn't sure what he was hoping for. If she were pregnant with his child, he only had nine months before it would "surface" and possibly complicate the custody proceedings. But what to tell Armstrong?

"Have you ever been in debt to an individual or an institution, either through written or verbal contract, except credit cards, auto loans, or mortgages?" Armstrong plodded on.

"Only to my father. So, yes."

"Have you ever defaulted on any loans?"

"Nope."

"Does anyone owe you any money for any reason?"

"I wish."

"Have you ever been imprisoned?"

"God no!"

"Have you ever been accused of any crime?"

"Accused? By who?"

"For example, has anyone ever accused you verbally of denting their car, hitting them, stealing from them, threatening them -"

"Jeez. When I was a kid-"

"I mean since you became an adult, Mr. Iorio."

"No."

"Good. Now, let's backtrack to your son. Where does he go to school?"

"P.S. 129 in Brooklyn."

"A public school. About how many children are in his class, would you say?"

"Oh, probably about thirty-two or so. That's a lot of cupcakes every year on his birthday, let me tell you."

"Has he ever had any problems in school? Been sent home for any reason, illness or maybe behavior problems?"

"Never. He really likes school. And he's in the gifted program, so I guess that keeps him stimulated."

"I see. Has the school ever had any violent incidents to your knowledge?"

"Yeah. Once in awhile some older kids from the junior high make trouble. But nothing coming from the inside. It's a pretty good school."

"Does your son have many friends?"

"Oh, yeah. Kids like him. He's very easy-going. Very accepting. Not like his old man."

"Have you met the parents of most of his friends?"

"Wow. Let's see. I know Jamie's mom and dad, Jonah's father, and Alex's whole family. But there are a couple of kids he plays with whose parents I don't know. Maybe Joe does, though."

"Are there any families of any of the children your son associates with that, in any way, would give anyone concern for the safety or well-being of your son?"

Sal sighed again. He was getting tired of this. He had no idea what anyone else would consider worrisome, but he certainly didn't. Most of these folks were working people with houses or apartments in the neighborhood. Probably among them were alcoholics and depressives and wife beaters. But he couldn't say for sure. "I don't know! I don't make them pass an interview just to befriend my kid," he snapped.

"We can finish this another time," Armstrong suggested abruptly.

"No. I don't have another time. I just want to get home to my family, eat a nice dinner, and relax with my kid. That's what this is all about, right? Me being able to be with my kid! Why is it so hard to do? He's doing great. Anyone can see that. He's well-adjusted. He's normal. He loves street sweepers! What judge in his right mind would take Bennie away from me?" Sal stood up.

"A judge who believes that your son will do better elsewhere. Do you think you've succeeded in convincing *me* your son should stay with you?" Armstrong asked.

"I wasn't trying to. I was concentrating on giving you all the facts. Isn't that what you wanted?"

Armstrong stood up too. He wasn't any taller than Sal, but his lankiness gave him that appearance. He walked around his desk and leaned against the front of it, facing Sal, who faced him squarely, hands on his hips.

"Please, have a seat." He gestured to the chair Sal had been sitting in. And still, that cool manner. Sal sat back down. Armstrong remained standing, looking down at him. "What I want is to discern the *truth* from the facts. Information alone is meaningless until we discover the truth it conveys. And yours isn't clear-cut. At least not to me, not as of yet. You seem to have done quite well by your son, and your ex-wife's history is unseemly, though we can't prove anything except that she willingly gave you custody six years ago and hasn't contributed one penny ever since. The judge won't like that. But biological mothers are given a great deal of leeway in Family Court, and when they have a change of heart and decide they want their babies back, some judges go for it. Now, you've had your son for six years. Perhaps his mother deserves a turn." Armstrong was baiting him, but Sal didn't realize it.

"Like hell she does!" he banged on the arm of his chair. "Listen to me, Armstrong. Bennie is not a toy we take turns with. He's a human being. Just because he's young doesn't mean people can fuck with his head and his life, the only life he's ever known, just because his 'biological' mother wants to get back at me. And no matter what she says about offering him a better life, I'm here to tell you she's doing this to screw *me*. And I won't let it happen! Not because of pride or any of that horseshit, even though it would break my heart and break an old man's heart. Screw that! Hell, if they get Bennie, I'll be the walking wounded ... but that's the breaks. I'm an adult. I'll learn to adjust somehow. It's *Bennie* I'm worried about. You don't know Angela. When she was home with Bennie she never, not once, took him to the playground. Joe did it. She never brought him to play groups. She put him in the playpen or the high chair and turned on the TV! Why? So she could do her exercises. She had no idea who her kid was, and she didn't care. She still doesn't. That's why she's never even visited him. It's one thing she never sends money. Maybe her old man's some kind of tightwad when it comes to my kid. But *she* could fly here every weekend if she wanted to. If she missed him so badly. And she doesn't! She never has! You tell me why, huh? Because to her he's just a 'distraction,' Armstrong. Well, maybe her twins are distractions, but not my son. There's nothing in my life more interesting than Bennie. And the older he gets, the more I enjoy him. There's nothing, not one thing I do, or have to do with or for my son that I don't enjoy." He paused to catch his breath and calm down. He'd better watch himself with this guy. Armstrong wasn't Larry. "Of course, under oath I'd have to admit I wouldn't care if I never watched another damned Godzilla movie in my entire life," he joked.

This time Armstrong smiled.

CHAPTER TWENTY-FIVE
Park Slope/President Street

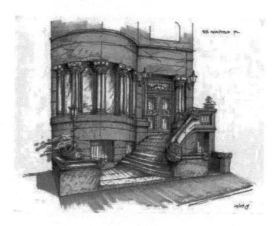

A classic no-win. If Armstrong turned down the case, Sal was screwed. If he accepted the case, Sal had to come up with a lot of money. On top of that, Sal worried about Armstrong's impending home visit. Most likely Angela's attorneys would demand that the court visit the home, and so Armstrong needed to know what they would see. And, he said, he might notice things about the house or household that could have a "deleterious effect" on the case.

And what would he tell Joe? The old guy was waiting to hear how it went, and when he heard about the cost he'd probably pass out. Maybe he should just wait the twenty-four hours until he heard from Armstrong. Because if he turned down the case, Joe would pass out anyway, but at least when he came to he wouldn't have to start figuring out how to come up with the money.

Sal wanted to relax and enjoy dinner with his family and forget everything. Just for the evening. Forget that Angela might very well steal his son. Forget that his father was soon going to get married and start a new life at the age of seventy while he was only forty-three and single. Forget that a woman he cared deeply about was out there somewhere, possibly pregnant, possibly with his child. Forget that he felt shitty about hurting Terry. And forget that Terry had hurt *him* by believing that he was capable of hurting her that way. Of using her.

Thinking about her as he drove back to Brooklyn from lower Manhattan, Sal finally allowed himself to review what had happened between them over the weekend. And it really was only two days ago. Unbelievable. He recalled Armstrong's surprise when he told him he had only known Terry since Friday. Amazing. And where was she now? At the hotel? In a plane? Back home? He didn't even have a home number for her, and Manny was terrible at keeping paperwork, so he wouldn't have it either. If she wasn't listed, he wouldn't be able to find her. This thought brought with it a slight sense of panic. He didn't know the name of her business either, though he could guess. And he could be wrong. How had he gotten into this mess? Whether she was pregnant or not, it was confusing, and he knew he really wasn't ready to just give it up. But he wasn't ready to call her and try to explain and patch it up, either. After all, not only did she have the gall to accuse him of something really disgusting, but she actually left someone standing at the altar. It was a bad sign. Someone who could be that flaky couldn't be trusted. It's one thing to back out of a marriage, people do it all the time. But another thing to let things just progress as if nothing were wrong and just not show up. There was no way in the world Sal could ever understand something like that. Beyond poor judgment, it was an almost crazy thing for an adult to do. And one thing he really thought he knew about Terry was that she wasn't crazy. Barely even eccentric, really. But then, maybe that explained why a woman as beautiful and rich as she was didn't have a husband. She was so ... guarded. So ready to prove to herself that he was out to screw her over. And yet, she hadn't used her diaphragm. Never said a word. One day she's outraged at the mere thought, the next day she decides to go ahead without even discussing it with him. Like deciding not to show up at her own wedding and never telling her fiancé. The two incidents somehow struck Sal as very similar. And very upsetting. And yet, he missed the hell out of her. And in his heart he knew she was the walking wounded. Her father never hurt her, was never "deliberately cruel," but he hadn't loved her right, either. That had to be like a hole in your heart.

Sal turned onto President Street and searched for parking. He missed her, and he worried about her. She had a goodness and gentleness that moved him, and if she was pregnant with his child, or any child, he couldn't stand to think of her going it alone. But what could he do?

When Sal got home, Joe had the table all set and Janet was at the stove. Sal watched them and wondered how they had managed to establish such an intimate relationship without him knowing. He had started to notice that

Bennie had been spending a lot of time over there, but it would never in a million years have entered his mind that anything was going on between Joe and Janet. And yet, Terry had asked about his aftershave and remarked that he looked like he was dressed for a date. This having never even met the man before. Maybe I have been blind, Sal thought. Too caught up in the day-to-day struggle to notice what I should about the people I love. Maybe it's true of Bennie too. Maybe he isn't doing as well as I think he is. Maybe having two strangers move into his house is the last thing a boy needs whose own mother disowned him six years ago.

"You look piqued," Janet said as she pulled the casserole from the oven. "Sit down and eat and tell us about your visit to the lawyer. Then I'll call the children down."

Sal sat down and poured himself some wine. Bennie had been kept in the dark about all the custody crap. No need to upset him until and unless it became absolutely necessary.

"I won't know anything until tomorrow sometime," Sal said and sipped his wine.

Janet looked puzzled as she scooped the baked ziti from the pan and placed a large portion on Sal's plate. Then she served Joe. Sal knew she held her tongue out of politeness. But Joe wouldn't bother.

"What happens tomorrow?" he asked.

"The attorney needs to think about whether he'll take on my case or not," Sal answered and started to eat quickly. Too quickly. He was hurrying so he could finish and disappear. But he had hurried home to be with them. It was insane. Wasn't there a place he could be these days where he felt calm and comfortable?

Joe and Janet exchanged glances. Janet spoke up, gingerly.

"Why would he turn you down?" she asked.

"If he believes Bennie really would be better off with his mother," Sal explained. "Now, please. Let's eat in peace and forget all this for one night. Okay?" He looked at each of them in turn. Then he called the children down to supper.

They had an uneventful meal, the children went back upstairs to play, and Janet cleared the table.

"Tea?" Joe asked.

"Sure. Whatever you grab is fine," Sal said and turned on the little television on the counter. But instead of making the tea, Joe just watched him. "What?" Sal said.

"Nothing, Sweetheart. Remember I told you when you called that maybe we could talk some more about my marriage?"

"Sure, Pop," Sal said, and watched the news. Out of the corner of his eye he saw Joe and Janet glance at each other. His heart sped up. Something was going on. Before he could ask, Joe volunteered, "We were thinking after we get married, maybe we would live ... in Janet's house," he said softly, as Janet walked closer to him, taking his hand.

Sal was startled. Then confused. "Why?" he asked, looking up at them from his seat at the table.

This time Janet spoke, knowing Joe was too upset. "Well, Sal, it's not that we don't want to live here with you and Bennie, it's just that I'm legally bound to the house. You see, when my daughter died, my son-in-law let me have custody of Courtney even though at first *he* wanted custody. I didn't think he was fit to raise the child alone, but I didn't fight him. He was unemployed when Sheila died, and she was trying to convince him to come to the United States to make a better life."

"What happened to your daughter?" Sal asked.

"She was hit by a bus," Janet said. "She died instantly," Janet added, reading the question in Sal's eyes.

"I'm so sorry," Sal said.

Finally, Joe filled the teapot and put it on the stove. "A cookie? Something?" he asked.

"Sure."

"My son-in-law, Wilton, was lazy, but he loved his little girl. I can't take that away from him. He knew that moving here was best for her, though he didn't want to come himself. A land of opportunity is only worthwhile for people who intend to take advantage of it. And Wilton didn't want to. So he said he would allow me to have legal custody of Courtney and move here, just the two of us, if we wanted to. But he was concerned that I provide the child with a stable life and not move around or get involved with men," she said, a bit sheepishly.

"It's okay," Joe said and patted her hand. She was obviously shaken.

Sal was puzzled.

Janet continued, feeling ashamed but needing to explain herself. "I wasn't a model mother to my own daughter. Wilton was worried about leaving Courtney with me. I -"

"You don't have to go into detail. It's okay," Sal said, rescuing her.

Janet was wringing her hands as she spoke. Her voice seemed to get softer and softer. "So he came here with us, and we pooled our money and bought the house, and he went back. And in the custody papers he made me agree to live in the house with the child until she is eighteen years old or unless an act of God makes it impossible to do so. So, for the next ten years, I must stay there. The only man allowed to live there is the man I marry, *if* I marry."

"I understand," Sal said, standing up and taking the whistling tea kettle from the stove top.

"It's just across the street," Joe said, helplessly.

But across the street might as well be across the continent when it came to his own custody battle. If Joe moved out, there was no way he could care for Bennie alone. He would surely lose the case. The silence in the room told Sal that Joe and Janet had already thought of it.

"We'll tell the judge that Bennie is moving in with us. Then, when the case is over, it's back to normal," Joe explained.

Sal ran his hand through his hair. Crap. He couldn't possibly tell Armstrong all this. It was a surefire loser. And he was already concealing the truth about Terry.

"We thought about having you all move in with us," Janet explained. "But the house is just too small. Only two bedrooms."

"*This* place is enormous," Sal said. "You guys could've taken the whole third floor."

"I know, Sal. I'm so sorry," Janet barely squeaked and started to cry. "I can't bear for either of us to lose our babies," she choked, while Joe held her and patted her back.

"I've decided: we won't get married until after the court case," Joe said, firmly. "We'll wait. Everything stays the same and no one will be any wiser."

"Pop, that can take a very long time. In fact, one thing the lawyer did say was that there's no point in his hurrying it up. Since we have custody anyway, we have nothing to lose by delaying." He paused to think. "I guess I could tell him to move quickly." *If I also told him why*, Sal thought. Then he poured himself some tea and sat back down with it, using the hot mug to warm his hands.

"The truth is best," Janet said. She sat down and reached across the table to hold Sal's hand. She squeezed gently, and he returned the gesture.

"Come, I'll walk you home," Joe said to Janet. Then, to Sal, he said, "I'll clean up when I get back. You go relax. You look all fahrblungeta."

Janet laughed. "Can you translate, please?"

"He means fahrblunget. It's Yiddish," Sal explained.

CHAPTER TWENTY-SIX
Flat Iron Bldg/Law Offices of
Armstrong & Birnbaum

"We have a great deal of ground to cover, Mr. Iorio," Armstrong said from the other side of his huge desk. "And I'd like my partner, Gerald Birnbaum, to join us, if you don't mind."

Armstrong had decided to take the case. Somehow, Sal had expected he would. And, he also knew he had to come clean and tell the guy all the crazy things that were happening and that could happen in the course of the next year. The last thing they both needed was any more surprises. If after hearing all of it, he was still interested in the case, then Sal would hustle for the money.

He didn't know why Birnbaum had to get involved at this point. Surely

Armstrong could handle the case himself. But hell, having them both in his corner couldn't hurt, so he told Armstrong, "No problem."

Birnbaum was younger than Armstrong, probably around Sal's age or a little older but not yet fifty. A nice-looking if plain guy in a nice suit. Balding, glasses, a nice smile and a solid handshake.

"Good to meet you," he said to Sal as they shook.

"Same here," Sal said.

"Don't mind me. Bill told me about your case and we put our heads together a bit and I just wanted to be up on the latest," Birnbaum explained.

"Sure," Sal said. Now he would have to tell his shitty story to *both* of them. And, much to their credit, they didn't flinch, didn't even raise an eyebrow when Sal told them about Terry very likely being pregnant and Joe very likely moving out.

"Does your ex-wife know about any of this?" Armstrong asked.

"Not a thing about Terry. Doesn't even know she exists. I did mention to her that Joe's getting married, though. I guess I shoulda kept my mouth shut."

"Well, it's never a good idea to reveal information you don't have to," Armstrong said, without criticism.

"But I also told her Janet was moving in, 'cos I thought she was."

"Good. Then she'll probably never even consider any other possibility."

"I doubt it."

"Of course, if questioned about the future of the household, we can't lie. Is there a wedding date set?"

"No. Joe wants to wait until after the case is over. So it won't be an issue."

Armstrong paused to consider his statement. He tapped his pencil and gently nodded his head as if he were listening to music somewhere far off in the distance. Sal recognized this as the way he puzzled out a problem, and so he kept silent. Birnbaum seemed to be working hard on keeping quiet. "So, if I delay the case, it's deleterious to your father and his fiancée. If I rush the case, it's not especially helpful for you."

"Rush it, Armstrong. Win or lose. I can't go on like this."

Again, Armstrong nodded. It was becoming obvious he had more to say, and it wasn't like him to pull any punches. So, Sal prodded. "What else?"

"Mr. Iorio, I don't mean to pry into your personal affairs, but I am compelled to ask you to ascertain if this woman is, in fact, pregnant with your child. I understand that your ex-wife doesn't even know of her, but things like this don't stay secrets. And, if this woman is angry with you, she may well use this information against you ... at a very inopportune time."

It was impossible, absolutely impossible, to imagine Terry doing something like that. What would she gain? But he knew it was useless to try to convince Armstrong of this.

"I'll try. But she probably left the city by now, and if she's not listed in the Racine phone book, I really don't know what to do."

Armstrong pondered again. "There are ways of finding her. We could hire someone if we needed to, but you'll save quite a bit of money if you do the legwork yourself."

"I'll give it a try," Sal said and stood up.

"A 'try' isn't good enough, I'm afraid. You'll have to *succeed*."

Sal understood that Armstrong was giving him an ultimatum.

CHAPTER TWENTY-SEVEN
Borough Park/D'Apeche's Bakery

"I have about three grand I can dig up for you," Josie said. Sal had come to the bakery to talk to her about the case and to ask for a loan. Man, how he hated to ask her for money. She worked so damned hard. But he just couldn't ask Joe for any more money for anything. The man had sunk everything he had into their house, the house he couldn't even live in once he got married. Schmuli had helped finance the business, and it never made enough money to pay him back. Sal's own savings were all in his IRA, which he couldn't touch, and a little in a college fund for Bennie. Even if he drained that, he wouldn't have enough for Armstrong, who was expecting his retainer.

"Let's see," Sal figured, "that'll buy me about fifteen hours of the good lawyer's time."

"Good? He better be fuckin' great for that dough!" she said, threw her apron on a chair, and sat down. "Man, it's hot in here," she said and wiped her forehead with a tissue.

"He impressed the hell outta me, I gotta tell you. Very thorough."

He looked at The Peach, sweating, pale, and looking overall pretty shitty.

176

He hadn't been there much for her lately and had only managed to see her father twice at the hospital. "How are *you* doing?" he asked, softly. "Anything definite with Denise?"

"Aw, Sollie, I'm about to give up. I just can't take it," she said and started to cry softly.

"What's wrong?"

"Pop is dying, and Denise is being so pushy, and now Joann knows."

"Joann *knows*?"

"She knows."

"You told her?"

"*Denise* told her!"

"So?"

"So? She's *my* kid! I got the right to tell or not. Who the hell is she?"

"She's the woman you love, you jerk! You're getting bent outta shape because she told your daughter something she probably already figured out a hundred years ago?"

"She did. She told me she knew all along. But that's not it. It's that Denise threatened to do it if I didn't. I don't like ultimatums."

"You've been fucking with her head for years. If it woulda been me, I woulda dumped you a long time ago!"

"Go to hell!" she cried out. "Fuck you coming here begging me for money and then dumping on me!" But her heart wasn't in it, and she cried into the small, crumpled tissue.

Sal got up and handed her another one. "Be happy, Jos," he said as he stood over her. "Be happy the woman you love loves you back. Be happy you know exactly where she is, right now, and can call her up any time you want. That's five hundred per cent more than I have right now."

Josie blew her nose again and took a deep breath. "It just makes it so final," she said softly and stood up.

"Makes what final?"

Josie started moving around the large kitchen, wiping counters, filling the sink with dirty dishes, and generally keeping herself moving.

"Jos? What's the story here? You don't *wanna* move in with her?"

Josie kept wiping the same spot on the stainless steel counter methodically, mindlessly. Sal walked up behind her and placed his large hand on hers to stop the movement. For some reason he whispered, "You don't love her, do you?" and he felt her try to start wiping again, but he held her hand tightly on the counter. "Do you? Quit bullshitting yourself, kid."

Finally Josie turned around and faced Sal. Staring up at him, her eyes all red and puffy, she said, very quietly, "It's just that ... that she was my first, Sollie. So I thought I loved her. She was patient and kind to me. She *understood* me and those feelings I had. And she stuck by me even though, let's face it, I'm no looker." She walked away from him now and turned on the faucet. With her back to him she continued, "But how can I tell her I don't love her after all this time? All I put her through? It's not right," she said and scrubbed furiously at a cookie sheet.

"Since when is it right or wrong to be in love? Besides, I think she knows anyway. So what's not right is you not being honest with her, Jos."

"I know," she said. She turned off the faucet, dried her hands on her apron, and reached for a pastry cooling on a rack. "Want one?"

"Nah. I'm not in the mood," Sal said. He sat down at the table and crossed his long legs.

"I don't get it, ya know? How come I loved Vinnie, huh? I know he was a bastard sometimes, and I was never really into having sex with him. But I loved him, Sollie. Somehow we *connected*. He could make me laugh, he could make me cry. He could make me crazy, too. *You* know how long it took me to finally get rid of him."

"I know," Sal said, softly. "But I never realized it was because you loved him. I always thought you were afraid of him."

"Sometimes I was. But mostly, I was just so connected to him. He moved me, Sollie. In a way that Denise ... just doesn't."

It was a difficult admission, and it hung between them.

"You have to break it off, Peachy," Sal said, finally.

"See, the thing is, I'm still attracted to her. I just don't *love* her. I can't move in with someone I don't love, can I?"

"You have to break it off," Sal repeated.

"And sometimes when she goes home, after we've been together all day, I'm actually relieved. Maybe I'm just getting old and set in my ways."

"You have to break it off," Sal said again, this time standing up and walking right up to her. "Hear me?"

"Okay, okay, cool your buns. I heard you the first time. I'm allowed to flap my jaw at you for three thousand dollars!" Josie walked over and sat down at the table with her pastry. "But I'm forty-three years old, and look at me! Who else would want me, huh?"

"Denise wants you. Why wouldn't anyone else?"

"Denise is a little wacko, that's why she wants me," Josie explained as she finished the cannoli.

"So, you don't think there are other wackos out there who will find you appealing?" Sal teased.

Josie laughed. "Every pot has a cover, huh?"

"Yeah. But I always wondered, with you and Denise, who was the pot and who was the cover?"

"You perv! Get the hell outta here! You come here asking for my money, then tell me to break up with my girlfriend, and then insult me," she said and leaped off the chair to slap at him with the nearest dishtowel.

Sal jumped out of the way and headed for the back door, laughing. "I'll come over the house to pick up the check later tonight. Then you can tell me the sordid details."

"Freakin' straight guys! You're all alike," she said.

"Give us a kiss," Sal teased, bending towards her and puckering up. "You know you want to."

"I'll give you a knuckle sandwich, you don't scram right now," she said and locked the door behind him.

CHAPTER TWENTY-EIGHT
Park Slope/The Purity Luncheonette

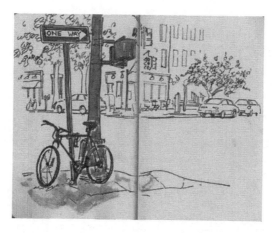

Manny had called and said it was important, so Sal met him for breakfast the next morning at the Purity Luncheonette around the corner. He was sitting in a booth reading the paper when Manny rushed over.

"Are you sittin' down?" he asked Sal.

Sal looked at him incredulously.

"I mean metaphorically," Manny said and sat down himself.

"Yeah, I'm sitting down *metaphorically*," Sal said, humoring him.

"Good, 'cos I have news. About Terry."

Sal's heart sped up. "Tell."

"She's still in town. I called the hotel."

"Why?"

"I needed to talk to her about our business deal, so I called."

"And she spoke to you?"

"Sure. It's you she's pissed off at, not me."

"She said that? That she was pissed off at me?"

"We didn't talk about *you*, we talked about the deal. And she's interested. For real, man!"

"When's she going back?"

"Saturday. I'm meeting with her tomorrow at the hotel."

"I'm coming with you."

"Whoa! Hold on there. This is a business meetin', not a lover's quarrel. I don't want her all pissed off at you and then screwing up our deal."

"Look, I gotta talk to her. It's important. My lawyer's making me do it."

"So, call her up yourself."

Sal had considered it. Over and over. But somehow he was sure she'd refuse to speak to him. It would be tougher for her to ignore him if he simply appeared. "Forget it. She'll hang up on me."

"Then she doesn't want to talk to you, Blood. Just drop it."

"Will you shut up a minute? There's something I gotta ask her, that's all. It'll take a minute, and then I'm gone and you can play her for a sucker the rest of the day."

"I don't think your lady friend is anyone's idea of a sucker. She knows a great idea when she sees it, friend."

"I'm this close to asking you to back off, Manny. To just drop this whole thing and leave Terry out of it, you know? As a favor to me."

"You want me to swear I'll do right by her, I'll swear. You want me to notarize it too?"

"What the hell's a notary do anyway?"

"He swears that you are who you say you are."

"I don't think so. I think *he* swears that *you* swear you are who you say you are."

"Get outta here! You mean you could go in there and say you were Gengis Kahn and he'd put his stamp on it?"

"I believe so."

"Some job! You lie, and he swears to it! I should look into it. Think it attracts women?" Manny asked, seriously.

"Like a magnet," Sal said. "Now, look. Why don't you just drop this whole insane idea, huh?"

"You think you're protecting her from me or something?"

"Yeah. That's exactly what I'm trying to do, in fact."

"When are you gonna get passed the past, Blood? You just can't accept that our business went bust, can you? And you still blame me, don't you?"

"Never, no, and yes."

"Okay, you wanna do this act and scene again, let's go. What's my part? Oh yeah, I'm the villain. The business bombed because of me. You had to go back to driving the cab because of me. Let's see. What else is because of me? Oh yeah, I forgot. Angela left you because of me."

"You're no damned good at being mean, Manny, but I don't appreciate it that you try," Sal said as he stood up. He dropped a few bills on the table. "Do what you want. But if Terry winds up losing any money, even one cent, I'm holding you accountable. Got it?" he said, pointing his finger close to Manny's face.

"Inagaddadavida, baby," Manny said, inexplicably.

CHAPTER TWENTY-NINE
Marriott Marquis/Broadway & 45th Street

He had until Saturday to talk to her. If she would even take a call from him ... or a visit. He toyed with both ideas for a long while, and finally decided he would just show up. Take a chance. If she wasn't there, he would come back later since he was working in Manhattan all day anyway. All he needed to know was whether she had gone to the clinic or not and when she would get the results. Then, of course, he would have to ask her if she was pregnant, to have a DNA test to ascertain if the baby was his. That's all. Armstrong wasn't asking for much, was he?

Sal drove into the city and pondered his options. The most appealing was simply to lie to Armstrong. Tell him he had spoken to Terry and that she wasn't pregnant. What were the odds that she was pregnant with his child, and if so, that Armstrong would ever find out? Pretty damned slim. Since they were going to try to rush the case anyway, a baby would take nine months to be born and then Terry would have to decide to have a paternity test. Would she? Was she pregnant? It was driving him crazy. Armstrong or not, the truth was that *Sal* wanted to know. And he wanted to see her again.

He got into Manhattan by nine and drove until eleven, then parked his cab in a lot and went into the hotel. The place was so huge and so hectic it felt like a carnival. There were more people in this one building than most small towns in America. He took the elevator to the eighth floor lobby and headed to the other bank of elevators leading to the rooms, but found himself floundering as busy tourists rushed by him, annoyed, and jostled him. Finally, not sure what the hell to do, he found a chair and sat down. He watched scores of people rushing in and out of elevators. Two ballrooms were just getting conferences started, and people in suits milled around holding their shot glasses of orange juice and wearing silly name tags.

He was afraid. His palms sweated. Like a kid at his first dance. What if she said no. No, I won't see you. No, I won't even answer you. He noticed a third ballroom at the other side of the lobby. The clown convention was getting started for the day. Sal couldn't resist. He walked over to the large doors and had to smile seeing hundreds of clowns, all in one place. Too bad Bennie wasn't there. This was a sight to see.

"Forget your make-up?" someone asked. "You can borrow mine."

Sal turned and faced a small female clown hardly larger than a child.

"Oh, no. I'm not a clown."

"Coulda fooled me," she joked.

Sal felt his spirits lighten. "Just 'cos I *act* like one most of the time ...."

"Me too. That's why I decided to look the part. Maybe you should give it a try."

Sal studied her make-up. She wasn't an entirely happy clown. Her colors were cheerful enough, but there was a downward curve to the eyes and mouth that made her seem sad at the same time. Or maybe he was reading too much into it.

"You're welcome to sit in," she continued. "Here, you can wear this." And she reached into her enormous clown pocket and pulled out a perfectly round red nose. Sal found himself taking it from her and rolling it around in his palms.

"Well, I have to get on in. You can keep that," she smiled, and tipped her stovepipe hat by pulling on some kind of string hidden inside her costume.

"Thanks," Sal said and walked away. The nose looked like a plump cherry in his hand. She must walk around with a pocketful of them, he thought. Occupational hazard, being caught without your red nose.

Sal walked to the elevators and rode up to the twentieth floor, turned left, and found Terry's suite. Without giving himself time to think, he knocked. Waited. Knocked again. Then he looked down and saw a tray on the floor. Room service. Looked like she had had dinner in. And then he looked closer: one plate, one fork. One meal. A relief.

"Who is it?" she asked, through the door.

"Look through the peep-hole and see for yourself," Sal said, as he popped on the nose.

For a moment there was silence. He knew Terry was making an instant decision, and he had to influence her.

"I've infiltrated the clown camp. I'm one of them now."

"Please go away, Sal. We have nothing to say to each other."

"We had plenty to say all weekend. Nothing's changed."

"Everything's changed."

Sal took a deep breath. If she wasn't going to let him in, he would have to ask her a bunch of personal questions right there in the corridor. He stepped closer to the door and started to speak softly. But Terry couldn't hear him. He raised his voice. "I need some information from you, Terry. I think you can figure out what it's about. Don't make me shout at you through a door."

"It won't be the first time."

"That wasn't my idea. Who told you to lock yourself in the bathroom?"

"Who told you to misrepresent yourself? Your lawyer? Or were you just using him as the excuse?"

"Is that what you've concluded these past few days? That I deliberately misrepresented myself to you? Then maybe you should explain why *you* lied to *me* about not wanting to have a kid with me!" he was getting loud. An elderly woman down the hall poked her head out her door and glared at him.

"I never lied."

"You sure as hell did! And I need some information. And this time it *is* my lawyer who's behind it. Because we're going to court for Bennie and we can't afford any surprises."

"Well, things are tough all over, I guess," she responded. It was obvious she wasn't going to open the damned door, and there was nothing he could do to make her talk to him. Nothing.

"So you'll talk to Manny, that maniac. But you won't talk to me?"

"Manny has an interesting business proposition."

"Manny's a lunatic, and you know it. Talk about someone interested in you for your money."

"Manny is honest about his interest in me."

"He honestly wants to sucker you into his next get-rich-quick scheme. But why are *you* so eager to get involved with *him*?"

"I don't have to explain myself to you. I'm running a *successful* business, remember?"

"A business your *father* handed you. Let's see you start with nothing, like my father, or me and Manny."

This time Terry didn't answer so quickly and Sal regretted the level he was sinking to. He could stand out there all day slinging insults at her. And she at him, no doubt.

"Terry, I'm sorry. I didn't come here to fight with you. I just need some information," he said, leaning into the door. He could hear her right on the other side. "It's not like you to be so withholding."

That seemed to get her. "You don't know what's like me and what isn't."

"I know you're not mean-spirited, even though you had it tough growing up. And I know you'll make a great mom ... if not now, eventually." But she didn't take the bait.

"I was about to shower."

"That wasn't the information I wanted, Ter."

"Not everything is about what *you* want, Sal. So long."

He heard her walk away from the door and he just stood there, not sure what to do. He couldn't bring himself to walk away, and he couldn't stand there either. Wasn't that what Terry said to him the other night? She didn't want him to leave, but couldn't think of a good reason for him to stay. It sure seemed to sum up their relationship. So he walked toward the elevator, got in, and went down to eight. It wasn't until he walked outside and people were staring at him that he remembered the clown nose, plucked it off, and dropped it into his pocket.

CHAPTER THIRTY
Park Slope/President Street

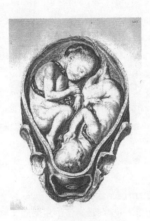

"Papa?" Bennie called out as he came downstairs and saw Sal sitting on the couch reading the newspaper. He had come home early to relax. It had been an exhausting day negotiating too many closed-off streets and avenues due to a water main break and the president's visit. Somehow, sitting down all day wasn't relaxing when you were driving.

"Hi, Bennie Boy. Did you finish your homework?"

Bennie sat down next to Sal. "Almost. I spoke to Mommy today, and she said we're going to have a visit and I'm gonna meet my brothers and go to a really big toy store in Manhattan where I can pick out anything I like!"

Mommy? Sal couldn't believe what he was hearing. He had never in eight years even heard Bennie say the word. It was almost not English to his ears.

"She called you?"

"Yeah. And you know what, Papa?"

"What?" Sal asked, working hard to keep his reaction under control.

"My brothers are twins, but they don't look alike. You know why?"

"I bet I can guess," Sal went along.

"Yeah? You know about fraternal twins?"

"Sure, Bennie. Everyone knows about that. Where was Grandpa when your mother called?"

"Taking his nap."

"Grandpa takes naps during the day, when you're home?" Sal asked.

"Sometimes. Anyway, listen, Papa. Mommy said to ask you to pick a day when I can visit, and then we have to call her up. When, Papa? They're going away pretty soon, and I don't wanna wait until they get back."

Bennie was seated on their mushy old couch. Sometimes it seemed to be swallowing up the child. Sal stared down at him. "Bennie, you don't even really know your mother and I don't think it's such a good idea to start now," he said softly, totally disarmed.

"But why?" he whined. "She said she wants to get to know me better."

"Just trust me on this, Bennie Boy. I know her better than you do."

"Is she mean?" he asked. "Does she hit?"

"I don't know if she hits, but she can be mean, yes."

"Then you come *with* me, Papa. To protect me," Bennie said, so sincerely it brought tears to Sal's eyes. Then they both looked up as Joe came downstairs still full of sleep. He could tell immediately that something was wrong.

"What's this?" he asked, meaning Sal's wet eyes. "Did someone pass away?"

Bennie jumped off the couch. "I'm gonna meet my mom and my brothers, Grandpa!"

"What?" Joe asked, dumbfounded.

"Angela called and spoke to *him*," Sal said.

Joe caught the implication. "I'm sorry," Joe shrugged.

"Can't you take a nap between two and three, Pop? *Before* he comes home?"

"At my age *I* don't take a nap, a *nap* takes me. So when is the visit?" he asked.

"I didn't say he could. I have to think about it."

"But I want to! Why not?" Bennie complained again.

"Because I said so. Now go finish your homework!" he ordered.

But Bennie wasn't so easily put off. He stamped his foot and protested. "She said I could visit her in California and go to Disneyland too! You better let me!" he cried. "Or I'll run away!"

"Don't talk to your father like that," Joe said softly, unable to muster any real anger at the child.

"I don't trust your mother, Bennie. I know it's not nice to say bad things about people, but I'm telling the truth. You can understand about trust, can't you? Remember when your friend Lee came to visit and he stole one of your little cars?"

"But I'm still his friend! And he doesn't steal anymore, Papa!"

Joe sat himself down in the armchair and let out a deep sigh.

"I can only promise you that I'll think about it, okay?"

But it wasn't good enough for Bennie. "No! Promise you'll let me! I wanna go, Papa!"

Sal saw Joe turn away to stare out the window. He knew the old man was crying. He did everything he could not to start himself. He squatted down next to Bennie so that they were eye level. He pulled the child toward him for a hug. Whispering in his ear, Sal said, "What do I love more, spaghetti and meatballs or you?"

"Me," Bennie said, not missing a beat.

"Oh yeah? Even though spaghetti and meatballs is my favorite food in the whole world?"

Bennie shook his head yes.

"Well, then, how can you be sure I love you more?"

Bennie shrugged silently.

"Because even though I love spaghetti and meatballs, I still get tired of it, but *you* I never get tired of! Why is that?" Sal smiled. "Because I love you more than spaghetti and meatballs. Now do me a favor and go finish your homework, and let me think about all this, okay?"

Bennie walked slowly out of the living room and up the long staircase. When he was out of sight, Sal turned to Joe, who had finally turned around and was facing the room instead of the window. Before he could speak, Joe did.

"She's his mother."

"Screw her! Who does she think she is to call him and manipulate him with bribes?"

"She's still his mother, and those are his brothers!" Joe said loudly. It had been years since they'd had a real argument. So long, in fact, that Sal couldn't even remember the last time.

"She had no right! To call up an eight-year-old after all these years and seduce him with some cock-and-bull story about toy stores and Disneyland!"

"She called the *house*! She didn't know Bennie would answer the phone."

"Would *you* have let her talk to him if you answered?"

"Of course! She's his *mother*!" Joe repeated.

"Then why didn't she act like a mother? Huh?"

"She made a mistake. A terrible mistake. Why can't you forgive her?" Joe asked, his voice shaking. "Why are you so bitter, Salvatore? It hurts me. I live with you and I watch and I hear and I ask myself: why is he still so angry? After all these years? Why?" he pleaded.

"She left us, Pop! Me and Bennie both. And for what? For a guy with a lot of dough! Money meant more to her than us back then, and it still does! She never loved us."

"And *you* loved *her*, my Salvatore?" Joe asked, this time quietly. "You loved *her* and not her pretty face? You loved *her*? Or you loved *winning* her like a prize in Coney Island?"

Sal was stunned. He dropped onto the sofa, saying nothing. Joe continued, "She's different now. Can't you see that?" he said more firmly, and started to pace around the living room. Sal hadn't seen Joe do that since his mother was sick. All those sleepless nights with Joe crying and pacing. "She has her own children. She learned a little something. She has a right, Sal. A mother has a right."

"Now you're taking her side? I'm breaking my damned back to support this family, to keep us together, and you tell me about Angela's *rights*!" he yelled.

"Bennie has a right too! Didn't you grow up with a mother and a brother? You're afraid maybe he'll like her *too* much? Maybe more than you? That he'll go to Disneyland and never come back? That he'll be so impressed with her money he'll forget you? He'll leave you?" Joe paused, not expecting Sal to react so strongly to his words. But Sal had suddenly begun to cry and was sobbing into his two hands. Joe came and sat next to him, petting his head. "Trust your son, Sweetheart. Have faith in him. Nu, you love him more than spaghetti and meatballs, but not enough to let him meet his own family?"

Joe continued to stroke Sal's head, and gently rub his back, just as he had done when Sal was a little boy, just as Sal did to Bennie to soothe him. But nothing could soothe Sal now. Everything was falling apart in spite of everything he had done to hold it all together. It had been a Herculean task to keep their little family together all these years. To maintain the house and keep up the mortgage payments, to raise the child and support the old man, to keep himself from sinking into despair when his business failed, to maintain hope of a relationship in spite of the ditzy women he seemed to attract, and to hope for more children in spite of the mess he had made with Angela all those years ago. It had been so hard and yet he had done it. It was just about the only thing he *had* done with all those years. And now it seemed it hadn't been enough after all because it was all falling apart anyway. And all he could do about it was cry in his father's arms.

CHAPTER THIRTY-ONE
Park Slope/President Street

He turned off all the downstairs lights and walked up to bed after dozing off on the couch in front of the TV. Joe was asleep already. He seemed to need more sleep as he got older, even though Sal always thought old people slept less and less.

He walked into Bennie's room and picked up the two stuffed dogs that had fallen on the floor. He tucked 'Barley' and 'Mayonnaise' under the blankets, kissed the boy on his head, and walked out.

But his fatigue had vanished and he lay awake, thinking. And worrying. If he let Angela have this one visit, maybe that would give her an advantage in the custody case. He would have to check with Armstrong, for sure, before agreeing to anything. And then what would happen if Angela disappeared again, forever? Then he'd have to deal with a kid with a broken heart. And yet, somehow he knew she wouldn't disappear again. What would be the point? No matter how hard Sal wished she had stayed gone, there was nothing he could do to banish her from their lives. Angela was now a *fact*.

Thinking of her this way actually helped. Because no matter how stubborn and pig-headed he was, and he knew it, once something was reality, he could deal with it. In fact, it was Angela who once pointed out to him that *until* he made up his mind, nothing on heaven or earth could move him, but *once* he made up his mind, nothing on heaven or earth could stop him. And she was right. Amazing how well she knew him back then. *Knew* him, but didn't love him. That's what hurt. Still. Joe had asked about his anger. That was it. That she didn't love him. Maybe never did. And maybe he knew it back then, even as a kid, and didn't care. He was too cocky. He wanted her, he got her. The question of love never entered the picture. They were just two confused kids from Brooklyn without a pot to piss in. Just a handful of hopes and hormones.

Sal reached over and turned off the small bedside lamp on the night table. He was starting to feel tired again. Staring up at the ceiling, watching the occasional car lights slide back and forth, he thought again about Terry … and he missed her. He wished they had never made love. He'd worried that this would happen. That missing her would be a physical pain, an ache. That's what happened after you touched someone you loved. You missed all of them, not just the personality, but the body. Now his hands had their own memory of her.

He turned on his side and closed his eyes. Where was she now? It was Wednesday. She was due to leave Saturday. She was probably asleep on that friggin' enormous bed. All alone. Except, maybe not quite. Maybe there was a tiny tadpole-like creature asleep inside her, doubling in size every few hours, developing its own personal obsession like brushes or street sweepers like Bennie, or maybe something else, something odd and uncommon that no one could anticipate. And maybe that sticky ball of cells waiting to watch Sesame Street and dig in the sand with spoons and take baths in the kitchen sink … maybe it was his child. The second child. The child he kept imagining and longing for.

He had to go back and try again. Get Terry to talk to him, no, to *listen* to him. He missed her. He longed for her. He wanted to laugh with her again and yell at her for feeding junk food to aquarium birds and to marvel at how she got Ted to talk! That was amazing! He smiled as he felt himself start to fall asleep. It seemed so simple to his tired brain; he was in love with her and all he had to do was tell her. He would tell her. He would tell her and she would listen. She would. She would listen. He would tell her.

CHAPTER THIRTY-TWO
Driving

"Did you think about it, Papa?" Bennie asked, as soon as he opened his eyes the next morning. He sat up in bed, clutching Barley the stuffed dog, to his chest. The child seemed almost breathless.

"I promise by the end of today I'll make a decision, okay?" Sal said and sat down on Bennie's bed. Bennie threw himself back down and turned over on his stomach. Suddenly he was sobbing into his pillow.

"What's the matter? Can't you wait 'til supper time?"

"I wish I was a grown up already," he cried.

"Come on, Sweetie," Sal cooed, and petted Bennie. "Being a grown-up isn't so great. We don't play Lego, we don't chase street sweepers, we don't even watch Godzilla movies unless it's with a kid. What do we do? We go to work and come home and eat supper and watch TV. What's so great about that?"

"You don't need permission to do stuff," Bennie said, calming down.

"But we also don't have anyone to stop us from making mistakes."

Bennie thought about that. The amazing thing about him was that Sal could usually reason with him. Even though he was so young, he was very thoughtful.

"I know it's hard to wait. Waiting is the number one enemy of kids. Always waiting for grown ups to do something you want them to. But sometimes there's pleasure in waiting too, Bennie. Maybe not this time, I know. But sometimes. The trick is to find the pleasure."

"Like Christmas," Bennie said, instantly catching on.

"Exactly. Now come on and eat breakfast or you'll be late for school."

Bennie kicked off the blankets and got out of bed. Sal grabbed him for a hug. Bennie took the opportunity, safe in his father's arms, to voice his worry. "Papa? Will you come with me to see Mommy if I go?"

Sal moved back a bit to look at Bennie's face, his eyes. To understand. "Are you afraid? That she'll be mean to you?"

"Her voice didn't sound mean, but ...."

"She won't be mean, Bennie. When I said she could be mean, I meant to *grown-ups*. We had a lot of mean fights before we broke up and we're still a little angry at each other, so sometimes we're mean to each other. But we *both* love you and would never be mean to *you*."

"But if I go meet her and my brothers, I still want you to come, Papa. Okay?" he asked and headed into the bathroom, dragging Barley along.

Sal sighed and stood up. "Cheerios or scrambled eggs?" he called into the bathroom.

"Cheerios."

After taking Bennie to school, Sal phoned Armstrong and asked for advice. The attorney told him he was legally under no obligation to let Angela see Bennie, but that a visit wouldn't have much bearing on the case. Too bad. He had hoped Armstrong would have told him not to let Angela see Bennie. So he kept pushing the guy. Finally annoyed, Armstrong said, "Mr. Iorio, I am giving you the objective facts. However, what you *want* to do in this case is entirely up to you."

"And what about what Bennie wants?"

Armstrong was silent a moment. Then, "I trust you will do right by your son whatever you decide," he said reassuringly.

Driving around the city all day, Sal pondered when to call Terry. What the hell was she doing all week, anyway? His simple plan of calling and telling her he loved her seemed increasingly ridiculous with every hour. He put in his "Barber of Seville" tape and decided to let this decision wait until later in the day. It was a very sunny winter day, almost scintillating, clear and brisk, and he intended to enjoy it.

The decision about Angela had made itself. Now that Bennie had spoken to his mother and knew she wanted to see him, Sal knew there was no way he could keep them apart. Even though he was legally within his rights to fight it, Joe was right. Angela was the boy's mother. And she was fighting much harder than Sal had imagined she would to see her son again. Maybe it was possible she was sorry about what she did. Maybe she did miss him. Maybe she had love to share with him and could be good to him. But would she be good for the long run? Would she always be there for him? Would she never abandon him again?

After telling Bennie his decision and having the little boy literally jump up and down with excitement, Sal phoned Angela to arrange the visit. Unless he wanted Bennie to skip school on Friday, it would have to be Saturday because after that Angela and company were leaving the country for a while. He didn't mind Bennie missing a day of school, but didn't like the implication: a visit with Mommy is like a holiday. So they planned for Saturday. They would meet in the city at F.A.O. Schwartz and take it from there.

At nine, when Bennie was asleep and Joe was watching TV in the living room, Sal went to his room and phoned Terry. He had promised himself he wouldn't think about it all day, and he hadn't. But now he just felt like he wanted to talk to her. And that made the decision for him. There was no answer, so he left a message: "Terry, this is Sal. Look, maybe this is ridiculous, but I realized something yesterday that I had to tell you. I love you, okay? I'm sorry for all the misunderstandings and stuff. I can see how you got the wrong impression. And, I guess I don't know you as well as I need to, either. But I've still got my boxing gloves on, Ter. I'm still fighting for you."

CHAPTER THIRTY-THREE
Where's Your Shorts/
5th Avenue @ Central Park

"So, Papa? When are we leaving for 'Where's Your Shorts'?"

Bennie asked as he walked into the bathroom.

"What the heck is that?" Sal asked, as he shaved.

"You know. The toy store Mommy's taking me to."

Sal put down the razor and laughed and laughed. "You mean F.A.O. Schwartz!" he said.

"Yeah! Is it very big?"

"Sure! It's so big it's even got an escalator."

"Yay!" Bennie shouted and ran out of the bathroom.

"Get your shoes on, Bennie!" Sal called out. "We're almost ready to go."

"Sweetheart, you're all right?" Joe asked, poking his head into the bathroom.

"Yeah, sure, Pop. I'm fine."

"You're doing the right thing, Sal. You're making me proud," Joe said, holding back tears. It seemed lately that the old guy cried at everything.

"Don't get your hopes up. This could be her first and last visit for another six years, you know," Sal spoke softly and wiped the last of the shaving cream off his face and dashed on some aftershave.

Joe looked puzzled. It was obvious this hadn't occurred to him. "Why would she do that?" he asked.

"Who knows? I can't figure her out. I just hope, for Bennie's sake, that she's for real. 'Cos if *we* get custody, she might get royally pissed off and disappear again. Ever think of that?"

"Jesus, Mary, and Joseph, " Joe said, and walked away.

"Okay, Bennie Boy ... you ready?" Sal called out.

Bennie came flying out of his room. Sal caught him and held him in place. "Let me look at you. Teeth brushed, hair combed, shirt tucked in. Okay, you look fine. Now remember what I said about manners: please and thank you. No whining or begging. If Mommy says no to anything, you don't make a peep, got it?"

"And you're staying the whole time, right, Papa?" he asked.

"If you want me to," Sal agreed.

"Good," Bennie said and headed downstairs.

"Why do you have to stay?" Joe asked, emerging from his room into the upstairs hallway.

"I think I scared him the other night. I wish I woulda kept my mouth shut."

"It's all right, it's all right. He's a little boy. It's only natural he wants his Papa with him." Joe smiled. But Sal didn't. "This won't be easy for you, my Salvatore," Joe said.

"I know what I'm getting into here, Pop. But thanks."

Joe patted Sal gently on the cheek. "Good things are coming for you too, my Sal. Good things for a good man."

Sal loaded Bennie into the cab, and they took off. Bennie's backpack was stuffed full of everything he wanted to show his brothers: Barley and Mayonnaise, his two favorite street sweepers, his Lego projects, and some books. It was so simple when you were little. You met new people and showed them the four or five things you loved, and that telegraphed everything about you. Adults traveled with so much more baggage, but it brought so much less joy.

At ten they pulled into a parking deck and walked over to Fifth Avenue. It was a cold but clear day, and already the avenue was starting to crowd with people in furs, shopping. Sal pointed out the Plaza Hotel so Bennie could see where his mother and family were staying.

"It looks like a castle!" Bennie noted.

They crossed the avenue, and Sal spotted Angela and her kids and another woman waiting outside the store. As they approached, it became clear that the other woman was the nanny.

"We should have met in the hotel so you wouldn't have to wait in the cold," Sal said as he approached.

"No problem. We just got here. The boys are almost out of control with excitement," Angela said, then looked down at Bennie. "Hi," she said.

"Hi," Bennie said shyly, clinging to Sal.

"I'm so glad you could come today," she said. Then the nanny brought the boys over. "This is Wentworth, and this is Geoffrey. And this is Bennie," she said.

"Wanna see my Legos?" Bennie asked.

The boys each nodded. They were small boys, both light like their father, but entirely different looking. Wentworth had Angela's sharp nose and large eyes, Geoffrey didn't. Neither of them looked anything like Bennie.

"Margaret, would you please bring the boys' duffel bag?" Angela asked the babysitter. "They brought a ton of things to show Bennie. I told them we could go back to the hotel afterward and play, but they couldn't wait."

The boys were squatting on the ground showing each other their various toys. Sal became uncomfortable. He wished he could just leave. "Bennie asked me to stay," he offered.

"It's fine with me," Angela said. "Thanks for bringing him," she added, sincerely. He could always tell when she was full of shit, and right now she wasn't. "He's beautiful, Sal. He was a beautiful baby, but sometimes when they get older they lose that beauty. Bennie still has it."

"Well, let's see what puberty brings."

"I bet he'll be tall, like you and Joe," she said.

"Good bet."

"Wentie and Geoff will probably be average height, the doctor says. There really aren't any tall people on either side of our families."

Wentie? Who the hell named a kid Wentie? Angela must have seen his reaction because she said, "Not my idea, I promise."

Sal had to smile. It was the first chink in the armor. The first sign that Angela was still deep down the same pretty little poor girl from Brooklyn, and that she was willing to let him know it.

"It's kinda cold out here. Why don't we get these guys inside?" Sal suggested.

"Sure. Margaret, let's gather up the toys and go in."

The children were almost in shock as they entered the store and were overwhelmed by so many toys. Little by little Bennie let go of Sal's hand and walked with his brothers. They steered the children around, letting them stop for as long as they liked wherever they liked. Bennie's shyness wore off, and soon enough he was talking to Angela like he had known her his whole short life. And she too. Like they had never parted. Like those six years were just a day or two. Like she had been there the whole time. Those absent years erased with one visit.

When they were upstairs the children begged to buy candy, and Angela had to negotiate with them. Sal pulled Bennie aside.

"It'll be for later, Papa. After lunch."

"Don't worry about the candy. Listen, Bennie. What do you think about your mom?"

"She's nice! And she's pretty too, Papa."

"So you still need me here to protect you?" he asked, dying to escape.

Bennie paused and thought about it. "I guess not," he said, tentatively.

"I don't want to leave you in the lurch, but I think you should get to know your mom without me around. I'll come pick you up later, okay?" he asked.

"Okay," Bennie said, again a little unsure. But Sal didn't care. Bennie would be perfectly fine without him, and he felt like a big jerk tagging along with them.

Sal explained the situation to Angela, they decided on a pick-up time at the hotel, and he left.

As he walked back to the parking deck, his beeper went off. It was Josie. Shit. Maybe it was her father.

"Sal?" she answered.

"What is it, Jos?"

"I need to see you," she said, shaken.

"It's the Old Man?"

"No, no. He's okay. I mean, he's not okay, but I just split with Denise."

"Are *you* okay?" he asked.

"She hit me, Sal," Josie cried.

"What? I'll kill her! Where is she?"

"Hold on. I'm okay. She didn't hurt me. She was just angry. You said yourself if it was you, you would have dumped me a long time ago."

"I would have dumped you, not hit you!"

"I had it coming."

"Bullshit! No one has it coming! I thought you learned something from Vinnie -"

"It's not the same. Look, Joann's covering the store. You got a little time to spend right now, maybe?" she asked.

The truth was, he didn't. He wanted to go to the Marriott and see if Terry had checked out yet. He wanted to catch her, maybe stop her. It was hair-brained but he couldn't help it. Maybe he could see her and get her to talk.

"Well, I have to pick up Bennie in a few hours ...."

"Oh, yeah! I forgot about that. How's it goin'?" she asked.

"They're a perfect match. He's a gorgeous, smart kid and she's a gorgeous, rich mommy."

"And the cheese stands alone."

"You got it."

"So come on over and hang with me, and then I'll take a ride back with you to get Bennie," she offered.

Sal could hear the desperation in her voice. She really didn't want to be alone right now. But he just couldn't drive all the way back to Brooklyn, then back to the city. He had to get over to Terry's hotel. "Jos, I really can't do all that driving. Why don't you come and meet me, and we'll have lunch or something?" he offered, doubting she'd go for it. And, even if she did, it still gave him time to track down Terry.

"Yeah? Where should we meet?"

"Uh ... you know the Marriott Marquis on Broadway and Forty-fifth?"

"Yeah?"

"Meet me on the eighth floor lobby. When are you leaving?"

"About half an hour."

"You driving?"

"Are you nuts? The way I feel right now?"

Sal looked at his watch. It was ten forty-five. "Okay. The train'll probably take you about an hour, so I'll meet you there about twelve-fifteen. Okay?"

"Okay," she said.

"You sure you're up for this? We could get together when I get back later, you know. For dinner."

"Nah. I gotta get out of here right now, Sollie."

"Is she threatening you or something?"

"Nothing like that. She's gone and ... I just can't stand all this aloneness."

"Okay. Twelve-fifteen on the eighth floor," he said and hung up. Then he drove across town to the Marquis, parked again, and went up to the lobby. If check-out was eleven, maybe he could catch her. It was a long shot, but what the hell.

The woman behind the desk checked the computer and said Terry had just checked out a few minutes ago. Sal found the concierge and asked if Terry had called a limo service or a cab or something to take her to airport, but the woman had no knowledge of it. She had to be taking some kind of service, Sal thought, as he went back down to the street. As he turned the corner on to Forty-Fifth Street, he saw a van that looked a lot like Manny's. Then he saw Manny himself and started to run toward him. Manny spotted him and held up his hand, as if to stop Sal. From the look on his face, Sal could tell he was serious. He stopped dead in his tracks. Manny trotted up to him in a hurry.

"*You're* taking her to the airport?" Sal asked.

"Yeah. Listen to me, Blood - "

"I gotta see her before she goes!"

"I said, *listen* to me, for once, okay?" he asked, his voice softer, his hand on Sal's shoulder. "Let her go."

"I can't! I can't just - "

"Just for now. Let her go. I got her number and address for you, so don't worry, okay? Trust me, will ya? And don't give me that look. Just 'cos I made a few bad business decisions doesn't mean I don't look out for you. I know how you feel about her."

"Did she say anything about me?" he asked.

"Nah. She wouldn't say anything to me about that kinda thing. Look, I gotta split before she misses me, but stay in the ring, Sollie. I'm in your corner," Manny said and trotted off down the street, a dancing bear in denim.

CHAPTER THIRTY-FOUR
Manny's Candy & Nut House/ Flatbush Avenue

A week later, Terry still hadn't called. Manny thought for sure she would, based on some things she had told him en route to the airport. Sal left one message on her home phone and that was it. To keep calling would be ridiculous and annoying.

"Why were you so sure she was gonna call?" Sal asked Manny. They were at the store sharing some licorice pipes.

"She said she wanted to talk to you but she needed to collect her thoughts first."

"It takes over a week to collect her thoughts?"

"She's not like me and you, Bro. She listens, she considers, she decides. *Then* she acts. Me and you, we do stuff then try to figure out why."

Sal couldn't really argue that one. And it was true that Terry did a lot more listening than most people he knew. He noticed that early on.

"Which reminds me. What did she decide about you and the business deal?"

"She's having some PR materials done to try to sell the idea of Pet Day. And then she said she thought a new line of Pet Greeting Cards would work well too. And pet astrology stuff. Like I said."

"She's financing all this?"

"She's having her accountant put together some 'numbers'. So, what's with Angela and Bennie? You hear from the lawyer yet with a court date?"

"He's trying to settle outta court first. Anyway, get this. Bennie calls his brother 'the worldwide web' 'cos the kid's name is Wentworth Wakefield. 'W.W.W.'... like the web, get it?"

"Yeah. Cute," Manny said and popped a Sen-Sen into his mouth.

"I didn't even know he knew about the web. He's using computers in school." Sal noticed that Manny was rolling his eyes. "What the hell are you doing?"

"I got these floaters on my eyes. They drive me nuts."

"Oh, yeah? I have a few of those myself."

"I got one, it looks like a hangman's noose. How about you?"

Sal stared up at the ceiling and focused. "Mine looks like Bizarro Superman's nose."

"Where do they come from?" Manny asked.

"Beats me. Look, I gotta get to work for a change. I owe my soul to a hot-shot lawyer."

"Hey man, I'm sorry she didn't call. I really thought she would."

"It's okay. I appreciate you got her number for me."

"I also managed to say some nice stuff about you too."

"Oh, yeah? Like what?" Sal asked as he stood in the door.

"I told her you were the only kid in school who ever made friends with me and didn't want anything from me in return."

"What the hell could you offer? You were so poor even stray dogs wouldn't hang out with you."

"But *you* did. And you never even asked me to beat up on anyone for you, either. Everyone else did eventually."

"Ah, they were a buncha knuckleheads."

"Sollie ...."

"Yeah?"

"You know I'm in your corner, right? No matter what. My money's on you, kid."

"Too bad you don't *have* any money. But thanks, Manny. And thanks for the licorice pipes too."

CHAPTER THIRTY-FIVE
Flat Iron Bldg /Law Offices of Armstrong & Birnbaum

"Have a seat, Mr. Iorio," Armstrong instructed. "We have quite a bit to discuss."

Sal sat down. Armstrong's demeanor was different. It looked like he was working hard at not smiling. And Birnbaum seemed in an awfully good mood too.

"I spoke to your ex-wife's attorney, Mr. Hall, and we spent a few days batting this thing back and forth, and we have arrived at what seems like a fair settlement."

"You mean we don't have to go to court?"

"Not if you agree to their terms." Armstrong had been standing and now sat himself down behind his mother-ship of a desk. He tapped his pencil.

"Okay, so?" Sal said.

"Firstly, you will retain full custody of your son, Benjamin," Armstrong said.

"Oh, thank God!" Sal burst out. He nearly wept. "Thank you, Armstrong!" He leaned forward to shake the man's hand.

"I'm not through. Secondly, your ex-wife will have regular visitation with the child. The details will be negotiated further, but she will want a minimum of one visit a month if she can manage it, part of his yearly Christmas and summer vacations, and every other Thanksgiving and Easter. Mr. Iorio, are you listening?"

Sal wasn't. All he cared about was that he still had Bennie. "Whatever she wants, it's okay. As long as we don't fight, ever again, over the custody issue. Is that in there?"

"We're not going to make that a term of this settlement, but I wouldn't worry about it. From what I can ascertain from her attorney, if she gets what she wants she won't bother you again."

"Fine, fine," Sal said and stood up. "I have to call Joe."

Armstrong smiled. "Let me finish. Please." He gestured to Sal's seat.

Sal sat back down, but could hardly contain himself.

"Your ex-wife will also be contributing one thousand dollars a month in child support -"

"Holy shit!"

" - in addition to which she will pay for summer camp for the child, and private school if you decide your son would benefit from it."

"Private school?"

"She will also provide you with a lump sum retro-active child support payment of one hundred thousand dollars immediately, for you to use *at your own discretion*. Do you understand what that means, Mr. Iorio?"

"Excuse me?" Sal was barely taking it all in.

"It means that the money does not have to be spent on the child or put into trust for him. She is setting up a trust fund for the child *in addition* to all of the things I just mentioned. So that money is yours, free and clear. To compensate you for the funds you already spent on the child."

"Armstrong, I -"

"Let me finish," he said, holding up his hand and smiling. He had dropped the formalities now and was clearly enjoying himself.

"Because you have custody of the child, he can't be claimed under your ex-wife's husband's medical insurance plan, so she will contribute fifty percent of all his future medical and dental expenses, including any mental health expenses should you ever decide to send the child for therapy. Oh, and she will also send you enough money to buy a computer for the child and to install a second phone line in your home for a dedicated modem so he can learn to use the Internet."

"Boy, you don't miss a beat, do you?"

"That's what I'm paid for."

Sal laughed. "How did you know I only have one phone line?"

"When I visited the house your son was on the phone and you asked him to get off because you were expecting a call. I also didn't see a computer anywhere. When I was negotiating with Mr. Hall, I just threw it in."

"Armstrong! You're incredible!"

Again, the man smiled. "Thank you. I do enjoy my work."

"How can I thank you?" Sal asked and stood up again.

"No need. Now, I have other business to discuss with you, but it can wait until you phone your father." He pushed the phone towards Sal and stood up as if to leave. Birnbaum did the same.

"Where you going?" Sal asked.

"To give you your privacy."

"Get outta here! I mean, *don't* get outta here! Stay right there. Joe will definitely want to talk to you."

And sure enough, the old man did speak to Armstrong, *wept* at him might be more accurate. "God bless you," Joe said over and over.

"Call Janet and let's celebrate tonight, Pop. I'll buy some champagne. Let me ask." Sal turned to Armstrong. "Joe said he wants you and your partner to come for supper. *I'd* like you to come too," Sal added.

Armstrong was obviously a little surprised by the offer. For once he was at a loss for words.

"Aw, come on!" Sal said. Then, into the phone, he said, "I'll work on him, Pop. Now go call Janet. And call Josie too. And Schmuli and Manny. And invite them all!" Sal said and hung up. "You just saved an old man's life," Sal said to Armstrong and started to put on his coat. "I gotta go. But please, come over tonight. Bring your wives, I mean, if you're married."

"We're both married, Mr. Iorio," Armstrong said.

"You can call me Sal."

"But before you go there's one more small thing I need to discuss with you. Do you have a minute?" Armstrong asked.

"Sure. But don't tell me to sit down again, whatever you do."

Armstrong laughed a warm laugh. "Sal," he said, warmly, "I'm retiring in about four years. Birnbaum here will step in for me, of course, but we're still going to need a second person. Someone we can groom to take on this specialized work we do. Someone who sees it more as a cause than a job and who wants to put in some time working with the Defense Group as well."

"Someone who loves kids," Birnbaum added. "A champion of children."

"Yeah?" Sal said, confused. Where was this leading? Was he asking Sal if he knew anyone for them? "I'm sorry, but I don't think I travel in the kind of circles where I would know anyone -"

"Did you know that you don't necessarily have to graduate from law school to be an attorney?" Birnbaum asked.

"What do you mean?"

"There are shortcuts. Could be very little college, in fact, and maybe very little or no law school."

"So?"

"So, after a few years' apprenticeship with Armstrong and Birnbaum, I am fairly certain *you* could pass the bar," Armstrong said and watched Sal's reaction go from befuddlement to comprehension.

"Me? Take the bar exam? You gotta be kidding! The last test I took was the GED."

"I'm aware of that. And you scored in the highest percentile."

"How do you know?"

"Due diligence."

"Let me get this straight. You want *me* to become a lawyer? With you? To work with you? You're kidding me."

"I'm absolutely serious, Sal. We need a man as passionate about the welfare of children as you are. A man as smart as you are, as quick to learn. Gerry and I loved how you handled your ex-wife the first time. It took ingenuity and guts. The kids we've been interviewing fresh out of law school don't know the meaning of those words. We believe you have what it takes."

"And how much college did you say I would need?"

"We're still researching that," Birnbaum said. "You could get credit for 'life experiences' and maybe not need more than a year or two to get your B.A. As for law school -"

"I can't believe this!"

Birnbaum continued. "You might even be able to get away with only one year of law school combined with your work here."

"You would be working for us throughout," Armstrong explained. "And we would pay you, of course. Commensurate with your experience. So your salary would go up every six months or so. Once you pass the bar exam, you will get a large raise. And once I retire, you and Gerry will work toward a partnership."

"Wow," Sal said. "I gotta sit down."

"We've given this quite a bit of thought, Sal. And you should, too. It's a serious commitment and very time-consuming, but the rewards are, well, I don't think that takes any explaining."

"After a few years with Bill and myself, you'll be unbeatable. You'll be able to smell a winner the minute it comes through the door," Birnbaum added.

"Was *I* a winner when I walked through the door?" he asked.

"I thought so. But your case hinged more on your ex-wife's absolute negligence than anything else. Had she made even a small effort over the years, it's difficult to say what the final outcome would have been. But her complete absence, emotionally and financially, was the wrench in the works and her attorney knew it. I just had to let *him* know that *I* knew. After that, it was just a matter of stating our demands."

"I gotta tell you Armstrong -"

"Bill."

"Bill. I really thought she had a good case."

"Their money scared you. I have to admit I was a little surprised that you never asked for any of it. We searched for it, you know," Armstrong said.

"What do you mean?"

"We looked for big-ticket purchases, large deposits, vacations. But we didn't find anything."

"You didn't believe me?"

"Let's just say we've never encountered anything like this before," Birnbaum said.

"My friend Schmuli said I suffer from tunnel vision," Sal said.

"In this case, it served you well," Armstrong said.

"That's not why I did it."

"We know that," Birnbaum said.

"I just washed my hands of her. I didn't want to think about her, and I didn't. Even when money was tight, it never even occurred to me to contact her. I never even thought about it as *her* money, anyway."

"You were too close to it to see it, Sal. But when *you're* in my shoes ...."

"So you've made my decision for me, huh?"

"I trust you'll make the right decision," Armstrong said and held out his hand. "But whatever you decide, it's been a pleasure," he added.

Sal shook his hand vigorously. "I'll see you tonight?" he asked, looking at them both. Then he threw on his coat and headed for the door.

"What time did you say?"

"Seven."

"Seven, it is," Armstrong said and sat back down at the controls of his mother ship.

"Oh," Sal said as he was leaving. "Just one thing. If I do accept your offer," he said, pointing to Armstrong's desk, "I'm definitely gonna need a larger desk."

CHAPTER THIRTY-SIX
Park Slope/President Street

At midnight, when everyone had gone, and Joe was asleep, Sal finally got into bed and did his best to calm himself enough to sleep. He had had too much wine, and the remains of a headache were still with him. But it had been worth it. When he had stood up to toast Armstrong, and then announced he was going to join Armstrong's firm, the expressions on everyone's faces were priceless.

"I so admire this man that I have decided to become a lawyer myself and join with Armstrong and his partner," he'd said. Armstrong was only a little surprised and very delighted. But the others had no idea what the hell was going on. "Is that okay with you, Armstrong?" Sal asked. And Armstrong had just played right along. What a moment! He would never forget it as long as he lived. The looks on their faces, the confusion. Then they thought they were being fooled with. But Armstrong definitely wasn't a practical joker and they knew it. Finally, Armstrong cleared it all up. Joe sobbed, and Schmuli smacked him so hard on the back that the wine in his glass spilled all over him. Manny said "No fuckin' way!" and Josie just stared at him, her jaw practically dropped down to her knees. Just thinking about it over and over again kept Sal awake. If there were times in a person's life when one era ended and another began, this was one of them. A new job with better pay. His kid safe and sound in his house, forever. No money worries. And his father free to get married. Now all Sal had to do was sell the medallion, buy a new wardrobe, and decide how he wanted his name painted on his office door. He toyed with Salvatore Soloman Iorio, then S. Soloman Iorio then Salvatore S. Iorio. Considering that his Bar Mitzvah date was only six months away, it seemed only right to be known as Sol. He would be S. Soloman.

Bill and Gerry explained that Sal could get his B.A. by attending a school that would give him credit for life experiences. He could end up only needing one year of college, and then he could apply for a Work Office Study program that might enable him to bypass law school entirely. And if that didn't work, he might be able to get away with only one year of law school. Sal figured if he had to compete to get into a law school anyway, why not get the degree?

CHAPTER THIRTY-SEVEN
Park Slope / President Street

The next day a letter arrived from Terry. Sal was too nervous to open it and instead tried to read parts of it through the envelope. He carried it around with him all day, and then, after supper, he drank two glasses of wine and tore into it.

Dear Sal,

I feel compelled to write you and explain a few things. There won't be any promises made in this letter, or any recriminations either.

Your reaction to the fact that I left Charles standing at the altar forced me to think about it again, and I had to ask myself how I had let it happen.

I know I told you that I realized I wanted to marry Charles so I could feel like a real daughter to Charles' mother, Rose. Belonging to a real family had become an obsession for me.

Shortly before our wedding Rose became quite ill and decided it was time to tell me she didn't think Charles was right for me. She said that she loved me and that I would always be like a daughter to her, whether or not I married her son. She was dying and I would be left with only Charles. That idea was so dismal that I finally realized I didn't love him.

Then Rose startled me with a deathbed confession; she told me that when I was around five, she and her husband, my father's partner, wanted to adopt me. She said she saw how difficult it was for my father to raise me alone after my mother died, and she didn't want him sending me away to school. She wanted me to have a family and she wanted a daughter. Apparently, my father wouldn't even consider it. Rose said she was never sure why.

She told me all this, Sal, only a day or so before I was supposed to marry her son. After hearing it I was very confused and furious with my father. Rose tried to console me by saying that my father loved me too much to give me up, but I don't think either of us really believed that. What finally gave me the strength and courage to walk away from Charles was knowing that Rose had loved me enough to want me to be her daughter.

Sal put down the letter to wipe his tears. He wished she were there with him so he could hold her in his arms and comfort her. What a raw deal for someone as great as Terry.

By this time it was the day before the wedding. There was no one I could talk to. I was in a daze. I got dressed and everyone arrived at the church, but all I wanted was to be with Rose. So I left and went to the hospital. When I showed up at her bedside in my wedding dress, she just smiled. By then she could barely speak. But she understood. She died a few days later.

I needed someplace warm to go to, and Rose had a sister in Florida who she was very close to. They took me in. Eventually I moved out, but stayed in Florida for two years as I tried to put my life back together and decide what I wanted to do. When my father died, I went back home and stayed there. I wish I could say I came to forgive him eventually, but I will never understand why he stood in the way of my having a family of my own. And, though I loved Rose, I will always wish she had fought harder for me.

That explains why I did what I did, as best as I can manage to explain it. Maybe I did "give up," but I think it was the right thing to do at the time.

As for you and me, all I can say is that it all happened too fast. I still think it's a miracle that we met at all and connected the way we did. But I suppose I just don't trust myself enough to take this leap of faith, knowing how I fooled myself before.

I'll be in Europe, on business, by the time you get this and I'll be gone a month, perhaps longer, so don't bother phoning me.

All the best,
Terry

PS - I almost forgot. I am NOT pregnant.

CHAPTER THIRTY-EIGHT
Park Slope/The Real House

Armstrong gave Sal a budget to furnish his office that was more than Sal made driving a cab in a month. They gave him an advance on his pay so he could afford his new wardrobe and sent him to Barney's. There he spent a thousand dollars on two suits. As soon as the money from Angela arrived, Sal would be able to pay back Josie and even Schmuli, who had lent him and Manny five thousand dollars to get their business off the ground back when. The rest he would spend fixing up the house, buying a new car, and filling out his retirement account since Angela was starting a fund for Bennie's college.

The first day he went to work, dressed in his five-hundred- dollar suit and silk suspenders, Joe hugged him and couldn't stop crying.

"Thank God I lived to see this!" he repeated. "Santa Maria! I only wish your mother could see you," he said.

"You look important, Papa," Bennie observed.

Sal took the subway to work for the first time since he was a teen-ager. He walked the streets with all the other suits, stopped at the newsstand and bought his paper, then descended the stairway. His attaché case was on order.

Armstrong had handed him a catalog and told him to pick one. Soon enough he'd be toting that as well. He looked the part. He was sure he could fool anyone into thinking he was a real lawyer. But he wasn't so sure himself.

The men held a morning briefing every day and set Sal in motion. He did research, made phone calls, and sat in on interviews with clients. He learned from Armstrong how to be professional: how not to get too chummy, at least not at first; how to instill just a little fear so that people were afraid to lie to you. He learned about the reputations of the judges and the importance of scheduling your case with the right judge, if you could help it. After only two weeks, they let Sal go solo on interviewing a potential new client. He sweated it out, but was pretty sure the client didn't notice. He made his recommendation to Armstrong not to take the case, and Armstrong agreed. Sal was catching on.

Riding home on the subway each evening, Sal read the Law Journal. He read over old bar exams to get a feel for them. And he studied everything Armstrong gave him. Between that and his Hebrew, he was exhausted. Joe's wedding was only a month away now. He had offered to help with the cooking, but Joe and Janet could see that he was overwhelmed and refused to let him. Instead, he offered to have the affair catered, an option he could never have afforded before. But Janet insisted that they wanted to do it all themselves.

Angela phoned weekly, and as far as Sal could see, she was treating the little boy right. No missteps so far. Still, he had his eyes wide open. For his Easter vacation this year, Sal would put Bennie on a plane to California. Angela had promised Disneyland, and it looked like she planned to deliver. Now that Bennie had a computer, he sent email to his mom often. Sal made sure to ask if Angela was reciprocating. She was.

One day, after shutting off his PC and changing into his PJs, Bennie asked Sal, "Why did you and mommy get divorced?"

Sal figured he'd get this question eventually. It only surprised him that it hadn't come sooner. "We made each other unhappy."

"But, then, why did you get married?"

"Because we were happy when we *got* married and then stopped being happy."

"What if Grandpa and Janet stop being happy?"

"Just because your pop made a mistake doesn't mean everyone in the whole world who ever gets married will make the same mistake!"

Bennie laughed and climbed on his father's lap. "Papa?"

"Yeah?"

"How come Mommy never called me when I was little?"

"Well, when we split up, we both decided it was best if you stayed with *me* all the time. And California is pretty far, you know. She couldn't just pop in any old time. But I know she missed you a lot. In fact, when she had the twins she probably thought she wouldn't miss you anymore, but then, well, I think having them made her realize she missed you even more. Maybe she didn't have the courage to call you after so long. Maybe she was a little afraid that you would be mad at her."

Benny was silent as he thought about this. "I wouldn't be mad. But what if she decides to stop calling me again?"

"That's never gonna happen, Bennie. Now that she knows you so well, she could never stand to be without you, believe me. Parents understand this stuff," Sal said, seriously.

Bennie was quiet as he slipped off Sal's lap, climbed into bed, and crawled below the covers.

"You ready to be tucked in?" Sal asked, pulling the covers up to Bennie's chin and tucking in the blanket. "You have a lot to look forward to," Sal said as he bent over and kissed the little boy on his forehead.

"I know it's not good to always think about tomorrow, Papa, but sometimes tomorrow seems like it's going to be more fun," Bennie said, and reached out to grab his father's hand, to keep him there. He had managed to get Sal's sleeve and was tugging on it.

"What is it, Bennie?" Sal asked.

"Except I don't want Grandpa to move out."

"I know. Me neither. But he'll be right across the street. You can see him all the time."

"Can I sleep over there, too?"

"Of course. It'll be like a second home for you."

"That's what Mommy said about *her* house."

"Well, then you'll have *three* homes! Some kid I got. A real big shot with three homes!" Sal teased, and stood up.

"But this is my *real* house, right, Papa?"

"As real as it gets. See you in the morning, Sweetheart," Sal said and walked out of the boy's room into his own.

He undressed, brushed his teeth, and sat down on his bed, intending to study his Hebrew. But something nagged at him. Now that he could finally afford his big house, he probably didn't need it. Joe was moving out and Bennie wouldn't be home as much either. Sal didn't want to think about being alone in the house night after night once Joe got married and Bennie was on vacation in California. He opened up his Hebrew workbook and studied his vocabulary.

CHAPTER THIRTY-NINE
Home: 40°,40.5 " / 73°,58.6"

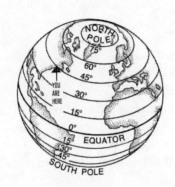

After the church ceremony everyone walked back to Sal's house for the party. Most of the food had been prepared in advance and just needed re-heating. Josie and Manny had left the church early to get things warmed up, put out the ice and the drinks, and set up the chairs. Little by little everyone filed into the old brownstone. Manny moved the sofa against a wall to allow for more floor space for dancing. Then he put on the music, which was mostly Frank Sinatra and Dean Martin.

"Congratulations, Joe!" Manny called out as Joe and Janet came through the door, hand in hand. Then he gave the man a big bear hug.

"How'd you get so big, huh?" Joe asked and slapped Manny lovingly on his cheek. It was the same question he had been asking him since Manny was thirteen and already over-sized.

Sal came in with Bennie and headed right for the kitchen. It was a warm day in late March, and the house was sweltering. He turned down the thermostat and threw open some windows and the back door.

"Hey, Manny! Open some living room windows, will ya? We'll get some air through this place," he called out and plucked an apron off a hook.

"Well, Brother-Of-Mine, looks like we finally got the old guy married off, huh?" Josie said as she came into the kitchen.

"Looks like it," Sal said absently. "Hey, hand me that jar of oregano."

Josie gave him the jar. "It's pretty crazy, huh, Sollie? We're forty-three and Joe is seventy, and *he's* the one getting married."

"You'll find someone, Peachy. Don't sweat it," he said, concentrating more on his sauce than her.

"Whatcha got there?" she asked, looking into the pot.

"The sauce for the spaghetti. It tastes a little bitter. What do you think?" he asked, and thrust the spoon at her.

Josie tasted it. "Add a little sugar. Or honey."

"I hate honey in sauce. Hand me the sugar, will ya?"

"What's all this other stuff?" she asked, looking at the trays of food on the table.

"Janet made a buncha food."

"Oh man, I can't stand all that curry crap, can you?"

"It's an acquired taste."

"Then you better start acquiring it, kiddo."

"I don't mind it. And Bennie seems to be getting used to it too."

"So, Sollie, tell me, whaddya think of this dress?"

Josie had lost some weight and was starting to buy new clothes.

Sal faced her, looked her up and down, and said, "It's nice," then turned back to his pots on the stove.

"That's all? Just nice? I *love* it. I mean, it makes me feel so pretty. I treated myself to something new for the first time in a long time, ya know?"

Sal dumped some sugar into his sauce and kept stirring. "Yeah, yeah. It's alarming how charming you feel," he teased.

"Screw you," she said and stuck a spoon in the sauce to taste it. "So, how's the lawyer business?" she asked.

Sal covered the saucepan then turned to face Josie. "The lawyer business is incredible. And it made me realize that no matter how shitty my break-up was, it could have been much worse."

"Yeah? How?"

"How? You should hear the things people do to each other! And how they use their own kids against each other! It makes me sick. At least Angela disappeared and left me in peace," he said and kept stirring the sauce.

"Not to change the subject, but let me ask you something, Brother-of-Mine. You think it's possible for me to ever be as thin as I was when I was nineteen?" she asked and sat down at the table, awaiting his answer.

Sal didn't bother turning around. "Are you nuts?"

"Now that's a vote of confidence," she said as she picked at the salad on the table.

"You want bullshit, hand me a shovel."

"Jeez, at least some encouragement ...."

Still stirring his sauce, Sal said, "Peachy, I think you can do any damned thing you decide to do. It's just that sometimes it takes you a long time to decide."

"You mean like with Vinnie."

"And Denise, and -"

The doorbell interrupted him. Since it had only rung in the kitchen, the people in the living room and dining room hadn't heard it.

"Could you get that?" Sal asked.

Josie walked to the front door and opened it, only to be face to face with Terry, holding two large suitcases.

"Hi," Terry said.

Josie was speechless.

"Surprised you, didn't I?"

"Shit, yeah. But I know someone who's gonna be *more* surprised," she said. "Come on in. Just drop the bags anywhere."

Terry came in and closed the door behind her. She dropped her suitcases in the hallway and followed Josie into the house.

"You got company, Counselor," Josie said, poking her head into the kitchen and then leaving immediately.

Sal put down the wooden spoon he was holding and turned around. Instantly his heart sped up and his face flushed.

"Hi," she said, softly, taking off her coat.

Sal was speechless. Finally he managed to ask, "What brings you here?"

"This," Terry said, holding up an invitation.

"Joe invited you?" he asked, stupidly.

"Well, I didn't forge it." She placed her coat on the back of one of the kitchen chairs.

She was wearing an old-fashioned style long dress with a high waist and boots that made her look even taller. With her hair up she looked so lovely it was almost painful for Sal to look at her without touching her.

"He didn't tell me," Sal said.

"I didn't think so."

"Can I get you a drink?"

"White wine?" she asked, and sat down at the table.

"Red it is."

"My mistake," Terry laughed.

Sal fetched the wine and poured some for Terry.

"I didn't see you at the church," Sal stated.

"My plane was late. In fact, I came straight here from the airport."

"Meet any interesting cabbies?" Sal asked.

"This guy had a last name I couldn't even pronounce."

"He needed to buy a vowel?"

Terry laughed.

"Probably Polish. They have a real vowel shortage over there."

Sal turned away from her and continued cooking and heating the food.

Terry sipped her wine. "I heard about all your good news," she said. "Congratulations."

"Thanks," Sal said. "No one was more surprised than me, I can tell you that," he said, with his back to her.

Terry smiled. "And no one deserved it more than you, Sal. I guess it was an easy decision."

"Yes and no. I mean, I had my doubts, but then I realized that Armstrong changed my entire life with one little phone call, and I -"

"How do you mean?"

"All he had to do was call Angela's lawyer, and bingo! He tapped into the mother lode! And then I realized that some day *I* could do the same for someone. I could change their life and the lives of their kids, and it started to really appeal to me."

He wanted to take her in his arms and hold her and tell her how much he had been thinking of her and how every morning when he went to work on the subway he fantasized having her beside him going to her own office and coming home to her every night for supper. How he wanted her to help him fill up his house and his days. But all he did was stand up and pull the first loaf of garlic bread from the oven and say, "So, how was Europe?"

"It's still there."

"That's reassuring. Maybe one day I'll get to see it."

"You're going to get to see *everything*, Sal. I'd put money on it," she said and stood up. She walked toward him, and he turned to face her. But instead of grabbing her, he held back. Instead of elation, he felt like crying.

Terry wrapped her arms around him and gave him a gentle hug. "I've missed you," she said.

"Me too," was all Sal could manage to say as he took in all the fragrances of Terry; her perfume, her hair, the wine on her breath.

"Hey, Sal! Joe's gonna open the presents," Schmuli said, as he walked into the kitchen. "Terry! It's good to see you!" he boomed.

"Same here, Schmuli. How's your family, and Ted?"

"Ted won't shut up now. It's like you cast a spell on him or something. When are you gonna come over and undo it? Reba's driving me nuts!"

"I don't think there's an 'undo' feature on that one, to tell you the truth."

"Maybe you'd like a bird?" Schmuli asked Sal.

"Yeah, sure. Lose a father, gain a foul-mouthed fowl. Nice trade," Sal said.

Schmuli shrugged and laughed. "Come, they're opening the presents." They all walked out of the kitchen as Sal grabbed Terry's hand.

"Come upstairs with me a minute. I need some help with something."

As Terry and Sal walked through the dining room and living room to get to the stairs, several people demanded they stay as Joe opened his gifts.

"I gotta go wrap mine!" Sal explained and dragged Terry upstairs to his room. He opened the door, and there on the bed was a large box wrapped in shiny silver paper. A large ribbon lay next to it. "I'll make the bow," he said and began to bring the ends together. "You put your index finger right here so I can tie it."

Terry hesitated.

"What?" he asked.

"Well, I can't remember which is my index finger."

"You're kidding me."

"No, really. It's a problem I have. I never could remember which finger is which."

"I remember trying to teach Bennie. There's no consistency at all. I mean, take the middle finger. Its name is based on its location on the hand, but none of the others are. The ring finger is named for what it wears, but what if you don't wear rings? And pinkie! I always thought it was a nickname, didn't you?"

Terry looked puzzled.

"Like it used to have a *real* name like 'Index' or something, but over the years people started calling it Pinkie, and so - "

"You've actually given this some thought, haven't you?"

"Yeah."

"I flew all the way here from Wisconsin to see you, and I'm in your bedroom for the first time. I was hoping for a kiss."

Sal smiled and bent down to give her a peck on the cheek. "You know, Joe used to have a friend everyone called Pinkie, but his real name was Lou."

"So you think that the pinkie finger's 'real' name used to be Lou?"

"It's a possibility. Anyway, it would make it much easier to remember if we just gave *all* the fingers real names." Sal held up his hand to demonstrate. "The pinkie is Lou," he said, and bent his pinkie as if it were taking a bow. "Then, there's Dave," he said and bent his ring finger. "And next to Dave is Bob." He bent his middle finger. "And then there's Vince, and then there's Fred," he said bending his thumb. "Don't you think the thumb looks like a Fred?"

Terry smiled, took Sal's upheld hand in hers, and brought it to her mouth. "I'm going to give Lou and the boys a kiss," she said and started to kiss Sal's pinkie.

"Oooh kinky!" Sal said and gently pulled his hand away. "But they're not used to being watched." He moved the present aside, sat down next to Terry, took her in his arms, and kissed her.

"You know that message you left me back at the hotel? As soon as I heard it I ran out and bought a tape recorder and taped it so I could listen to it over and over and hear you say you loved me. I must have listened to it fifteen times by now."

"You didn't shop at one of those slimy electronics stores on Broadway, did you? The ones that are perpetually going out of business?" he asked, as he pulled away from their embrace.

She just gave him a look.

"Sorry."

"Rose would have adored you, Sal. When I imagined you two meeting, I knew I had to come back. You're the only two people who ever loved me."

"The only two people who ever *said* they loved you. Your mother loved you, but you were too young to remember her. And, no matter what he did, your father loved you too, Ter." She started to protest. "I know, I know," he said, holding up his hand to cut her off. "But some people have trouble showing their love. And you can't assume that your father didn't love you just because he didn't want you living with his partner's family."

"Then why not give me a chance at happiness?"

"Maybe he loved you too much to give you up. And you were his only connection to your mother."

"But he sent me away!"

"He did what he thought was best for you."

"I've always wanted to believe that. But to believe that would mean believing in a very sad kind of love."

"Everyone loves differently. There's no formula."

"Too bad. It would make things so much easier if there were," she said softly and sat back down on the bed. She realized they were supposed to be wrapping Joe's gift, and she reached for the bow. Sal placed his hand on hers, to stop her.

"Ter," he said softly, and took her hand lightly in his. "I've been doing a lot of thinking, and I realized something about me and Angela. Something that was worrying me all these years. Something that made me not trust myself anymore." Terry looked at him, puzzled. "Joe said it. He said I never loved Angela. That I was a cocky kid who wanted to *win* Angela, but I never really loved her." He stopped and sighed deeply. Then he stood up and paced the room. "I was such an idiot. How come *I* didn't realize it?"

Terry said nothing.

Sal sat back down next to her. "It explains so much, know what I mean?"

"I'm not sure."

"See, I've been so afraid these past years since the divorce that I could make the same mistake again. I've been afraid to get serious with anyone -"

"You were so wounded, Sal, you -"

"No, no, Ter. The thing is… I feel liberated now!"

"I don't understand."

"Look, you realized you didn't love Charles *before* you married him, right?"

"Yes."

"Well, I never loved Angela either, only, it took me about …." he paused, calculating. "About twenty-two years, four months, three weeks, and two days to realize it!"

"You may be an autodidact, but you're not exactly a fast learner," she joked.

"I could never figure out how the mess with Angela happened. All my *other* relationships work out. You see how many old friends I have. You know why?

"Why?" she played along.

"Because I love them, Ter. And I'm *good* at love. The reason I wasn't good at being married to Angela was that I *didn't* love her. I *wanted* her, but I never loved her. There's a difference between a horny teen-ager with something to prove and really loving someone. Like how I love you." He paused. "The truth is I've never been in love before. I mean it! I was married for sixteen years, divorced for six years, have an eight-year-old son and a seventy-year-old father. I have a mortgage, and now I even have a profession. I have suspenders, Ter! I carry an attaché case now, did I tell you? And cufflinks!" he said and jumped up to scoop a pair off his bureau. Terry took them from him and held them. "And even so, here I am, forty-three years old and -"

"*And* with cufflinks," she teased.

"And with cufflinks! And yet I have never really loved a woman. I mean, Terry, in spite of all my other doubts, the one thing I *know* I'm good at is love! This is something I can do! And now that you're here, I can show you," he said, softly, squeezing her hand.

"I have something for you," she said, and took a gift from her bag.

"For me?" Sal asked and started to unwrap it. It was a small framed photo.

An aerial picture of Sal's neighborhood. At the top there was a label that said "40°, 40' Latitude|-73°, 58' Longitude." Sal stared at it.

"It's a picture of your neighborhood. And that's the latitude and longitude of this house," she explained. "Or close to it."

Sal said nothing. He was very moved but wasn't sure what this meant.

"The first day we met you said that home wasn't just the intersection of latitude and longitude," Terry explained.

"Wow. I don't even remember that."

"Well, I can't forget it."

Sal pulled her to him, and they sat hugging until Schmuli's booming voice called up to them. "Nu! Are you two ready yet? We're all waiting."

Terry kissed Sal lightly on his lips. "Yes. I think we are," Terry said and led Sal downstairs.

Art Credits:

COVER ILLUSTRATION: © Christine Marie Larsen: ChristineLarsen.com

Chapters 3,7,17,26,31,35	© Rene Fijten: www.renefijten.blogspot.com
Chapters 23,29,32	© Patricia Clements: www.patriciaclements.com
Chapters 2,4,11,25	© James Anzalone:ParkSlopeSketch.Blogspot.com
Chapters 1,8,14,19,27,28, 34,38	© Stephen Gardner:www.gardnerillustration.com
Chapters 18,21	© Lapin: www.lesillustrationsdelapin.com
Chapter 15,24	© ClareCaulfield:ClareCaulfield@googlemail.com
Chapter 22	© Christine Larsen: www.ChristineLarsen.com
Chapter 12	© kevinjduke@yahoo.com
Chapter 33	© Clambake.com
Chapter 36	© mysitemyway.com
Chapter 9	© Dorling Kindersley: www.dkimages.com

My heartfelt thanks to all the artists (and others) for their generosity in allowing me to use their art work. Please visit their web sites!

Correspondence, love letters, rave reviews welcome!

Made in the USA
Middletown, DE
29 October 2023